CZAR RISING

Also by

Geoffrey Sambook

TARNISHED COPPER

CZAR RISING

by

Geoffrey Sambrook

Published in Great Britain by Twenty First Century Publishers Ltd.

A catalogue record of this book is available from the British Library.

ISBN: 978-1-904433-77-4

To order further copies of this work or other books published by Twenty First Century Publishers visit our website:
www.twentyfirstcenturypublishers.com

Acknowledgements

Many people have helped in the writing
of this novel, in Europe and in Russia.
I think it's fairer to respect their right to anonimity.

Dedication

With thanks to Jenni, Rebecca and Victoria.
They give a lot of support, even if they don't always realise it.

Prologue

March 2000
Bitter End, Virgin Gorda, British Virgin Islands

The stars were the only pinpricks of light blinking against the dark tropic sky. The inky waters of Gorda Sound heaved gently in the swell, and the boats moored on the buoys bobbed quietly up and down. It was two a.m., and the myriad cruising yachts in the marina and on the buoys out in the Sound were largely dark and silent. Here and there, the odd light was visible, twinkling through a porthole or in a cockpit where the holidaymakers were keeping the evening going, but the black Zodiac inflatable was unnoticed. Engine throttled back to keep the noise down, crewed by three figures, also in black, it crept in through the mouth of the Sound.

Standing out amongst the chartered forty and fifty foot sailboats were two big yachts, each around 120 feet, anchored a couple of hundred yards off the end of the marina pontoons – there were no berths alongside for boats of that length. Their lights were doused apart from a soft glimmer from the bridge of each, where the crewman on watch sat idly through his spell of duty, reading, playing on a Gameboy, occasionally glancing across the few hundred feet separating the two boats. They were bored, watch keeping largely redundant here – what was going to happen, in Gorda Sound in the British Virgin Islands? Down below, in the big staterooms of the luxury yachts, the owners slept peacefully. They were among the world's super-rich; why wouldn't they sleep sound and deep?

There was an almost imperceptible squeak as the rubber Zodiac nosed up to the stern of one of the two big yachts. Silently, quickly, the figure at the front lashed the dinghy to the stern anchor chain and all three of its crew scrambled nimbly up, pausing only briefly at the rail to check there were no lookouts. On rubber-soled feet they sprinted along the deck and then ducked in through a companionway. Again with only the slightest pause to check they weren't being observed, they ran on down the passageway. They clearly knew the layout of the boat, as they stopped directly outside one of the staterooms. From pockets in their black windbreakers, they each removed a Glock 9mm pistol and a silencer tube which they attached to the guns. Slowly, silently, the man in front opened

1

the door. As they stepped through, the movement in his room awoke the figure in the bed and he looked up. He saw three men, masked and clothed all in black. What were his last thoughts, as each of the men took aim and fired? Who knows, but the soft coughs of the silenced pistols were hardly louder than the gentle lapping of the water against the side of the boat. The figure in the bed fell back onto the pillows; one of the world's billionaires died in his luxury yacht, blood spurting from his throat and his brains spattered over the costly linen pillows and sheets.

The three men returned the way they had come; back in the Zodiac, they eased their way across the Sound – no stranger to piracy and blood-spilling here: this is where Drake and Hawkins waited in hiding to ambush the Spanish treasure galleons heading up from the Main back to Europe. Back through the narrows and out into the Sir Francis Drake Passage, the man at the stern opened the throttle and the little inflatable bounced over the calm seas until they saw the outline of a power boat ahead. Boarding, they stripped off their masks and black windbreakers, and dropped them and the guns they had used into the deep, dark waters. In a guttural Chechen, they greeted the boat's helmsman, who helped them with the Zodiac. Then, as the helmsman opened the throttles, they headed off towards St Thomas. Cigarettes are fast boats, and this one had 800 horsepower. They trusted the holidaymakers were all moored for the night, because at their speed, the radar wasn't too effective, and an unexpected sailboat tacking across in front of them could have created a nasty mess. The killers passed around a bottle of vodka, the helmsman concentrated on keeping the boat straight.

They took the first flight out of St Thomas in the morning, changed aeroplanes in New York, and were back in Moscow by the following morning. They never bothered to read the newspaper accounts of what they had done – all they knew were their orders and the money they got paid for their unthinking violence. Just a nagging curiousity, that the last time they had seen the man who had been their target, they had been bodyguarding him, as an important man, vital to their country's economic growth. Still, in the fragmented, violent world they knew from their homes in Grozny, alliances had always been fickle.

Part One

Chapter One

In the mid nineteen forties, Victor Lansky had been born to an English girl and her Polish immigrant husband, an émigré who had fought for Western freedom in the Free Polish Forces with their British and American allies through the Second World War, through the baking heat of the Western Desert, the muddy hell of Monte Cassino and eventually on to Hamburg in 1945.

Freedom? He'd expected to continue to his homeland, to see Warsaw liberated. But the shameful, self-interested accommodation of Yalta had stopped the progress of the West at the Elbe, and instead of returning to his family's lands, Wladislaw Lansky found himself back in Britain in late 1945 as an embarrassment to his one-time allies and comrades-in-arms, with a war-time bride and an eighteen-month old son. What did a Polish aristocrat do in post-Second World War London? Working wasn't what he'd been bred to do, and in the end he became a porter at the Covent Garden fruit market. Victor grew up with his father's bitterness an all-pervading memory of his childhood in the shabby house off the Commercial Road in the down-at-heel East End of London.

Victor's childhood otherwise was unexceptional, were it not for the one thing he took from his father – a conviction that eastern Europe, the land of his ancestors, owed him his living. He left school as soon as he could, despite his teachers' assurances that academic success was there for the taking, and got himself employed by a scrap-metal merchant. His job was to tour the metal-bashing factories of the industrial midlands and north of England buying scrap. It was the beginning of the nineteen sixties, the go-go "you've never had it so good" England of Harold Macmillan and business was good for Secondary Metals Ltd, of East London. Victor started to have some cash.

And then, he made his first big step in the world. At the time, the accepted way of cleaning the plastic coating off scrap copper wire was to take it up on to the Yorkshire Moors, or out to the heathland of the West Midlands and burn it. In common with their competitors, Secondary Metals usually paid the travelling gypsy families to do it for them. But environmental concerns were already beginning, and more and more the police spotted the spiralling black smoke. It was starting to be a problem, for the whole industry. Victor's solution? Forget letting the gypsies play cat and mouse with the police; he did a deal with the Governors of Winson Green and Strangeways prisons, in Birmingham and Manchester. For a few shillings an hour, he got the services of a captive workforce to strip his wire by hand. And at the end of the week, when his trucks rolled back into the prisons to collect clean, recyclable copper, the plastic residue was left for the gaols to dispose of. An elegant solution, one which enabled Secondary Metals not only to sidestep their problem, but also to claim the twin high moral grounds of being friendly to the countryside and providing employment for prisoners, letting them do something positive for society. Tendentious claptrap, of course; all Victor cared about was that it was cheaper and more secure than the old way, and it put more money in his pocket.

But it raised his stock with his bosses, who began to take notice of the Polish kid, as they thought of him. Scrap metal has an image of rag and bone men, of Steptoe and Son. Actually, it's a sophisticated business, recycling base metals into new products. The skill for the trader is in knowing what he's buying, and what the market price is at any given time. The more responsibility Victor was given, the more he thrived on it. Soon, he looked after all the scrap buying Secondary Metals had, and, in a cash-based business, his pockets started to bulge. Copper's not like steel or iron, which have stable fixed prices. Copper is traded on a futures market, the London Metal Exchange, where the price fluctuates minute by minute, sometimes moving more than ten percent in one day alone. Victor had to learn to use this market to hedge his copper purchases, and over the years of his early twenties, he began to understand that he could earn as much or more by speculating on those price movements as he could from buying and selling scrap copper. Secondary Metals had an account with a London Metal Exchange broker by the name of Commet to execute their LME trades; Commet was a well-established member of the market, a subsidiary of Metals and Commercialisations SA of Luxembourg, a large, well-known conglomerate in the mining and metal processing trade. It was originally established to enable its parent to execute its own hedges on the LME, but over the years it had grown to offer a brokerage service to other clients in the non-ferrous metal business.

Victor became quite a good client of Commet, his hedging and speculation combining to give him good volumes to trade. The dealers got used to hearing the East End voice, with its indefinable overlay of Polish vowels, on the other end of their phones, buying and selling, usually making profitable trades. And in turn, Victor got to know them, got to know whose opinion to listen to, and whom to ignore. And then, one day in late 1969, a strange voice on the end of the line:

"Good Morning, Commet."

"Good Morning to you", replied Victor, "This is Victor Lansky of Secondary Metals. Who am I speaking to?"

"My name's Mack McKee. How can I help you?"

"Mack, I don't think we've spoken before. I need to trade some copper. Can you do that, or can you pass me over to one of the others?"

"Sure, I can help you." The voice was confident, even brash. "What do you want to do?"

Not true, in fact. McKee couldn't really trade copper, he was a new employee, a graduate trainee, actually the first Commet had ever had. But he was a confident young man, and the fact that technically he didn't have the experience to do a deal wasn't going to stop him. He'd spent his first three weeks at Commet checking dealing cards against telex customer deal confirms, and he was bored with that. He'd watched how the account executives took orders from their clients and passed them through to the copper trader for execution. If they could do something that simple, then so could he. In those days, there were no regulatory concerns about being a "fit and proper person", or anything like that. "What do you want to do?" he asked.

"I want to buy two hundred tonnes at nine eighty-two. Can I do that now?"

McKee could see from the screen in front of him that the price was actually lower that Lansky's buying level, so "Yeah," he said, "that's done. Two hundred tonnes you buy at nine hundred and eighty-two pounds."

"Thanks, Mack, I'll speak to you later." And Lansky hung up. McKee clicked his phone off, and laid the handset on the desk. He sat and watched the screen for a moment or two, delaying passing the deal on to the copper dealer at the head of the trading desk. As he watched, the price dropped another three or four pounds; the deal he had just done was making more money for Commet. But even in the first few weeks of his career, McKee was a lateral thinker. Pulling the customer phone list towards him, he looked for the Secondary Metals number. Making the connection, he said, "Is that Victor Lansky? This is Mack McKee from Commet. We spoke a few moments ago."

"Yes, Mack, what can I do for you?"

"The copper you just bought – I can improve the price to nine-eighty."

"Well, thank you. An improvement is pretty unusual. But most welcome."

"I like to try and give the customers a good service. To show we value their business. Don't forget to ask for me next time."

Now McKee passed the deal on to the copper dealer, still showing a profit of a couple of pounds a tonne. The dealer looked hard at him. "You shouldn't be doing deals," he said. "I can't be looking out for your mistakes. Just concentrate on doing what you've been given. You can have my job when you know how to do it. And that's not yet."

McKee glowered at him, but said nothing. Yes, my friend, he thought, I will have your job – and sooner than you think. The customer likes me now, and I made a profit for Commet. Would a word of congratulation have cost too much?

And the customer did like him. McKee and Lansky, from very different backgrounds, discovered they had something in common – both had an eye for the main chance. They hit it off from the first time they met, after McKee badgered his boss to let him take Lansky out to lunch, promising it would result in more business if the client got to know him better. So McKee booked a table at The City Circle, near the Guildhall. The food there was nothing particularly special, but McKee loved the idea of the service. The waitresses wore diaphanous, see-through tops, and very short skirts. This was the early seventies, and pretty risqué in the City of that time. They made a strange pair. The dark-haired McKee was six foot six tall, and broad shouldered with it. He'd played number eight in the rugby team in his university days at Sheffield, but was already beginning to thicken around the waist. Lansky was thin and spare, flashily dressed with a loud tie. They spent the afternoon and four bottles of heavy red wine getting to know each other. Lansky recognised in McKee a reflection of himself – a gambler, a man with an eye out to make some money for himself. The age difference was only five or six years, but Lansky had the experience of the business on his side. At around six-thirty, they stumbled out of the City Circle, loathe to leave the waitresses, but persuaded finally the restaurant wanted to close, and crossed the road to one of the numerous quasi-private drinking clubs that abounded in the City at that time. McKee bluffed his way in, using his boss's name, and by the time they finally made it out that evening, they'd become friends.

Mack McKee had been right. The business from Lansky did increase, becoming increasingly speculative, as McKee egged Lansky on to trade more and more. Lansky was successful, and Secondary Metals grew. He was made a partner, and then bought into the company as the founders took their money and retired. By the early eighties, he too was looking to get out. Secondary Metals had a scrap processing yard in the East End of London, a prime site for development. So Victor Lansky made the sideways step, and became a property developer. Still everything he touched seemed to turn to gold, and his portfolio built comfortably. Letting go of the excitement of the speculation on the copper market was a wrench, but what the hell. He was getting older, did he still need the market?

McKee moved on as well. As he'd predicted to himself, he did get the copper trader's job at Commet, and made a lot of money for the company. Through the late seventies and early eighties, he took more and more responsibility for Commet's progress, particularly for the company's push into Japan and the Far East, where he and Commet really made their reputations. By 1984, he was Managing Director of Commet and one of the main men in the London Metal Exchange world. Later in the decade, he was elected to the Board of the LME, and cemented his place as the most influential player in the game. Then he got caught up with an old acquaintance, the American Phil Harris, in the Kanagi copper scam of the late eighties/early nineties. McKee and Harris made hundreds of millions of dollars, but McKee died in his blazing Aston Martin, when it plunged over the side of a gorge in the Alpes Maritimes. There were those who doubted it was a genuine accident, but Mack McKee was dead anyway. Victor Lansky was amongst the crowd of mourners at the big man's funeral; their paths had diverged over the last few years, but the friendship had remained.

Chapter Two

Late Summer 1994

Mayfair, London

Victor Lansky walked into his Mayfair offices on a bright summer's morning. Now in his late forties, he dressed in a more subdued but coolly expensive way than in his flasher youth. Tailored suits from Savile Row, heavy silk ties from Herbie Frogg; still slim and lithe, he was every inch the successful property man. He greeted the attractive receptionist, and walked through into his private office. As he sat down at the desk, the intercom bleeped, and his secretary's disembodied voice came out of the box.

"Victor, good morning. I've had three calls for you this morning from a man called Oleg Malenkov. Says he's got a proposal to make to you, but he didn't leave a number. Said he'd call back again later. D'you know him?

Lansky thought for a moment. "No, never heard of him. Did he sound Polish?"

A snort of laughter came from the speaker. "I may have worked for you for six years, Victor, but I don't pretend to do accents. Let's just say he's some sort of east or central European."

"OK. We'll see when he calls back. Anything else of interest?"

The secretary reeled of his schedule for the morning, a series of meetings with planners, builders and others in the world of property. Getting involved in his day, Lansky almost forgot about the call; until, an hour or so later, the girl again buzzed him.

"Mr Malenkov on the phone again for you."

"OK, put him through." And then, as the connection was made, "Mr Malenkov? This is Victor Lansky. How can I help you?"

"Mr Lansky, good morning. My name is Oleg Malenkov. I have some matters to discuss with you." Lansky's secretary may have had difficulty placing the heavily accented voice, but for Lansky himself, recognition was instant. The man on the other end of the phone was a Russian. The man continued, "Can we arrange a meeting?"

"What do you want to talk about? Why should I be interested?"

"Mr Lansky, I have a very serious proposition to make to you. It is not something we should discuss on the telephone. I promise you I am not wasting your time. You will be interested, I am sure."

Lansky paused, torn between logic, which told him he had a good business, a lot of money, and that unsolicited telephone calls rarely turned out to be worthwhile, and the gambler's instinct, which told him he had nothing to lose by listening to a proposal. Gambling won.

"OK, Mr Malenkov. I can give you some time this afternoon, if that suits. Otherwise, I am going to be travelling for the rest of the week, so it would have to be next week."

"This afternoon would be fine." The voice may have been accented, but the English was correct. "I shall come to your office at around four this afternoon." And with that, he hung up, leaving Lansky holding a dead telephone.

Lansky rocked back in his chair. Russian..... As a Pole, he couldn't pretend to love them. But as an Englishman, as he was to all intents and purposes, apart from when he was with his father, he was aware of the changes that were happening as the Soviet system slowly wound to its death. The phrase "Russian Mafia" was just beginning to gain currency as tales of corruption, violence and staggering profits started to appear in the western press. And, of course, he knew people in the metals business who had had a raft of strange contacts in Russia. But, nevertheless, what did he have to do with a Russian?

Punctually at four p.m., Oleg Malenkov presented himself at the reception desk in Lansky's office. He was short, swarthy and unappealing, but his clothes looked expensive, and would have been stylish on another man. The formalities of introduction over, he lounged back in the chair opposite Lansky's desk, pockmarked face and stained teeth leering across at his host. He said nothing. The silence lasted just longer than was comfortable, then Lansky broke it.

"Mr Malenkov, you told me this morning you had an interesting proposition for me. Perhaps you would care to expand on that a little. I am a busy man, and I suppose you are too, so let's not waste time sitting staring at each other."

Malenkov continued smiling for a moment. Then, in heavily accented but grammatically correct English, "Mr Lansky, we have heard much about you. You have made a lot of money, first from metal dealing, and then from property." He gestured with his hands to take in the restrained opulence of Lansky's office. "We have almost made the reverse journey from you. Since the changes in my country, the move to a form of capitalism, we have made many investments in property, both in our home region and more recently in Moscow itself. Now, we perceive a substantial opportunity is developing in the world of metal. We would like to discuss this opportunity with you."

Lansky looked blankly across the desk. "Mr Malenkov, I'm always interested in opportunities, but they don't often just walk in off the street. Maybe you would like to describe what is on your mind, then we can have a serious discussion as to whether it interests me or not."

Malenkov slouched even further down in his chair. "OK, I give you the background. My brother and I are from the town of Krayanovsk, in Siberia, to the east of Irkutsk. It is an industrial city, formerly a gulag city, one of those developed by Stalin and Khrushchev to keep Russian industrial production well out of the range of your western missiles during the 1950s. It has a number of heavy industrial facilities, but the one with which we are concerned is a 750 000 tonne a year aluminium smelter. This smelter was built as part of the Russian military production; it has always been operated by governmental appointees, whose knowledge of the industry is minimal. Indeed, their knowledge of the basics of commercial life is also minimal. My brother and I are, how shall I put this, in a position to be able to offer commercial advice to the managers of the smelter." He paused, and looked directly at Lansky. His hooded eyes were hard and cold. "We believe they are most unlikely to ignore our assistance." What does that mean, Lansky thought to himself. And why is this guy talking to me about it?

"Anyway," continued Malenkov, "the situation in Russian industry right now is interesting. All over the former Soviet Union, what we now must learn to call the CIS, there are heavy industrial production units with no commercial infrastructure. They are accustomed to the State central organisation providing them with raw materials and taking away their finished products. The management responsibility has been to ensure production is not interrupted, and that quality is maintained." He looked sharply across at Lansky. "Despite what the West believes, the quality of Russian primary industrial goods is as good as, if not better than, their western equivalent. Wages, of course, across the CIS are far lower than in all Western Countries, and lower also than in many developing nations." He looked again across at Lansky. "Sounds promising, eh? Better quality, lower costs, and a big gap in the infrastructure for commercial knowledge. This is the opportunity my brother and I see in the aluminium smelter in Krayanovsk." Again, Lansky thought, why is this guy talking to me? Malenkov just stared at him, then pulled a toothpick out of his pocket and started digging at his teeth. Lansky stared back. Clearly, he was expected to comment. But the silence wore on; Lansky had spent years outfacing rugged scrap metal traders. He wasn't going to crack first. He just looked straight across the desk. Eventually, Malenkov pulled the toothpick out of his mouth, examined the end of it and flicked it disdainfully on to the floor.

"So," he resumed, "you may wonder why I am telling you this, when I have such an opportunity to make money. Is it because I like you so much?" He grinned, the crooked yellow teeth leering. "Can't be, we don't know each other. Or at least, not yet. Well, Mr Lansky, there is a small problem that we believe you may be able to help us with." He cackled. "It's called cashflow. You see, my country is rich beyond belief in raw materials, and the equal of any other in terms of industrial know-how. But to put these together, we must have money. And money is what Mother Russia is short of at this moment." Lansky still said nothing, just looking across at the Russian.

"We've looked at many people," the latter continued. "None of them really look like what we want. But you, Mr Lansky, you seem to be just the right person to join us in our little enterprise." Still Lansky stared at him. Then, finally, he responded.

"In what way, Mr Malenkov? You are proposing a metal deal, as far as I can understand. But these days, I'm a property developer. My metal trading life ended when I sold Secondary Metals. That's all in the past – another life, you might say. If you want a financier for your project, why don't you go to the banks, or Metalex or Commet?" He named the two biggest players in the international metals market.

Malenkov cackled again, showing off his stained and jagged teeth. "Ah, if it was that easy! You are a man of the world, I am sure you can guess that there are some small complications. Always in the best deals there are complications. Metals, property, everywhere things are never as straightforward as we would like."

For the first time, Lansky smiled. "That I can agree with. But still, you don't explain what you want with me."

"Let me be very frank with you." That raised a big flag in Lansky's mind. In his experience, anyone who claimed to be frank was more often than not the precise opposite. But he gestured to Malenkov to continue.

"OK, what I've told you is very simple. We have access to an aluminium smelter which can produce good quality metal at very cheap prices. We will install our own management, and we will export the finished product to the west, where we will be able to sell it at the international price." He looked hard at Lansky, the cackling jocularity gone. "At current prices, we can make around $1000 per tonne profit. Our smelter will produce, realistically, 700 000 tonnes per year. Work it out, Mr Lansky. That is a very great deal of money – more, I guess, than one can make in property dealing, even somewhere like London. But there are two issues to resolve. First, we have to buy the smelter, and ensure that we retain control. Secondly, we have to be able to secure the supply of raw materials – alumina and electric power, principally. Mr Lansky, Russia is not like the west, particularly now as the certainties of the last seventy years are being overthrown. Ownership – or rather, the concept of ownership – is not as clearcut as it is to westerners. Right now, force is an important element." He grinned thinly this time. "I think you will recognise the phrase, possession is nine-tenths of the law. In Russia today, possession is ten-tenths. And to retain possession, you have to be the strongest. The law comes from the barrel of a gun."

Chapter Three

Krayanovsk, Siberia, Russia

Summer may be the preferable season in Siberia, but there's not much in it. Deep-frozen, perma-frosted winter or sweaty, midge-ridden summer. And in the gulag cities of the Former Soviet Union, drab, utilitarian and now, as the system crumbled, teetering on the brink of anarchy, the barrel of a gun was a reality in the lives of most inhabitants. In Krayanovsk, it was very, very frequently held in the bear-like paw of Leonid Malenkov, Oleg's big brother. No-one really knew where the Malenkov brothers had come from, but there was no denying that they had rapidly become a serious force in the murky underworld created by the imploding society. Leonid was the brawn, while Oleg was the smoother face, the diplomat to handle negotiations that needed something more than violence. There were rumours of a previous KGB career, that they'd tacitly been released to run amok in central Siberia as a reward for services rendered to the strong-man Regional Governor, but nobody really knew. And with their coterie of Chechen enforcers, nobody was really going to ask too many questions.

As Oleg sat in Lansky's office, his brother, seven hours ahead, sat in the Turkish baths with three companions and half a dozen girls, in various states of undress. In the communal room next to the bath, they sat around a table strewn with the remains of their dinner, and a raft of vodka bottles, some full, some empty. Leonid was in expansive mood, confident he would soon be getting a positive report from his brother in London. He reached forward, across the table, and speared another piece of smoked fish. Chewing it noisily, he knocked back a half-tumbler of vodka to accompany it. He belched.

"We're close, my friends. In a short while we will get a phone call from my little brother Oleg to tell us he has secured our western money. Then we can begin the real business. You," he pointed vigourously over the table at one of his companions, "you will then really become the General Director of the aluminium works. And we will have our money machine."

"You're very confident, Leonid. Do we really know that this Polish Englishman will take our bait? What if he says no? Where will the money come from then?"

"I am confident. We have spoken with many people in the metal business. Lansky is a gambler, and he likes money. He also believes there is unfinished business for him in the East. He wants back from Russia what he believes was robbed from his father when the Soviets overran Poland. And he also knows the metals business, even though he has been out of it for some time. Trust me, my friends, he will bite. And it will be good for him too." Leaning back in his chair, he put his arm round the girl next to him. "Come on, we have food, we have drink." He picked up his vodka. "A toast. Mother Russia's wealth has too long been been taken by the Soviets. Let it come back to those of her people who have the courage to set hands on it!" Solemnly, they raised their glasses and drank.

The mobile phone on the table in front of Malenkov trilled its ring. Glancing at the screen, he answered it eagerly. "Oleg, how are you? Do you have good news for us?" The others watched, as he listened to the voice four and a half thousand miles away in London. His expression went from benign to puzzled to furious as they watched. "What do you mean, he's not interested? Little brother, I sent you to London to conclude a deal, not to call me with failure. You cannot let him go."

In London, Oleg protested, "Leonid, I did my best. I told him all the money he would make, that we have everything in place to make the deal work. All he has to do is put up some money and we can all profit. But he wouldn't listen. He just kept saying he was in property now, and that he has enough money. What more could I do?"

Leonid's voice rose to a roar. "I don't care what excuses you make. He must agree. Do not fail me, Oleg." And he flung the telephone across the room, where it clattered into the wall. Nervously, the girls looked at each other. Then, as Leonid sat clenching his fists, as one they stood up and ran from the room.

The other three men looked anxiously at each other. They knew Leonid's temper, and they all wanted to be somewhere else just then. But they also knew that leaving would not be tolerated. So they sat, edgily, waiting for the explosion.

"How dare he refuse? I have offered him the chance to make his fortune. He cannot say no! This operation must work." He stood up, and in his fury grabbed the edge of the table and upturned it, spilling the food and drink across the floor. He stormed through to the cold plunge pool, and flung himself into the ice-cold water, still muttering to himself.

Back in London, Oleg paced his hotel room nervously. After the phone had gone dead when his brother had hurled it at the wall, he had begun to realise quite what a problem he had. He couldn't simply let it go; his brother had invested all his interests in this project. This was the chance to move away from simple extortion and murder. This was to be how the

Malenkov brothers were to become businessmen, the acceptable face of Russia. If he failed to get Lansky involved – or more correctly, Lansky's money – then, brother or not, Leonid would exact a terrible price for failure. Oleg knew his brother: he'd made up his mind that this scheme would work, and nothing would deflect him from his purpose. Not for the first time in his life, Oleg felt the cold draft of fear when he thought of his brother's temper. All their lives, Oleg had had to be the mediator, the one to whom it fell to calm Leonid down. But when Oleg himself was the target – unconsciously, he rubbed his left shoulder. Under the expensive western shirt, the scarred flesh bore testimony to a terrible beating Leonid had given him at the age of fifteen, for failing to collect protection money from a bankrupt trader. It hadn't interested Leonid that the man couldn't pay – as far as he was concerned, he'd given Oleg his instructions, and he expected them to be fulfilled. And if he failed now, it would be worse, far worse. Could he try Lansky again? The man had seemed certain that he wasn't interested in the proposal; how could Oleg persuade him to change his mind?

The ice-cold water of the plunge pool seemed to be cooling Leonid down. He hauled himself out, and stripped off his soaking wet clothes. Wrapping a towel round his hairy body, he stalked back into the other room, where the staff were furiously clearing the mess he had made overturning the table. In fact, the temper was a device, a way of reminding the world of the violence just under the surface. Leonid had grown up in a rough school. An alcoholic father, a weak mother who relied on him to protect the family. He'd learned early on that violence gained him respect, and he could use it to get what he wanted. It had served him well over the years, and just like this evening, always provided a refuge when things didn't immediately go his way. He knew the fear his brother would be feeling, and he still trusted him to achieve his target. Leonid stooped down and picked up a miraculously unbroken vodka bottle. Cracking the seal, he downed a healthy gulp. Time enough tomorrow to see what little brother could do. He went looking for the girls.

Chapter Four

Mayfair, London

Victor Lansky was no fool. He'd turned Oleg Malenkov down, but he knew that wasn't the end of the story. After the Russian had left his office, he sat staring at the wall for a while. The proposal *was* interesting: a potential profit of the size Malenkov had indicated would be of interest to any businessman. It was obviously dubious; if not, the Malenkovs could have gone to any major metal miner or producer, who would have loved it. But just *how* dubious was it? Time to speak to a specialist. Lansky reached out his hand to the phone, and dialled the familiar old Commet number. His friend Mack McKee may be dead, but there were others there who could help him. "Rory Davis, please," he asked the receptionist who answered the phone. And then, when he had been put through, "Rory, hi, it's Victor Lansky. Formerly Secondary Metals, if you remember."

"Yeah, sure I remember Secondary Metals. How are you?"

"I'm good, Rory. I think the last time we met was at Mack's funeral, right?"

"Yes. A lot of things have changed since then. But what can I do for you? I thought you were right out of metals these days, and making a fortune in property."

Lansky laughed. "I'm not sure about a fortune, but life has been pretty good since we sold out of Secondary. But look, I've been approached with a metal deal that on the surface sounds interesting. I'd like to pick your brains, if I may."

"Of course, Victor. If I can be of any help, I'd be delighted. Do you want to talk on the phone, or should we meet?"

"Can I invite you for dinner some time this week?"

They settled on a date a couple of days ahead, and Lansky hung up, leaving Davis somewhat puzzled.

The death of Mack McKee had left Commet in something of a mess. The big man had been at the centre of the company and its growth for many years, and had been an astute enough corporate politician, despite his buccaneering air, to ensure that there were no obvious rivals to him. The profits from the Kanagi affair had been good, but in the aftermath, with no leader to point the next direction, the company had blundered on with no real dynamic. Rory Davis, fifteen years McKee's junior, had been appointed Managing Director by the Luxemburg parent, more because he at least understood the way the business ran than because they saw him as a good corporate leader. From Davis' point of view, he would rather have remained as the head trader, looking after the metal dealing books, than to have to shoulder all McKee's various responsibilities. Still, he was doing the best he could in the circumstances, but Commet was not in truth the force it had been with McKee at the helm. So as he stepped out of the cab outside the Mayfair restaurant Lansky had chosen, Davis was intrigued but also sceptical of what the Pole wanted. The last thing he needed as he tried to stabilise Commet under his leadership was one of McKee's cronies coming back to haunt him with a bright idea. The restaurant was chic, discreet and full of the well-heeled of London. The maitre d' led him across to the table where Lansky was already seated, waiting for him.

"Rory, how are you," said Lansky, getting to his feet and shaking Davis by the hand. "Thanks for taking the time out to come and see me, after my somewhat elliptical approach. It may be a few years, but you haven't changed a bit." True, but it was a bit of a back-handed comment; Davis had lost his hair at an early age, and had always looked older than his years. Time was catching up.

Davis smiled. "It's always a pleasure Victor."

They sat down at the table, and ordered some drinks, as the waiter handed them the menus.

"Look, Rory, why don't we get the ordering out of the way first, and then I can give you an idea of what I wanted to talk about."

"Sounds good to me."

That done, Lansky leaned back in his chair.

"So, I guess after all this time it was a bit of a surprise to hear from me?"

"Yeah, it was. I'd assumed you were right out of the metals business after selling Secondary. I mean, I know you and Mack still used to meet from time to time, but I always thought that was just personal friendship, nothing to do with Commet."

"Yeah, you're right. Mack and I got to be good friends over the years, but my activities on the LME stopped once Secondary was gone." He grinned. "I get my gambling kicks from punting properties these days, not metals. But, actually, I do want to pick your brains on a matter relating to metals." He continued, as Davis looked across at him quizzically, "How much do you know about the metals business in Russia? Or I guess we should say the CIS?"

Davis paused reflectively for a moment. "That's an interesting question, and very much up to the minute in the metals market. Everybody's very keen on the potential of huge money out of Russia, just because they're such a big producer, particularly of aluminium and nickel, and the old

Soviet infrastructure seems to be just imploding. So the thinking is, that creates some pretty interesting opportunities, for those who are brave enough to take them. I guess in broad terms, there is a great chance of making a lot of money, but in order to do it, you've got to put in some cash investment first, and your problem is that the security for that cash is pretty dubious. So I guess you've got to be sure of your relationship with your local partner." He made a dismissive gesture with his hands, "Without a local partner, forget it. You'd just hand over your money and never see it again. And the problem, of course, is that your local partner is going to have to be a gangster, otherwise he won't have the strength to protect the investment." He grinned. "Bit like a horse race – choose your runner, put the bet on and then go to wait and see what happens at the finishing post."

"Interesting. And yet you do think there is a serious profit potential there. Who's taking the gamble right now? Are you guys involved, or Metalex?"

"Metalex have always been very strong with the old State authorities, and that's stood them in a pretty good position in the nickel business, where the handover to private owners has actually gone pretty smoothly and a lot of the commercial management are still in place. But the big money is in aluminium – or it should be – and that's a tough one. I know there are a fair number of Western companies who will deliver raw materials to the smelters in return for a simultaneous release of finished metal at a recognised port, under the control of a Western freight agent, but the problem with that is that it's an ad hoc business, each deal on a case-by-case basis. The one nobody's really cracked yet is how to set up a long-term deal, to guarantee a consistent supply of metal. If you could do that, you could probably make a thousand dollars a tonne, just by delivering it to an LME warehouse. More, if you sell directly to end consumers in Europe or the US. And no, up to now we're not involved, although it's a hot topic, and keeps coming up at management meetings over in Luxemburg. They want to be involved, they know they have to be involved, but it's tough for a public company to deal with that kind of people. If it works, the shareholders would love it, but if it doesn't, somebody at the top would be paying with their head." He smiled across at Lansky. "That kind of concentrates the corporate mind."

Lansky smiled back. "Yes, I see the problem. But why haven't Metalex tried? They're a private company, so it should be easier to handle." Metalex were the biggest and most powerful of the metal trading companies; privately-owned and secretive, they were based in Vienna in Austria, a jurisdiction which gave them the opportunity to keep their own secrets to themselves, rather more so than would have been the case in London or New York. And as Davis had remarked, they had traditionally been close to the old Soviet masters of Russia's mineral wealth.

"Well," said Davis, "rumour is that they've been trying to get involved, but so far they haven't seen the right combination of assets and people to give them the confidence to make the investment. And, as I said, they're pretty happy with the nickel position." He looked quizzically across the table at Lansky. "But why the interest, Victor? You're a property man these days. Surely you're not thinking of getting back into metals? And in Russia? Can't property create enough problems to keep you happy?"

Lansky smiled. "You're right, of course. I made a stack of money from my scrap business, and I've made that stack bigger through the property investments. And yes, on the surface, getting involved in Russia right now would seem to be absurd. But still....I've received an approach which I think I need to think about, rather than just reject out of hand. Don't forget, my family are from the east, and the Russians stole everything in 1945. I've got a lot of money back, but if I could get something out of Russia, that would be a kind of poetic justice, wouldn't it?" He held up a hand to stop Davis interrupting, and went on, "And before you tell me, I know that's sentimental claptrap. If I go into any deal, it will be on a solid business basis before I invest a single dollar."

Davis was beginning to be interested. "What's the approach, Victor? I mean, who are they, and what are they actually suggesting?"

"Basically, money up front, in return for which I get to be a joint owner with them in the Krayanovsk aluminium smelter. Sounds good, huh? But there are rather a lot of added problems, chief amongst them being the fact that under current Russian law, foreigners are not allowed direct ownership of Russian assets. So anything anybody does has to be done at a hidden level – which implies a huge amount of trust in one's Russian partners."

Davis interrupted. "So actually, what you're saying is that you give them money to enable them to run the smelter, in return for which they give you a stake in the plant – but only you and they know you own that stake? Sounds very dubious to me." He grinned. "Just the kind of deal Mack would have loved. But who are your Russians? Are they really in a position to offer anything solid?"

"As yet, I don't know. I'm getting some research done, but I'm just trying to get some background on the overall business before I go back to them. Obviously, I just said no to the initial approach, but the reaction I got makes me certain they'll be back. I don't know why, but they seem to see me as a good prospect. What are they like? I guess they're some sort of gangsters, so really the question will be whether they have the strength to keep hold of what they've got. I'm not under the illusion these are nice people, Rory, but you can't deny the fragmentation of the Soviet Union is creating some good opportunities. Look, you know as well as I do that some of the scrappies I used to deal with are as dubious as hell, so it wouldn't exactly be a first to mix with the dark side."

"That's true, but that particular dark side was to do with not paying taxes, or delivering lower quality than the contracts wanted. This one is probably more to do with killing people, if what we hear about Russia is even only half true. Do you really want to get involved in that?"

Lansky looked at Davis for a moment before answering. The truth was that the folk memory ingrained in him as a Pole meant that he really didn't care if Russians were getting killed. In fact, it was almost more of a positive. Best not get into that here, though. "That's why I'm investigating them a bit. I need to know exactly who and what they are. What I want you to help me with is whether you think it's realistic to envisage moving around 700 000 tonnes a year into the Western market?"

Davies sat back in his chair and twirled the stem of his wine glass while he thought for a moment. "Well," he said, "it's a big quantity and it depends what you want to achieve. Your easiest bet would be simply to sell it on the LME and then make deliveries straight into the LME warehouses. That way you've got less hassle, because you'll get paid in two days – normal LME contract – and you won't have to worry about the financial status of the customer. The LME isn't going to go bust, so you're sure of your money. On the other hand, the more you put into the warehouses, the more people will perceive a surplus of metal, and the price will go down. And if you want to be in it for the real long-term, then maybe you want to build up supply relationships with consumers – people who really use the stuff – 'cos that will give you continuity. They'll pay a premium to the basic LME price, as well. So, you have to balance it up: security and immediate payment from the LME, or a long-tem business, with higher prices but extra credit risks. If it were me, I'd go the LME route, but that's partly because that's where I'm comfortable. If you want to get into the genuine physical supply business, then you're competing with the likes of Metalex and you probably need a much bigger corporate structure to handle it. More money in it long-term, but let's face it, anything in Russia, with gangsters, probably has a limited life anyway, so what is long-term?"

Lansky leant forward and rested his elbows on the table. "Ye-es," he said, pensively, "I suppose in anything like this it's important to know what your way out is when it gets too rough. Don't want to end up like Mack – sorry, that was in bad taste"

"Yeah, but it's a valid point. We don't really know what happened to Mack, but a lot of people think it wasn't an accident. For sure he was mixed up in something fairly unsavoury with Phil Harris, Jamie Edwards and the Japanese, but the court case never really got to the bottom of it. Phil and Jamie have sure got a lot of money, though. I still see Jamie occasionally when he's over in London. My guess is just what you said – Mack should have got out earlier, but he was chasing the last buck."

Lansky's eyes sharpened again. "One thing, Rory, that I should have said before; all this conversation stays strictly between us. Not for repetition. To anybody."

"Of course, that goes without saying. But look, if you want to move forward, let me know if there's anything we can do to help. As I said, Commet won't get involved directly with the Russians right now, but with someone we know and trust in the middle, maybe that's a way in for us."

"OK. I'm not sure what I'm going to do yet, but if there's anything for you, I'll certainly be in touch. And thanks for the help this evening."

"That's OK. Always a pleasure to meet an old customer. You should come by the office next time. I'm sure some of the boys would like to say hello."

And the conversation drifted off into reminiscences of the old days and the old contacts. At the end of the evening, though, as Lansky strolled back the few streets to his apartment in Mayfair, he felt he'd made some progress. True, he hadn't come to any decision, but talking things over with Davis had focussed some things in his mind.

Chapter Five

Mayfair, London

Oleg Malenkov had had an uncomfortable few days. Since Leonid's outburst over the phone, the only communication he'd had had been a brusque comment from one of the henchman to the effect that it would be wise for him not to come back to Siberia until he'd got Lansky's agreement to their proposal. He would have been happier had he known that Lansky was making enquiries about the deal, but having heard nothing from the Pole himself, he'd spent most of his time in his hotel bar in front of a bottle of vodka, feeling sorry for himself. He really didn't know how to proceed. This Western society was clearly different from Russia, and although Leonid trusted him as the smooth face of the Malenkov empire, in an environment where he couldn't resort to threats when persuasion didn't get what he wanted, he was somewhat adrift. Having failed so far, what he really wanted to do was to march into Lansky's office with a couple of Chechen heavies and simply tell the man what he was to do. That's how it worked in Krayanovsk, but Oleg understood that it wouldn't in London. That option gone, he was at a loss as to how to proceed. He took another deep swig at his glass, as the mobile phone in his pocket began to ring. Flipping it open, "Hello?" he said into the mouthpiece. Then, "Mr. Lansky, what can I do for you?"

"Mr. Malenkov", came the voice at the other end, "I find that perhaps I have some more questions to ask you concerning your proposal. Do you think we could have another meeting?"

For Oleg, it was his prayers answered. He had the sense to understand that he should sober up before seeing Lansky, so proposed a time two days hence. He knew this time he had to conclude the deal, otherwise Leonid's vengeance would be vicious. The Gods had offered him a second chance; this time he had to be sure to take it.

As he put the phone down, Lansky was still not sure of what he wanted to do. The conversation with Rory Davis had helped focus his mind on how profitable it could be. On the other hand, though, he was acutely aware that Davis had been right, there was a major difference between the peccadilloes of the scrappies he used to deal with and the serious lawlessness of the Malenkovs. He'd had a quiet word with some acquaintances who were involved in development in the growing Moscow property market, and the reports had been universally bleak.

The Malenkovs had a reputation for savage violence in pursuit of their aims, and for ruling their fiefdom with a rod of iron. They controlled large parts of the life of Krayanovsk, and there was a feeling amongst the informants that it was only a matter of time before they started taking over industries. That was the bit that interested Lansky; it implied some sort of move towards legitimacy. He tried – not altogether successfully – to convince himself that they were just like the robber barons of 19th century America, who had metamorphosed into the higher echelons of society as they had divorced themselves from their dubious backgrounds. Would he not just be involved in a similar development? But his thoughts always came back to the violence. True, those who suffered were Russians, which mitigated it in his eyes. But could the Malenkovs be controlled? Or would the violence just spread to engulf the whole business? And always, back to the same question: why had they come to him?

Oleg wasn't going to make any mistakes this time. He'd had a long phone conversation with his brother, finally convincing him that threats would not work here in the West; they had to negotiate, to be prepared to take time and persuasion to achieve what they wanted. He had made sure that this time, Leonid was not going to demand instant success, he'd persuaded him that it was going to take much more explanation of the circumstances. Lansky would only play if he knew what he was getting into. The strong-arm technique of raising investment in Krayanovsk – "give us some money, we'll return more to you in the future, or we'll shoot you" – was not going to work in London. He had permission from Leonid to describe how they intended the business would work, and what role it was envisaged Lansky would take. It was a bright September day, and Oleg felt he was almost like a western investment banker, as he walked down Mount Street in his smart suit, carrying his polished Gucci briefcase. He was going to a business meeting, to pitch an investment opportunity without a gun lurking just off centre stage. It was a strange new feeling.

This time, when he got into Lansky's office, there was no lounging back in the chair, no picking of the teeth. He sat upright, and although there was nothing he could do to change his overall appearance, he'd taken the trouble to be clean-shaven; this time, the expensive clothes didn't look so out of place.

"So, Mr Lansky", he began, "you have been kind enough to give me another opportunity to explain our project in Siberia and how it could be of interest to you. I thank you for your kindness in taking the time to see me again. I have with me" – he indicated his briefcase – "some description of the plant and some basic figures. Would you like to begin by looking at those?"

Lansky was surprised at the change in presentation and demeanour, but was happy to let the other begin his explanation. "No. I would rather we had first a discussion of why you believe this project to be of interest to me, and also of some of the background of your …. enterprise." Lansky smiled to himself; enterprise was probably a more neutral, less emotive, word than activities would have been. "Before we get into any specifics of the actual smelter itself, or the way the metal is going to be moved into the western market, I want to get some better sort of feel for the people involved, for how you think I may fit in with them. You understand? I only want to look at the financials if I am confident there is a realistic base to move forward."

"I understand perfectly, Mr Lansky. I believe last time I was here, I gave you some idea of how things in my country are changing. Very well. I recap a little here. The problem Russia has is access to capital. Investors are exceedingly cautious about risking their money in such a situation. In truth, we are looking into the unknown, because the world has never before seen a powerful, industrialised nation effectively imploding. I believe there is a saying in English – 'nature abhors a vacuum'." Lansky nodded his understanding. "Well, I believe this is what we are seeing in Russia. There is a vacuum where the law and the normal behaviour of civilised society should be. Into that vacuum are being drawn entrepreneurs, people like my brother and me, who can see the way to opening society to something more like the capitalism of the West, where success does not depend upon Party membership, but rather upon one's own efforts. While we can see this way forward, we cannot be independent, because we do not have the money to push forward our industrial development. For that money, we have to look outside Russia. The first step in our plans for development is to buy industrial assets from the Russian state, which no longer has the money or the appetite to own them. Look, Russian industry was a servant to military necessity for many years; now, the government no longer has the same military requirements, and they are prepared to sell off these assets to selected buyers, at attractive prices." He smiled thinly. "Frankly put, my country is bankrupt, and they don't know how to get enough money to feed the people, except by selling state factories at knock-down prices to those whom they believe have the strength to develop those assets. It's a high-risk policy, but truly, they have no alternative if they want to avoid a military coup – without money to feed the people, that would be the only feasible solution. So we need to buy factories from the government. You may assume the Malenkovs are amongst those on whom the government will look favourably in the asset auctions. We need not discuss now why that is the case – time enough for that later, if you wish." Lansky made a mental note to raise that subject again; it was precisely in the area he wanted to understand. Oleg went on. "So, my brother and I could probably raise the money we need within Russia, but that would still leave us with a problem. The products of our factories will need to be exported to the west, and for that we need western partners." He smiled again. "We are not naïve enough to believe we can expect western companies to make purchases direct from Russians except at heavily discounted prices. So, in order to make it more interesting for our western partner, we intend to offer them the opportunity to be part of the consortium which buys the factories. That way, they will also benefit from the advantageous price we get from the government. And it will give us a much more secure relationship with our customers. We do not believe any of the other Russian groups preparing to buy assets have thought of this partnership aspect." He sat back in his chair, and looked across at Lansky. "That is the outline of our proposal to you. Obviously, there are many details, but this is the principal of our scheme." He looked expectantly.

Lansky leant forward; the bright halo of sunlight through the window behind him made it difficult for Oleg to distinguish any expression on his face. "That's all very interesting, Mr Malenkov, and I can see that there may well be some basis for further discussion. Although I'm no longer in the metals business, I can still recognise a good opportunity when it's put in front of me. But before that, perhaps you would give me some more background on your - consortium, I believe you called it. You see, I have a problem. I am not naïve either, so I have made some enquires into you and your brother, and into the viability of the business you are proposing. If we take that first, then I can see a good opportunity, for me or for another western partner. For sure, the West needs the product of the Krayanovsk smelter, and provided the supply is secure, it will not be a difficult task to make the sales. That much is clear to me. But – and I hope you won't mind if I speak frankly" – Malenkov nodded him to continue – "you and your brother have a certain reputation for murky activities. There are accusations that you are part of the Russian mafia, that your present state of strength in your region is based on violence and the proceeds of violence. In short, you have got to where you are by criminal activities." He held up his hands towards Malenkov. "You understand I am not making any accusations myself, I am just suggesting to you what is said generally about you."

Oleg looked hard at him before replying. "Mr Lansky, please try to imagine the situation in Russia right now. All of the certainties of our former lives have been swept away. The Soviet era may not have been a time of plenty for most of my countrymen, but it was a time of certainty. Contrary to what many in the west believe, at least since the demise of Stalin the people have always had enough to eat. Many jobs may have seemed ridiculous overmanning to western eyes, but unemployment was low. It wasn't a great life, but it was a relatively secure one. It was only when the military spending ballooned so enormously that shortages began, and that, together with the Afghan war, drove the country to bankruptcy." He smiled thinly. "Maybe you are surprised, Mr Lansky, that a man you see as a common gangster understands the how and the why of the Soviet collapse, maybe better than some of your western commentators. Anyway, after the futile attempts to match Reagan's spending on weapons, the writing was on the wall for the Soviet system. There was no longer any money to support it. That is from where came the vacuum I spoke of earlier. Have you any concept of what happens when a society breaks down entirely?" Lansky thought back to the stories he'd heard from his relatives of Poland in the immediate aftermath of its ravaging, first by Germany and then by Russia. That must have been a society in meltdown. Oleg continued. "So in that environment, only the strong will survive. We had to grab all the chances we saw. Everybody was doing it, and to keep your head above water, maybe sometimes you had to do things you didn't really like." As he had agreed with his brother, Oleg was using any means of persuasion he could to achieve their purpose. Westerners tended to be squeamish about the business methods used by the Malenkovs and their henchmen, so Oleg was prepared to spin this tale of how hardship had driven them to do things they didn't like. In truth, they had an almost total disregard for the life of anyone who got in their way. "So we had to resort to the law of the jungle to survive and to build our business. But now, we are in a position to move into bigger, industrial activities. Let's be frank with each other. We have not been angels, but many of the stories you have heard are exaggerated. And anyway, we are asking you to join us in the next phase, not to become part of our past." He reached down for his briefcase. "I think it is probably time to consider the concrete deal we are looking at."

"OK, we can talk about specifics." Lansky didn't really believe all that Oleg had been telling him, but he was prepared to let himself be persuaded. At least for the moment. "But in fact, I have one more question first. I understand that under current Russian law, it is not possible for foreigners to own Russian assets. This is to ensure that the buyers of industry in the auctions will be Russian, to prevent western companies simply buying Russia at a knockdown price. If that is the case, how would the partnership you propose work? It seems to me that the overseas partner would be making what is technically an illegal investment."

"*Technically*, you are correct. However, we believe we have a way around this annoyance. I will come to that in a moment." He drew a sheaf of papers out of his briefcase. "You can see from here" – he pointed to various lines on the top copy – "that assuming our labour costs remain the same, and that we can buy raw materials at international market prices, then we can estimate a profit of approximately one thousand US dollars per tonne of aluminium. The other variable costs are of course power and transportation from Krayanovsk to the port of export, probably St Petersburg. As we can discuss at a future time, we have some plans which will also enable us to fix these costs, thus guaranteeing our profit margin. The Krayanovsk smelter has a practical annual production capacity of 700 000 tonnes, so the profit margin we expect is seven hundred million dollars per year, or around fifty-eight million dollars per month. This is serious money, Mr Lansky. And to buy this income will not cost that much. Our information is that the government will sell this factory for one hundred million dollars – approximately two months profit. Not a bad deal, I think you will agree."

Lansky – like everybody else - had heard the rumours of how Russia was being raped senseless by its own government to pay for the political support of the strong-arm gangs, but this took his breath away. Cash in hand and let the future of the country go screw. And tendentious arguments about paying for food stacked up only until the numbers became clear. Another thought came uninvited into his mind: how much of the money being raised in these asset sales would find its way into the personal bank accounts of the present ruling elite, rather than the State Treasury? Well, corruption was everywhere; best not follow that thought for now. But the staggering numbers were interesting. Lansky was a rich man; he'd made several millions from Secondary Metals, and those millions had been multiplied by his successful property ventures. But a decent share of $58 million a month, on an ongoing basis, that was a different league. That would put him near the top of the tree. True, some Russians were going to be killed – almost for sure – to get that money. Sad, but there you go, he thought to himself. He was beginning to warm to the whole scheme.

"And so what participation would you anticipate that I might have in this venture? Assuming I'm interested," he added hurriedly, not wanting the Russian to take him for an easy mark.

"We envisage a fifty/fifty joint venture between you and us. The cost of the smelter will be, as I said, one hundred million US dollars. We do not expect initially to have to add any working capital, since we will be generating so much free cash that we can be self-financing from the beginning. We also recognise that there is an extra risk for you, as you are a foreigner and will have to rely on us to protect the investment internally, so we would propose that you actually contribute forty million dollars to pay for your fifty percent share. This is what you would pay. In return, you would earn half of the income of the factory – as I said before, fifty-eight million per month, so your share would be twenty-nine million every month. Of course, you would also have to undertake to source the necessary raw materials in the international market, and to sell the monthly production quota. So it will be an investment which imposes considerable demands on your time." He grinned again. "Actually, I guess it will be a full-time job."

"Yes, I think it would be. But tell me, what exactly do you mean by 'protecting the investment internally'? You really mean hiding it from the authorities, don't you?"

For a split second the smile slipped, and the old Oleg was back. But he forced himself again, and came back, politely. "In a way, that is what I mean. We're all men of the world; you know as well as I do, because you mentioned it earlier, that strictly you can't own any part of the plant. When the Malenkov brothers buy something, they make very sure nobody can take it away from them. So while we protect our own interests, we will also be protecting yours. We will rely on each other. We'll be partners. We help each other. You understand?"

Lansky understood only too well. It wasn't just an investment, it was moving into the whole murky Malenkov circle. If the stories were true, people got killed for opposing the brothers. Still, he would stay in the comfort and relative safety of London, wouldn't he? Or at least, in the west. Obviously, the brothers expected him to take the lead in negotiating supply contracts for raw materials, but that would mean dealing with reputable western mining companies, in London or Sydney or New York. The grubby side, the dangerous side, would remain the fiefdom of the Malenkovs in their Siberian stronghold. He wouldn't be too directly involved in the Russian part of the venture. That comforting thought lasted only until Oleg's next remark.

"So, I think the next step to help you decide, if you are still interested, would be a visit to the smelter, so you can see for yourself that it exists, and is functioning. That would also give you the chance to meet my brother, and some of our colleagues."

Chapter Six

Autumn 1994

Luton Airport, London

Lansky felt some trepidation as he parked his Porsche in the car park labelled for clients of Jetways Aviation, next to the private aviation terminal at Luton Airport. In one sense, he felt he was being bounced into the trip to Siberia; at their last meeting, he had still not committed himself to the Malenkovs' project. On the other hand, without meeting Leonid and seeing the smelter with his own eyes, he wouldn't be able to make up his mind. He wasn't fooling himself; he was prepared for the elder Malenkov brother to be a rough prospect. But then, for $29 million a month, he could put up with a little unpleasantness. His real concern was to be sure he would be able to distance himself sufficiently from the less salubrious activities of his putative new partners.

Flying in private jets is a liberating experience, compared with the cattle-truck crush of scheduled airlines, even in first class. In the Jetways reception lounge he was met by a smiling, smartly-uniformed hostess, who took away his overnight case and passport, and in return brought him a glass of champagne and a copy of the Financial Times and Country Life magazine. "The pilot will be here in a couple of minutes, to introduce himself," she said. "The rest of the crew are just checking over the inside of the aircraft, and then they'll be ready for you to board. It's just you from here, and then you're picking up another two passengers in Moscow when you refuel. That's right, isn't it? No last-minute change of plans?"

"No, that's absolutely right. The others had some things to take care of in Moscow, so they went over there at the weekend. We pick them up, and then it's on to Krayanovsk. First time I've been to Siberia, actually. I'm not quite sure what to expect."

The hostess smiled again, reassuringly. "The pilot and co-pilot have both been there before, so you'll have no worries on that score. But I think it's a new one for the cabin crew. We're getting more and more Russian business these days, getting to be almost as big as the Gulf, which used to be our bread and butter." She laughed. "All the Sheikhs seem to have their own planes these days. No need for us."

Lansky smiled back at her. "As long as the Russians don't get too rich, then….."

No walking down endless corridors to board the plane; ten minutes later, after a brief welcome from the pilot, a Mercedes limo pulled up to the door to take Lansky the five hundred yards across the tarmac to where the aircraft was waiting. It was an HS 125 executive jet, and another smiling hostess was waiting at the top of the stairs to welcome him.

"Mr Lansky, it's a pleasure to have you on board. You're the only passenger today, as you know, so please feel free to make yourself at home. Our pilot, Captain Cork, whom you met earlier, expects to be ready to go in about fifteen minutes, so just settle down and wait for take-off. Can I bring you a glass of champagne?"

Looking around him, Lansky saw seven leather-covered seats, and another hostess, red-headed, standing smiling in front of the cockpit door. As he sat down in the middle seat on the left-hand side, the first girl appeared at his elbow with his drink. "There you are, Mr Lansky. My name's Jackie, by the way, and this is my colleague Zoe. Anything you want during the flight, just ask either of us."

The pilot's voice came over the intercom. "Good afternoon, Mr Lansky. This is the Captain, Nick Cork, speaking. We're just finalising our checks prior to starting up the engines. Should be just a few minutes, and then we have clearance for immediate take-off. Flight time to Moscow Sheremetyevo should be about five hours, and then we'll have a brief stop for refuelling and to pick up your colleagues; after that we'll be on our final leg to Krayanovsk. Settle back and enjoy the flight. I'm sure Jackie and Zoe will do everything they can to make your flight a pleasure." Jackie appeared again, holding a bottle of champagne. "Can I top you up?"

"Please. But don't I have to surrender my glass for take off?"

The hostess laughed. "We don't need to bother about the conventions of public transport on here. Just hold on to it so it doesn't fly across the cabin, and you'll be fine."

Although his business had made him a rich man, this was Lansky's first experience of private jets; he was already sold on the concept, even before they taxied out onto the runway, and then, with a roar of power, the little plane lifted off into the autumn sunlight.

Unfortunately, even the smooth Jetways operation couldn't do anything about the chaos of Moscow's Sheremetyevo airport when the jet touched down in the middle of the night. The Russians had no concerns about keeping down night-time noise pollution, and with flights operating all through the night to myriad domestic destinations, the terminal building was heaving as Lansky was pushed and jostled in the queue for immigration control. He was a well-travelled man, but this was an eye-opener for him. The departures board had names he'd barely heard of – Dushanbe, Igarka, Norilsk, and long lists of others, in Roman letters as well as Cyrillic. The people crowding for the departure gates were carrying everything from boxes of electrical goods to cages of live chickens. The noise was indescribable, and although fascinated by the sight of such humanity on the move, Lansky was relieved when he finally fought his way through to the private aviation lounge. There, sitting waiting to greet him, was Oleg Malenkov, with a large, broad-shouldered, bullet-headed man in a double-breasted suit at his side.

"Victor, my friend, it is good to see you again. How was the flight from London? Our friends from Jetways took good care of you?" He gestured to the man next to him. "This is Georgi, one of our colleagues from Krayanovsk who has been helping me with some business in Moscow this week. He will be joining us on the flight home."

Georgi put out his hand to shake Lansky's. "Welcome," he said, in a heavily accented voice. "I hope you enjoy your visit."

Lansky smiled back. "Thank you. I hope it will be rewarding."

"OK," said Malenkov, "so the aeroplane should be ready again in around one hour, when they have finished formalities and refuelled. Until then, we must wait here. We can have some food if you wish, or some drinks?"

"I'm fine, thanks. The aircrew kept me well-stocked with food and drinks all the way. What time of day will we arrive in Krayanovsk?"

"Around nine in the morning. It's three hours ahead of Moscow, and the flight will last around five and a half hours." Malenkov grinned. "So that will give you a chance to get some sleep. When we land, the car will take you directly to the hotel, so you can have a shower and so on. My brother Leonid will come at about midday and we will have some lunch, then we can all get to know each other a bit more. The tour of the plant and meeting with the management will be tomorrow."

Lansky settled back into the armchair, grateful for the rest. Another five and a half hours on the aeroplane wasn't really what he wanted, but hopefully he would sleep. Sitting opposite him, Georgi leaned forward to pick up the drink from the low table in front of him. As he did so, his double-breasted suit jacket flapped half open; Lansky was shocked to see the grip of a pistol sticking out of a shoulder-holster under the jacket. His old doubts about the Malenkovs surfaced again. Maybe the most sensible course would be to stand up now, and walk back through the lounge door and find a flight straight back to London. But then, the hundreds of millions of dollars………no, he was a big boy. He'd go ahead for the moment, everybody knew business in Russia was a wild game. He could always back out later, if he needed to. He smiled to himself. At least the gun wasn't aimed at him. Oleg caught the smile.

"You find something funny, my friend," he asked?

"Not really. I was just thinking how odd it was to be sitting here at midnight in Moscow airport, heading for a place I had never heard of until a few weeks ago. I'm just a London property developer."

"Ah, yes. Well, we hope Krayanovsk will soon be like a second home to you. And soon you will be a great industrialist, not a developer."

"Let's hope it all works out how we want. It would be a long way to go for nothing."

They lapsed into silence, Oleg and Georgi concentrating on the drinks in front of them, and Lansky closed his eyes.

He must have dozed off, because the next thing he knew was a hostess gently touching his shoulder.

"Time to go," she said, and he saw Oleg and Georgi standing by the door. I wonder how Georgi gets his toy through security, Lansky thought to himself. Naïve, he realised a few moments later. When they got to the scanner, Georgi simply said something in Russian to the security man, and walked calmly round the outside of the machine. Oleg and Lansky were ushered through the right way, and then they were all walking down the passage and on to the plane.

The runway lights flashed past, and then the little jet eased into the air again. Lansky looked across at his fellow-passengers. The thick-set, heavy Malenkov, and the muscular, shaven-headed Georgi. A Russian Mafioso and one of his gunmen. He shook his head to himself, and wondered what he was doing. He didn't need any more money, he certainly didn't need to be associated with these guys, but it kept coming back to the deal, and what it could mean. He dozed fitfully for an hour or so, then finally dropped off to sleep.

When he awoke around three hours later, the cabin crew were serving breakfast to the two Russians. Seeing he was awake, the red-headed stewardess came over to him. "Good morning, Mr Lansky," she said brightly. "Welcome to Siberia. If you look through the window, you'll see it's as empty and snowy as the brochures told you." She beamed at him. "What can we get you for breakfast? Your companions" – she gestured towards the two Russians – "are having scrambled eggs and smoked salmon. But I could do you something else if you would prefer it."

"No, that sounds good. Just give me a few minutes to wake up properly."

"Sure. Fifteen minutes, while you freshen up?"

"Perfect."

Lansky was surprised how wide-awake he felt, as he was tucking into his breakfast, twenty minutes later. The view through the window was as the girl had said; from a clear sky, he could see the empty white waste rolling away in all directions. Just then, the captain's voice came over the PA system.

"Good morning, gentlemen, this is Nick Cork again. I hope you had the chance to grab a few hours sleep, and are now awake for the beautiful morning outside. However, enjoy it while you can. We shall shortly run into some cloud, and the forecast we're getting for our arrival at Krayanovsk is for wind and light snowfall, so not a particularly welcoming weather pattern. The headwind has been stronger than forecast, so we still have about an hour and a half left to run. But we should be fine for a straight-in approach and landing. Krayanovsk is not a particularly busy airport, so we don't expect any air traffic delays. Sit back and enjoy your breakfast."

Sure enough, within half an hour the aeroplane was flying through thick cloud, and the changing engine note as the pilot throttled back to begin his approach was all that warned them they had almost arrived. Malenkov came and sat in the seat next to Lansky.

"Victor, I left you to sleep, but now there are some things we should talk about before we land and meet Leonid, my brother. First, just so you know, the airport at Krayanovsk is about 45 minutes drive from the town." He smiled thinly. "It was formerly a Soviet airbase, and the authorities wanted to keep the military at some distance from the workforce of the town. Our masters did not want the different parts of the military/industrial complex to meet too much. Leonid himself will not be at the airport to meet us, but a car will take you to the hotel where we have reserved a room for you." He smiled again. "You must understand that the hotel is not London five star standard; in fact, it is quite basic. But we own it, and we have told them you should have a good room, the best they have. Obviously, you pay nothing. After around one hour, to give you time to shower and change and so on, Leonid and I shall come to the hotel with some of our associates, and we will have lunch and some discussion. After lunch, we will not go to the plant, but maybe just have meetings with some management people. This evening, we will have a dinner and a visit to the Turkish bath. I guess you have not experienced a Russian Turkish bath. You will find it very relaxing, especially after the long travelling you have done. Tomorrow, we will go out to the plant, for a good tour, and then you will meet quite a number of our associates. Over the next days, you will get to know all the important ones of them. They have different roles in our organisation; some of them will be part of the aluminium business, and obviously these ones you should begin to get to know. Others have more of a role in security, and although part of their job will involve protecting your investment" – he held up his hand before Lansky could interrupt – "assuming you decide to make it: I know you have still to make the decision – but, anyway, you will understand that their expertise is different. What I am saying, Victor, is do not be too disturbed by these people; you will not have to have direct contacts with them. They are around, but think of them as being in the background."

Lansky grinned. "Yes, I think that may be best. So we are seeing the plant tomorrow?"

"Yes, and depending how long we take there and in discussions with the management, then we shall either visit the dam and the power station tomorrow afternoon, or the next morning. We must have enough time for the power station, because it is important that you are happy with our electricity supply. It is a key part of the investment we propose." The stewardess approached and asked them to strap themselves in for landing. Malenkov returned to his own seat, leaving Lansky with his thoughts.

The little jet touched gently down onto the runway and ran on under the looming grey skies. The ground was covered in snow, and bare birch trees mixed with brown-tinged pines stretched out into the distance. As the plane turned off the runway, the terminal building became visible to the passengers through the cabin windows. It was single-story, of rough concrete and looked, to Lansky at least, completely deserted. As the aircraft came to a halt in front of the building, a jeep appeared from round the back, with two heavily-overcoated soldiers sitting in it. It pulled up to the door of the plane, just as the stewardess went to open it. The other girl came towards Lansky.

"If you give me your passport, we can deal with all the formalities from here." She smiled at him. "It's a lot warmer in here than out there." As she said it, her colleague unlatched the door and let the folding stairway down; a blast of icy air penetrated the cabin. "Don't worry. We can close the door again while they go off and process the paperwork. And Captain Cork just had a message from the control tower that your car will be here in about five minutes."

Lansky sat staring through the window while the soldiers went through what seemed to be an endless shuffling and stamping of papers. The world outside was grey – grey sky, grey tarmac and buildings, grey light. He could see sleety snow blowing in the wind, and drifts of snow piled up against the walls of the terminal. It was an unprepossessing welcome to Russia. As he watched, a pale blue Mercedes pulled out from behind the terminal building and drove slowly over to the aircraft. The stewardess opened the door again and the soldiers handed all of the documents back to Malenkov. The latter grinned at Lansky.

"OK, let's get off and into the car. I will accompany you to the hotel; Georgi has some things to do here at the airport, so we leave him here. You will have to trust me with your passport for the moment. I shall give it to the hotel when we check in; they have to record your stay and report to the authorities. You will get it back from the hotel reception tomorrow morning. Formalities are a bit stricter then in your country, huh? Ah, yes," as the stewardess handed Lansky his overcoat, "put it on. It's cold outside. I think maybe while you are here we will have to get you a fur coat – it's the only thing that can deal with a Siberian winter!"

Lansky did just that and turned his collar up against the wind. He still grimaced as he walked down the steps into the drifting grey snow. Malenkov ushered him into the back of the Mercedes, and the driver accelerated away from the aircraft, rounding the terminal building and heading for an open barrier in the perimeter fence.

"Well, that's the easiest immigration formalities I've ever come across", he said. "Much better to have them come to you, rather than you go and queue for them, as normal."

"Yes, that's one of the benefits of our position with the local authorities," replied Malenkov.

The driver pulled out through the gates, the back of the car fishtailing slightly on the snowy road surface as he picked up speed. Lansky looked around curiously, but the landscape was a continuous bleak grey, only the few straggly trees breaking up the monotony. The car bumped uncomfortably over the pot-holed surface of the road.

"It's a bit different from Mayfair." Malenkov broke the silence. "The development of Siberia will be an enormous undertaking. The wealth to finance it is under our feet – the richest mineral deposits in the world. Our project will be part of the new beginning. We can get very rich from this dull landscape, my friend. All we need is the key to unlock the safe, and then we can begin. Isn't it exciting to be part of it?"

Lansky was starting to see the dichotomy of Oleg Malenkov. Was he truly the thug, the gangster, or was there in his character the genuine visionary, desperate to see the development of his country?

In the distance, buildings appeared, which, when they got closer, turned out to be new construction; seemingly, large, wood-framed houses.

"You see," said Malenkov, "this is where the new rich of Krayanovsk are starting to build their dachas. Krayanovsk, as you know, was originally a gulag city – a prison. So there are no old big houses, just the apartment blocks for the prisoners." He smiled. "But although it was a prison, you will see no fence. The Siberian taiga is far more effective than any walls or wire for stopping escape attempts. Venture out there" – he pointed out at the bleak landscape – "and you will not survive long. These gulag cities were left to function pretty much on their own. Here, the only real contact with the rest of the Soviet Union was for the raw materials to be delivered, and the industrial products, like the aluminium, to be taken away. Stalin knew what he was doing when he created these places. Of course, he was only continuing the way of the Czars."

Like most westerners, Lansky had never really thought about the logistics of dumping hundreds of thousands of people in a deadly wilderness, and then forcing them to become the engine of your economic growth. Looking around him at the barren, endless snow wasteland, it was a horrific prospect.

Malenkov seemed to read his thoughts. "Yes, my friend, it was a hard, hard time. The survivors here are very tough people. My grandfather was sent here as a middle-aged man in the 1930s. My brother and I are the second generation of our family to be Siberian. Not actually from Krayanovsk, from a similar place, further east. Leonid and I only came here as the country began to open up to entrepreneurs like us." Lansky kept quiet. Entrepreneurs was not what he had heard the Malenkovs called before. "Our father could not in the end handle life out here – he was already a teenager when he was brought here with his parents, and he did not have the strength to cope. In the end, he became an alcoholic. That's a serious problem in these places, even now. Still, helps to keep the workers from getting too restive and asking for improved conditions."

"So you learned something from Stalin, then?"

"Victor, you may say anything you like to me. We are – I hope – going to be partners, and we shall get to know each other well. But be careful if you joke about things like the Stalin era. It is still very raw in some people's minds, and they may resent these kind of remarks from a westerner. But yes, we did learn some things from the Soviet time, and yes, we do still rely on some of their ways." He smiled thinly. "First, we must make the money for ourselves, then we can think about changing industrial relations."

As they had been speaking, the roadside had begun to become more built up. They were coming into the city. All along both sides of the road were four-storey blocks, clearly constructed from pre-moulded concrete slabs. But not well constructed. Even from inside the car, Lansky could see chips and even open gaps where the joints should be. The window frames were rusty, again ill-fitting, and the whole picture was one of unremitting bleakness. Again, Malenkov seemed to sense his thoughts.

"This is how everybody lived. *Everybody*. From the plant managers to the fork-lift drivers. The size of apartment purely dependent upon the number in the family." He laughed. "But do not think that means a room for each child you have. No, the families are packed together in two or three rooms; originally they had communal washing and cooking facilities. That was improved in the 1960s, so most now have their own water supply and gas for cooking. But heating, electricity – all centrally controlled. Originally there was a party representative in each block, responsible for making sure nobody thought bad thoughts." He grinned. "Most people came here in the first place for thinking bad thoughts, so it probably strikes you as strange that they still wanted to control them, even as they were suffering their punishment. But these places were truly a reign of terror. Of course, things improved through the 70s and 80s, and theoretically all that is now in the past. But you can't change people just like that. There's still a strong wish to be told what to do – the worst thing the gulags did was to rob people of independence of thought." Again came the wolfish smile. "But, of course, that also helps us, since we're prepared to tell them what to do."

The car pulled into a small driveway, which led to an oblong, three storey building. *Hotel Krayanovsk* was emblazoned across the double glass doors leading into the reception area.

36

Lansky was ushered straight past the reception desk and up to his room, while Malenkov, having reminded him that he would be back with his brother in around an hour, walked back out to the car. The room was as Lansky could have predicted – spartan, with just a bed, a cheap desk and chair, and a wardrobe. The bathroom was also basic, and the décor throughout was plain and functional. He sat at the desk and looked out of the window. Grey, everything was grey, with the small flakes of snow still blowing in the wind. He could see the blocks of apartments, stretching away into the grey murk. Although it was warm in the room, he shivered at the prospect outside. Shaking his head, he picked up his briefcase. Time enough for melancholy later, for now he had to be ready to meet Leonid Malenkov.

Chapter Seven

Krayanovsk, Siberia, Russia

Lansky may have been feeling a little nervous of meeting Leonid, but the latter was full of enthusiasm. He sat with his brother in their office in the centre of town.

"Little brother, you have done well. Did I not say you would be able to convince him? This is a big day for us – we are beginning to move forward at last, into the international world."

"Maybe. Don't forget, he has so far committed to nothing. He has just agreed to come and look, and to talk to us. We must not take him for granted."

Leonid chuckled. "Ah, Oleg, always you are cautious. Certainly the Englishman has not yet signed anything, but do you think he would come here to say no? We must be positive, we must give him confidence that we can all work together well. The others will meet us the hotel for lunch?"

"Yes, we will arrive at 12:15, and I have told them to be there around 12:45, so we have a chance to speak to Lansky first. That's what you wanted, isn't it?"

"Yes, I would like to meet him first; we, after all will be partners. The others just work for us." Although his brother was so confident, Oleg knew they still had serious work to do to convince Lansky to part with his money.

The Mercedes was outside to take them back to the hotel. As they walked in through the doors, they saw Lansky emerging from the lift.

"Victor, my friend, "called Oleg, "now at last you and Leonid will meet." And turning to his brother, still speaking in English, "Leonid, let me introduce Victor Lansky, our friend from London."

Lansky could see the family resemblance – the swarthy complexion, the short stature – but Leonid was if anything even coarser in appearance than his brother. Where Oleg's hair was neatly trimmed, and his clothes were of sophisticated western cut, Leonid looked like a hard, tough Siberian gangster.

"Mr Lansky, Victor, it is a pleasure to meet you. My brother has told me about you, and we are very grateful that you have come to Krayanovsk to discuss our proposal and to see the possibilities of our factory. I hope this will be the first of many meetings."

"It's very good of you to extend the invitation to me. Hopefully, we can come to a good solution, but in any case I am happy to be able to make the visit. I think it will be an eye-opener for me to see how industry functions here. I guess it will be very different from what I am accustomed to seeing in the west."

"Come, my friend," said Oleg, "let us go through to have some lunch. Our colleagues will be joining us shortly."

They went into the dining room, where they were shown to a large table at the back of the room, set for nine people. The two Malenkovs gestured Lansky into a place at the end of the table, and then sat opposite each other, on either side of him. The table was set with dishes of salad and pickles, and plates of various different colours of smoked fish.

"Help yourself, Victor", urged Oleg. "We will have some meat and fish when the others are here, but, please, just take some of these snacks for now."

The waiter filled two glasses in front of Lansky, one with beer, the other, only marginally smaller, with a clear liquid, which Lansky, with a sinking feeling, realised was vodka, when he saw the bottle. And as he feared, the vodka almost immediately came into play.

"So, Victor," began Leonid, "we meet for the first time. I would like to welcome you formally to our town, and to give you my hopes that our association will be a long one, and a very successful one. Let us drink a toast to our future relationship." And he raised his glass, saluting his guest. As Lansky clinked glasses with the brothers, he did pause for a moment. Siberian gangster Leonid might be, but his command of English was impressive. As he drank, he realised he was expected to respond.

"Gentlemen, thank you for your welcome. I hope our discussions go well, and that we are able to reach a conclusion which is satisfactory for all of us. Meanwhile, I look forward to my first experience of Siberia." Solemnly, they all drank.

"Oleg tells me you have seen all the projections he has made for our development. While you are here, we will try to show you the actual factory and power plant so you can see how it all works in reality." He smiled. "My little brother is very good at the theoretical part, that's why he travels to Moscow and the west, whereas I am more involved in the real management of the smelter. Of course, you understand that my name does not appear in the board of directors. We can describe my role more as enabling everything to run smoothly. As yet, we do not have all the shareholding in our hands. But don't worry, we soon will have, particularly if you decide you would like to participate with us. Most of the board members are friendly towards us, and we have for sure their support. As they have ours, of course. Soon, you will meet the most important of our colleagues. As I think Oleg may have told you, the quality of the production in the Soviet times was very good, at least, we are told, the equal of western metal, so we have as much as possible kept the production people as they were. So the potlines and the casthouse are still run by the same managers as before, which we believe is the best way. These people know their business, and we have managed to convince them that they should give their loyalty now to us. We will look after them."

With a foreboding feeling that he might not be too happy with the reply, but nevertheless seeing that he had to say something, Lansky asked "So who are the other board members? Were they also involved with the smelter before?"

"One was. He was the man who originally approached us and suggested this was a good enterprise for us to look at. The others are mostly long-term associates of ours. And one man is formerly professor of mathematics and accounting at our Siberian University. He is overseeing the finance of the company. He is a good man; he makes sure no money is wasted or – what is the English? – misappropriated, I think?"

"Yes, that's a good word, and it's always important in a business to have somebody aware like that. But how long have you been negotiating to take the plant?"

"We have been building our interest for almost one year. Obviously, as you know from Oleg, we are currently not producing very much metal; we still need to ensure the supply routes for our raw materials. It is not an easy time in Russia. We cannot yet operate like a western smelter and use credit to acquire our alumina and other necessities. Nobody internationally will give us that credit. So for the moment, all we can do is work on a tolling basis. So we can receive raw materials from a western partner, for example Metalex, and we can transform these raw materials into aluminium, which we then give back to Metalex. For this service, they pay us a tolling fee, which we can use to pay the workers and maintain the plant. However, we want to be free of this way of working, we want to be in control of our own business. As you know, this is why we have contacted you in the first place. We believe that if we work together, your knowledge of the west can help us make our enterprise more solid."

As Leonid was speaking, Lansky reflected on the truth of this. Gangsters they may be, but the underlying proposition was a valid one. The numbers in the proposal were genuinely attractive, and when Leonid was speaking like this, and when Oleg earlier had been describing how he wanted to realise the mineral wealth of Siberia, it all seemed very plausible.

Oleg leaned across and pushed one of the plates of fish towards him. "Come, Victor, have more smoked fish. It will help to give you the taste of Siberia." And they all laughed together, like business associates the world over, when one of them makes a feeble sort of joke.

Lansky took some of the fish, tasted it, and immediately wished he hadn't. Smoked salmon it was not.

"Yes, I understand the constraints you have. In theory, it should not be too difficult to change things. Once the initial deadlock is broken, and you have begun producing to capacity, then the deal becomes almost self-fulfilling, because you will have a cash flow which will enable you to fund raw material purchases. So the trick will be to bridge the gap. How long does it take from raw material arriving until you can ship out the finished product?"

"Normally around three weeks, but we can get more accurate figures when the production head comes here shortly. And then you will have a chance to discuss this further with management in the plant. It depends also on how many pots are in use. As you know, the smelter is more efficient when it is in full production than it is now, when it is only partially operating. Running on a full cycle, maximum production, the time can be down to around twelve to fourteen days. So, anyway, there will be many questions like this we need to discuss, but I think we are better to wait for this until the others are here. For now, I want you to understand that we are proposing a genuine partnership with you. I know, because Oleg has told me, that you have heard some bad things of us. I know that there are many stories about us in the western press, calling us Russian Mafia, and names like this. I do not pretend that we have always been perfect, but many of these stories are exaggerated. Anyway, this is all in the past. Now, we concentrate on developing our industrial business. We want to make a lot of money, sure, but we know things will be different, that international standards must apply to what we do. We know this, and we are happy with this. It is what we have chosen to do."

Somehow, the overt defensiveness made Lansky uncomfortable again. He had begun to believe in the Brothers Malenkov, industrialists. That speech of Leonid's raised all his concerns again. But, as he knew at the back of his mind, if it was straightforward, he probably wouldn't have had the opportunity put in front of him. He realised he had to make some reply.

"Yes, I think that's very important. In order to be acceptable to the international market, you will have to make certain that they can't point the finger at you for bad practices or untransparent financial statements. In fact, that raises an interesting point. I've obviously seen the numbers Oleg showed me, but do you actually have audited accounts, that can be presented to western companies? Because that's one of the first questions they will ask. It's all right for us to talk amongst ourselves about how the business may perform, but outsiders will not move without the official paperwork."

This time, Oleg replied. "We know this, and it is a problem. The concept of audited accounts is a strange one here. Bear in mind that under the Soviet system such a thing was unnecessary, even meaningless, because everything was owned by the State, in one way or another. So there is no background in preparing such information. We hope that it will be available relatively soon, but in the meantime, we need to work together to try and find some way around it for the present."

"OK, that's clearly an issue we will need to address before we go too much further. Maybe we will need to incorporate a western company which can act as the trading counterparty. That might help, but we will still need our trading partners to be sympathetic, which is always OK when things are going well, but not so good if problems develop."

Oleg chuckled. "One reason we want your partnership is to help prevent problems from developing."

Leonid gestured over the shoulder of his brother, who had his back to the doors of the room. Oleg turned in his chair, following the signal. "Ah," he said, "here are our associates. Excellent."

Briefly, a thought of "Reservoir Dogs" came unbidden into Lansky's mind. Resolutely, he put it aside, and stood up to meet the oncoming Russians. The introductions were made, although the names and functions were a bit of a blur to him, and they all sat down, the Russians talking noisily to each other, leaving Lansky isolated at the top of the table. The waiter loomed over his shoulder. "Meat or fish?" he asked, in atrocious English. After the smoked fish, there was only one answer for Lansky – "Meat, thank you." The man went round the table, asking the same question, presumably, in Russian, followed closely by his colleague with the beer and vodka.

Suddenly, Oleg turned to Lansky. "Victor, so these are our colleagues. I'm sure you will not remember all the names and titles immediately, but I hope these gentlemen will all soon become very familiar to you. We are at the moment talking with Alexey" – he gestured to the man sitting next to his brother – "about the question of turn-round time and the production cycle. He was formerly the production manager at the plant for ten years, and is now our director of production. He is a very important man in making sure the plant works properly. He will prepare his full reply for tomorrow, when we will be having some more formal discussions. Our finance director – the former professor," and here he pointed to a thin, bearded man at the far end of the table, "will also be able to report on his conversations with the outside accounting firms about when we can expect to conform to western standards. You see, we take your comments seriously! Now, let us enjoy our lunch."

The food came and went, most of it pretty tasteless to Lansky, the glasses of beer and vodka kept being filled, and the conversation between the Russians got progressively louder. Lansky was left largely to his own devices, apart from the odd remark from Oleg, while Leonid was deep in conversation with the production man, Alexey, sitting next to him. All the while, through the window at the back of the dining room, Lansky could see the snow still drifting down in the grey light. Suddenly, the loud Russian conversations, the beer and the vodka, and the long flight got to him.

"Oleg, the jet-lag is really hitting me now. Do you mind if I go upstairs for an hour or so?"

"Of course, no problem. I will tell the others we will postpone the meetings until tomorrow, when we make the plant tour. But do you want me to cancel this evening's dinner?"

The true answer was yes, but nevertheless Lansky answered, "No, of course not. I am looking forward to it. What time should I be ready?"

Oleg looked at his watch. "It is now three o'clock. I will come by in the car at seven to pick you up and we will then go to the Turkish bath and dinner. Will you be down in the lobby at seven?"

"Certainly. I'll see you then." And he made his excuses and left the table.

As Lansky made his way to the door, Leonid turned to his brother. "Well, little brother, what do you think now? Will he play?"

"Leonid, relax. We have time, and he is here in our domain. I think he likes the idea of the money, but I also think he is still nervous of associating with us. We must play on the way we intend to become respectable, and make him think that we will do everything to become acceptable to the west." He shrugged. "But he has to want to do it. We cannot force him. So let our accountant" – and he pointed to the professor – "let him be very convincing about his conversations with accounting firms. I think Lansky will be comforted if he sees that we take them seriously. But now" – he addressed the table as a whole, now – "we must not be drunk when we meet him this evening. We all have things to do now, so let's meet again this evening at the Turkish bath. Then we make sure he has a good time."

Up in his room, Lansky took out his mobile phone. There was a signal, but a weak one. He needed to talk to Rory Davies again; what he had heard from the Russians about the plant sounded reasonable, but he wanted to check over a couple of things. After all, he was a scrap trader and processor, and a property man. He was happy looking at the financials, but he wanted a bit of background on smelter operations.

The weak signal made the call difficult, but in the end he got the information he wanted. As he lay down on the bed to doze, a couple of floors below him a thickset man took off his headphones and stretched his neck.

Chapter Eight

Outskirts of Krayanovsk, Siberia, Russia

Lansky saw the pale blue Mercedes pull up to the hotel, and was at the car door as it stopped. Before Oleg could get out from the other side, Lansky had opened the door and got in.

"Victor," said Oleg, "I hope you are feeling more refreshed."

"Yes, thank you. I'm sorry I had to duck out earlier, but a doze has done me the world of good. I'm looking forward to this evening, and starting to get to know your colleagues."

"Good. I know you cannot really have learned the names at lunchtime, so I will remind you. The two most important for your purposes are Alexey Louzhny, the production man, and the finance director, Anton Vronsky. These two you should get to know well."

The car was rolling through the dimly-lit streets. All Lansky could see through the gloom and the falling snow was block after block of workers' apartments. It was a dull, grim prospect. Something struck him.

"Oleg, we've driven a bit from the airport this morning, and now out this way this evening, but I haven't seen any shops at all. Where are they? Where do people buy things?"

Oleg looked at him for a moment, before replying. "You are still naïve about our country. There are not really shops, as you would understand the word here. There are some kiosks, where they can buy vegetables, a little meat, and of course vodka, but really the concept of shops, of retail places where you can go and choose things to buy, it never existed here. Never forget this was a prison. Until Stalin's death, the people were frankly slaves. They worked, they were fed enough to keep them alive, but that was their whole life. Since then, they have notionally been free, but only now, in the last year or two, has anybody begun to think of them as consumers, a market which may buy things. Look" – he pointed through the car window – "there. That's a food kiosk, that's what has been a shop here." To Lansky, it looked a bit like a European bus shelter. Oleg continued. "On the outside of the town, they are beginning to build what will be a small shopping area. People are finally beginning to realise that things can be sold here. Look, in some parts of Siberia, say up in the north, at Norilsk, where the nickel and copper mines are, the workers are actually paid very well. Far higher than the national average. There, they have many shops, and restaurants and clubs, because the miners have

44

money to spend. But that's because the work is very hard, brutal, and since the slave labour finished, they have to pay more. You know that's where the remnants of the German army from Stalingrad ended their days. But the last of them was dead by 1955, and they had to attract some other workers who could handle the mining work. So they had to pay them properly. Here, the work is not very skilled, so there is no need to pay too much. I know what you have been told of us, but in fact the aluminium smelter is the highest-paying employer in the town. And when we have full control, we shall continue like that." He cackled. "The cost is peanuts compared with what we can make, but it keeps the workers happy."

The apartment blocks outside the windows were beginning to give way to scrubby pine trees, and the streetlights were becoming even more infrequent. Lansky smiled to himself. What would his Polish father have thought? He was riding with a Russian gangster, whom he didn't really know, going to a destination he had only a sketchy idea of, in the middle – literally – of the Siberian wasteland. It wasn't only the German army that had been sent to the mines – for sure, over the centuries, some of his ancestors had made the same journey.

The car pulled in through a pair of gates and braked to a halt in front of a low, squat building. Parked outside were four or five other cars; Oleg ushered Lansky past them and through the entrance doors into the building. Inside, they walked through a well-lit lobby, and down a long corridor, which led them into what appeared to Lansky to be a well-equipped changing room, looking rather like the locker room of an upmarket golf club.

"OK, Victor. You will find towels over there" – he gestured across the room – "and you can leave your clothes on these hangers. Don't worry, everything will be safe. Petty thieves will not cause trouble to friends of the Malenkovs. Leonid and the others are already here, so as soon as you are ready, we will go into the steam room."

A couple of moments later, clad just in a towel, Lansky followed Oleg through the door into the baths. A wall of steam and heat hit him, and although he could here voices talking and laughing, he could see nothing initially through the steam. Following the Russian, he walked across the marble floor, and began to make out shapes through the fog, which resolved themselves into the figures of Leonid and his cronies. Indicating the space on the seat next to him, Leonid beckoned Lansky. "Victor, welcome to our baths. Come, sit down here next to me and enjoy the steam."

Lansky complied, thinking how much more surreal it was becoming. Not only driving to who knows where with the Russian mafia, now he was sitting almost naked amongst them in a Turkish bath in the middle of Siberia. He was beginning to find the atmosphere irksome. It was very hot, and steam mixing with sweat on his torso was making him uncomfortable; he tried wiping it away with the end of his towel. Leonid noticed. "Relax, Victor, you must just let the steam wash out your skin. Don't fight it and you will soon begin to feel comfortable."

Lansky followed his advice, and began to relax. He began to feel drowsy, and then, half dozing off, he heard higher-pitched voices. "Ah," said Leonid, "here come the girls." Lansky looked up, to see four blonde girls approaching, all clad in nothing more than the same white towels as the men. Giggling, they sat themselves down amongst the men. Leonid moved along the seat, creating a gap between himself and Lansky, and gestured to one of them to come over and sit there. As she sat down, she said, in passably good English, "Hello. My name is Olga." She was attractive, long blonde hair and deep blue eyes.

"Hello Olga", replied Lansky, "My name is Victor. I'm from England."

"Welcome to Siberia. You like Turkish bath?"

"Its growing on me since you appeared."

She looked puzzled. "Growing? I don't understand. What is growing?"

"Sorry. My English was too fast for you. I am enjoying the Turkish bath, and I am pleased you have joined us."

"Thank you."

The steaming lasted about half an hour, and then the Russians started standing up and moving off through the mist. Lansky heard splashing of water, and the girl stood up and pulled his hand. "Come," she said, "we must go for the bathing." He followed her, as she kept hold of his hand. Through a stone archway and then a wooden door, they came out into a large hall with a plunge pool in the centre of it. Four or five people were already in it. The girl dropped her towel, and gestured for Lansky to do the same. He was momentarily mesmerised by her body, then she signalled him to follow, and dived into the water. Lansky followed, and then wished he hadn't. It was icy cold, and soon made him forget about the sight of the girl's naked body. Spluttering, he came to the surface and took the few stokes to the other side, where he heaved himself out of the water. Olga, still in the pool, laughed. "You are not yet like real Russian man. We must teach you to love the cold." And she swam across and pulled herself up to sit next to him on the side. Suddenly, he became interested in her body again, but she sprang to her feet and wrapped a towel back around her. Picking another off the pile, she tossed it to him. She had noticed how he had been looking at her, and giggled.

"Let's go through for some food," she said. "And it's warmer in there." She pointed to another doorway, and led him through it. In the room was a big round table, laden with salads and smoked fish. On a cabinet at the side were bottles of vodka and what Lansky assumed to be Georgian champagne. Two or three of the Russians were already seated at the table, including the man Lansky recognised as Anton Vronsky, the finance director of the plant. The girl was right, the room was warmer, and now that the icy chill of the plunge was wearing off, Lansky could feel his skin tingling with the warmth. It was a pleasant sensation, and, what with the presence of all the girls, he was beginning to warm to the concept of the Russian Turkish bath. He took the tumbler of vodka Vronsky held out to him.

And so the evening wound on. Food, drink, steam room. Lansky's initial concern about the effect of drinking and steaming wore off as his head became more befuddled by the vodka. Russian, English and a tortured mix of the two got louder and louder. Music started pumping through the building, and Olga and one of the other girls abandoned their towels and started dancing together, to loud cheers from the men sprawled around the table. The other two girls disappeared through the door with two of the Russians, to emerge, flushed, about half an hour later.

Then, suddenly, the girls disappeared, as did most of the men. Lansky found himself left with the Malenkov brothers and Louzhny, the production man.

"OK, Victor, we have had a good evening. Tomorrow, we have work to do, so we have sent away the girls to stop then distracting you. You need some sleep to prepare for our meetings." Oleg seemed stone-cold sober, as he said this. His brother took over. "Tomorrow, Victor, we need to make some decisions. We are ready to move forward. We just wait for your final word. You see this evening how we look after our friends; let us hope we can continue like this."

Even with his fuzzy head, Lansky could sense that there may be an implied threat in that statement. Oleg was right. He needed to sleep, after the flight and now the vodka. Tomorrow he would need all his wits about him.

They changed back into their clothes, and at the door of the building, as the blue Mercedes pulled up, Oleg opened its door for Lansky, and said: "Victor, the car will take you back to the hotel. We will send it tomorrow morning to pick you up at ten o'clock, so have a good night, sleep well and we will meet again tomorrow."

Lansky knew he was in no fit state to think rationally, but as the car drove steadily through the outskirts of the town, he could not help but reflect on that last statement of Leonid's. Had it been a threat? Was that his first real sight of the steel underlying the Malenkovs? Or was he being over-sensitive to the words?

Chapter Nine

Krayanovsk Aluminium Smelter, Siberia, Russia

Shortly after ten the next morning, Lansky was in the car, driving once more through the drab surroundings of the town. The sky was still grey, and the few people to be seen in the bleak streets were wrapped in thick clothing, trudging into the snowflakes that were still drifting in the cold wind. Lansky estimated they were going in almost directly the opposite direction from the airport, but the streetscape was just the same as he had seen yesterday. There were small vans buzzing around, and the occasional heavy truck or bus belched out clouds of black diesel fumes. Idly, Lansky wondered how they treated the fuel to make it function in the cold. He had some memory in his head about diesel getting too thick to flow much below minus ten degrees. Must be some form of additive, he mused. He actually felt quite well, considering the previous evening, grateful it was vodka they had been drinking, rather than something which produced a heavier hangover. He settled back in the seat.

In an office in the smelter, the Malenkovs sat with the electronic eavesdropper from the hotel and another man. The latter was heavyset and exuded an air of menace.

"Well," said Leonid, "that tape is still not conclusive. It shows he is seriously interested, enough to call his associate and get some more background, but we need to get him to make a firm commitment. You know we have only got another couple of weeks until the Government will tell us we have had long enough, and if we can't finish the deal, they will get someone else to."

"Yes, I know. I think we are very close. We need to get Vronsky to persuade him how honest our accounting is. And from that phone call, he seems very concerned to know how long the production cycle is. Yesterday evening, I told Louzhny to make sure he knew the answer to that question, and to make sure it was the answer Lansky wanted to hear. I think he understood me, so he knows what he has to say. Are we going to show him the power station as well today, or just the smelter?"

"It depends. As soon as we have his agreement, we want to send him back to London, so he can start getting the money together. So we show him as much as it takes to convince him. I think we may have to take him to the power station and the dam, and if Vronsky and Louzhny need to spend time with him, I guess we'll have to go there tomorrow. Then hopefully, the next morning he will fly out. OK, he should be here soon, so let's go into the Boardroom and tell the others to be ready."

Lansky was actually feeling a bit nervous as he was shown into the room. The conversation he had had with Rory Davis had been useful, so he was confident his thoughts were on the right lines, but he also knew that this was crunch time – he was going to have to make a decision which could risk pretty much all the wealth he had built up over the years. He could have simply said no, and walked away, fortune intact. But the gambler in him would not let him do that. He had to play the hand through to the end.

Oleg welcomed him to the meeting, and went round the table, giving the names and functions of all those present. "So", he went on, "you have seen the outline of our plans for this enterprise, and you have seen some fairly detailed financial projections. Perhaps so that we do not spend time going over the same things again, we could ask you to tell us what further information you would need, in order to make a decision about whether or not you wish to join us."

"That seems fair to me. I must say first that I have found your proposal intriguing. Clearly, there is a substantial profit to be made from the business. I have spoken at some length to contacts of mine in the aluminium business and they confirm that it would be perfectly possible to supply the bulk of the Krayanovsk metal into the western market. Those who have used the metal confirm that the quality is acceptable, and the brand has been registered with the London Metal exchange for some years now. That means that it will have pretty wide acceptance with most users. I know that later today, I shall be making a tour of the plant, although obviously as a commercial man rather than a technician my understanding of the processes will be those of a layman. So, after some considerable thought since I met Oleg for the first time a few months ago, I am well-disposed towards the investment. However, as you rightly suggest, Oleg, there are a few points where I need some clarification." While he was speaking, there was a murmur of translation coming from the far end of the table. They clearly didn't all have such a good command of English as the Malenkovs. He continued. "There are four principal issues we need to think about. Three of these are what we might call production issues, and they are, in no particular order: the provision of electric power – we all know how energy intensive aluminium smelting is, and I need to be sure that there are sufficient safeguards to keep the power flowing to the plant. Next, I need to know the process time of the plant – in other words, how long is it between raw materials arriving at the factory gates and finished product leaving. The third of these issues is the question of transport logistics – how long does it take the finished metal to get to the port, and how safe is the journey? The other point, and this is very important, is one I outlined to Oleg before: are there any audited accounts for the company which can be presented to western trading counterparties and banks? If not, then how soon will they be available, and what might we be able to use in the interim?" He looked round the table. "Well, gentlemen, those are the issues. I look forward to you answers." And he sat down.

The Malenkov brothers exchanged a glance, then Oleg got to his feet.

"OK. So, we can try to answer your questions. For the first one, we shall be going to look at the hydro plant on the river, probably tomorrow morning. This plant provides all the electricity to the smelter, and is also one of the main power sources for the town as well. The minority share of it is currently still owned by the regional government, but my brother and I, together with some of our associates, hold a significant majority share, which we anticipate increasing, in the holding company. It was through taking this stake that we first became aware of the possibilities of the aluminium plant. This ownership has advantages for our smelter investment. First, since it is a major electricity source for the town, the regional government are obliged to ensure that it remains operational. If it doesn't, then there would be uproar and demonstrations throughout the town. So the regional government will maintain it. Secondly, as we own a substantial share, we are able to ensure that the smelter remains one of the main offtakers, and will therefore be protected against any problems. The dam on the river is quite old; it was built during the 1930s, in the Stalin era, but the power generation plant is newer. It was originally completed in the 1960s, and was fully renovated and modernised during the last years of the Soviet time. So technically, it is in top condition, and as I said before, we have sufficient strength of ownership to protect our investments."

Lansky was impressed. He had known the power source was hydro, and therefore cheap, but not the extent of the Malenkovs involvement. Again, their project seemed to be stacking up well.

Oleg continued. "I shall also reply to your point about transport. The finished aluminium leaves Krayanovsk by railcars, which take it to St Petersburg, where it is loaded for shipment overseas. We have heard of examples of Russian train cargoes being stolen, but the Krayanovsk smelter has had no problems in this respect since we have been involved with it. On the trains, we have armed guards who are in our employ. So far, that has prevented any criminal gangs from trying to steal our metal. We are not naïve; we know there is this risk in the state of Russia at the moment, but we believe that we take the most effective precautions possible." Armed guards, thought Lansky to himself. This really was beginning to sound like something out of the Wild West. "The trains normally take between one and two weeks, as they must go via Moscow and often they have to wait because of the heavy traffic between there and St Petersburg. But our guards stay with the cargo all the way, and then return with the empty railcars. Because at present many products are being sold and exported from Russia, there is a lot of pressure on railcar availability, so we always ensure our wagons come directly back here for reloading."

"And you directly employ these guards?"

"Yes, mostly they are former soldiers, many of them veterans of the Afghan war, or Chechens. Victor, they are not nice people, but they do a very important job for us, and so far they have always done it very effectively. You will recall that in some of our earlier discussions I have pointed out to you that it is impossible for western companies to get too involved in Russian business without Russian partners – this is exactly one of the reasons. We have the expertise to handle the problems of our confused society. I understand why you need to be comfortable about the transport situation, but really, in this kind of area, we do know best."

Lansky nodded thoughtfully. "Yes."

"So, we need to talk about the cycle of the production. Alexey" – he gestured towards Louzhny – "perhaps you would like to explain how this works?"

As Oleg sat down, Louzhny stood up and took his place at the top of the table.

The Kremlin, Moscow, Russia

A few thousand kilometres and several time zones to the west, in the Kremlin, in Moscow, the President sat with his economic advisor.

"So," he said, "where do we stand now with the asset sales programme? And how much money do we need this week?" He was tired, worn out from the constant struggle to keep his country afloat in the global economy. After the break-up of the Soviet Union and his push into power as the presidential candidate of the strong-arm gangs who were the only people in the country able to keep any sort of order, he had eventually agreed with his backers that the only way out of the mess was to begin selling off the industrial infrastructure of the country. Initially, he had harboured hopes that he might be able to attract foreign investment, but that hope had been crushed by the Duma's resolute refusal to pass legislation allowing foreign ownership of Russian assets. That left, as the members of the Duma knew full well it would, the gangs as the only real prospective buyers. The President hadn't really intended to sell his country to the mafia, but from somewhere, the people had to get money to buy food to eat, and the only ones with money were the gangs. The President was an old Party apparatchik, who had sensed the changing winds before his colleagues, putting him in pole position when the Soviet system ran out of money. He had been walking the tightrope since. He was in late middle-age, white-haired and careworn. His advisor was younger, slimmer, and from that finishing school of Russian politics, the now-defunct KGB. Defunct, but still a vital arm of the State under its new, post-communist set of initials, the FSB. Yuri Ansonov, the advisor, was playing a long game.

"Things are progressing, Mr President," he said. "We are very close to concluding our final deal in the oil industry, at which point the State will have transferred its oil production facilities to our two favoured bidders. That will realise an immediate payment to the State treasury of approximately five hundred million US dollars. The buyers have been able to secure the money against future sales of crude oil to western traders."

The President sighed. "It seems crazy, Yuri, we know the value of the assets is far greater than that. And yet, the private sector can arrange these sorts of financings, which the State cannot."

"That's true, Mr President, but we are constrained by our need for speed. We cannot risk rioting in favour of a restoration of the Soviets. *We* know the regime was bankrupt. The people have been told, but they don't know what that means. All they know is, they want food to eat every day, and securing that has to be our prime political aim."

The President nodded slowly. "You are of course right, but it shouldn't have to be like this. We are giving them freedom, but selling their country out from under them."

"Not entirely. We are ensuring that the ownership of all assets remains in Russian hands. We are being forced to do in months what should be a process over years. But this is just the first stage. We will survive, and develop how we wish in the future."

"I sometimes wonder whether I shall survive to see that future. But let us continue. Where do we stand with the Malenkovs in Siberia?"

"I spoke to Oleg yesterday, to remind him they only have a short time left as preferred bidder. He assures me they will very soon be in a position to make their final dispositions to enable them to conclude the deal. That will be a big step, because once the first aluminium plant is in private hands, I am sure we will be able to do deals for the others. That will ensure Siberia remains loyal to our intentions."

"I suppose we shouldn't think about how the Malenkovs may raise the money. But you know all about that, don't you? They were amongst your KGB heavy units in the old days. I doubt if they've really changed their tune."

"The Malenkov brothers are Siberian entrepreneurs," the advisor said smoothly. "They intend to develop Siberian industry, and to take it to a level which was impossible under the Soviets. They were it is true in the past associated with me through the security services, but that should not be used to try to undermine their position in the new society."

"Yuri, don't bullshit me. You and I both know what they are. You and I both know that I need them, just as I need you, to try to get some sense into this basket case of a country. But don't give me that self-serving shit. They are a pair of thugs; but I can't rule without them and their like. But remember, Yuri, when I no longer need them, then maybe I no longer need you either." The threat implicit in this was left hanging in the air for a moment or two. Then he continued. "Anyway, make sure they come through with their money in time. We cannot afford to wait. The Duma knows my position is precarious, and some of its members would like to push me over the edge. This is a very dangerous game we are playing here. If the Malenkovs cannot perform, you know I can always go to my friends at Metalex."

"With respect, you know that will not work. For political reasons, this has to remain Russian. Whatever your personal antipathy to the Malenkovs, and whatever reasons you have for supporting Metalex, they cannot be allowed to step into this deal. We have been round this subject so many times. If Metalex get it, even with a Russian partner, that will undo all we are trying to achieve."

Yuri Ansonov picked up his papers and left the room. Down the heavy oak-lined corridor, he went into his own office. It was indeed a dangerous game, but the President didn't know the half of it. The grip of the former KGB hierarchy was tightening and tightening on the bankrupt state, and Ansonov was at the heart of it.

Chapter Ten

Krayanovsk Hydro-Electric Dam, Krayanovsk, Siberia, Russia

The minibus stopped at the dam; Lansky followed the Malenkov brothers out, to stand on the cold, windy sweep of the road across the top of it. Shivering in the icy air, he walked forward, to look over the edge; he recoiled in shock. The concrete face of the dam dropped away vertiginously for what seemed to him to be hundreds of feet. At the bottom, columns of water spurted out to plunge into the dark pool. A few hundred yards downstream, ice was already beginning to form on the surface. The river was contained between two steep, wooded banks. Through the murky grey air, he could just about make out the buildings of Krayanovsk, crowned by the fumes belching out of the chimneys of the smelter.

Oleg walked across the dam to join him. "This is the key, Victor. The power this dam generates will ensure we can always have enough electricity to run our smelter. We control this dam, and that's why nobody else can buy the smelter. If we do not get it, then we simply turn off the electricity, and whoever else buys the plant will have nothing. Power is everything. Like our country." He laughed at his own joke.

"How did you get to own the dam? I would have thought that the town of Krayanovsk would also be interested in who controlled its electric supply. Did the town, the community, not have a say in who bought it?"

"Good question, Victor." Oleg glanced over towards his brother, who was still standing on the other side of the dam, looking upstream across the icy headwaters. "Leonid was able to come to an arrangement with a friend of his in the governing party which gave us the majority ownership. We guaranteed to keep supplying the town with domestic power, as a separate issue from the smelter supply. We gave them what they wanted, and they knew that we had the ability to carry it out. If the town or regional authorities had control, they would just be squabbling all the time about how to operate. This way, the Kremlin was sure that Central Siberia would not be left dark and cold. It was a good deal for everybody – and once we have the smelter as well, it will be even better." Leonid called, and beckoned them over to where he was standing, next to a brick-built shack at the edge of the dam. "This is where we go down into the dam," explained Oleg. Seeing the look of surprise on Lansky's face, he

54

continued "It's OK, we just go down the stairs through the middle of the dam, past all the turbines and machinery, so you can see how it works." Lansky didn't say anything, but he didn't relish the idea of climbing into a dam built by Soviet engineers in the 1930s, with God knew how many millions of gallons of water pressing their weight up against it. Ah well, it had stood for sixty years, it would probably survive the next half hour. He wasn't going to hang around in there, though.

They clambered down iron staircases, passing dank grey concrete walls, lit only by dim bulbs hanging from the ceiling. The hum of the turbines was audible from the moment they stepped down into the structure, and became louder and more insistent the lower they went. Eventually, they stepped through the door at the foot of the stairs and were in the brightly-lit control room. Three or four men sat around, watching an array of electronic instruments. In the centre of the room, one man sat in front of a control console, dominated by a big panel covered in flashing green lights. Oleg gestured to Lansky to come over to the console. "This is where they control the power," he said. "All these green lights indicate that all flows of water are clear, and there" – he pointed to six large dials at the side of the panel – "are the indicators of the turbine speeds. You can see they are all showing about half power. That is because there is a lot of excess capacity built into this dam. We only need to run at half available potential to create enough power for the town and the smelter. Eventually, the town will expand, which will be easy to handle as far as electricity is concerned."

Lansky had to ask the question that had been disturbing him all the way down through the dam. "Oleg, this is a Soviet era construction. Have you done any upgrading to modern standards?"

Oleg smiled thinly. "It is true this dam was built in the 1930s by slave labour. People who were dissenters from the Stalinist orthodoxy. But the engineers who designed it and supervised its construction were not gulag-fodder. They were trained and skilled. They ensured it was properly built. Standards of Russian construction at that time were high. It was only later that quality and safety became compromised. This dam is as strong as, I don't know, say the Hoover dam in the United States from the same period. So no, we have not had to do any major reconstruction work. The structure is sound. Obviously, turbine technology has advanced, and at some point in the interests of greater efficiency, we shall replace the generating equipment. But in terms of reliability and safety, we can easily and confidently continue to run as we are." He laughed. "Honestly, Victor, do you think I would climb down here if I thought it wasn't safe? And would I bring our most important western guest here? I know you have some knowledge and understanding of Russia's history, but you must never forget how much more complicated it is than you can ever imagine. We have a long tradition of slave labour which you do not. It is natural therefore that you mistrust products of that environment. But it's not that simple. Come, follow Leonid. We will go and look at the turbines."

Down again they went, the turbine hum getting louder and louder, until they debouched into a cavernous room, with six massive metallic monsters, like half cylinders set on their sides on the ground. By now the noise was deafening, and Leonid could barely make himself heard above it. "Our turbines," he shouted. "This is where the power comes from. The river is now running right underneath us, turning those wheels in the machines to make the electricity. We power the whole town from here." Lansky sensed the pride in his voice, and understood it. To have come from the Malenkovs' origins to controlling the light, power and heat of the city was indeed a big step. No matter how they had achieved it, it was an impressive journey.

Despite Oleg's confidence in the integrity of the dam's structure, Lansky was relieved finally to come back out into the open air at its foot. Looking upwards as they walked along to the river bank, he was staggered by the size of it. Even more than from above, the scale of it was awesome. They were still a good hundred feet above the level of the river, and yet the sheer concrete face of the dam soared into the grey sky above them. Immediately above and below them were the various different sluices which allowed excess water to be drained off. Oleg pointed at them. "You see these sluice gates?" He had to shout to be heard over the roaring sound of the flowing water. "They are used to control the flow of water through the dam and the turbines. Those green lights on the board in the control room – they all represent one of these gates. There are two things to consider. One, obviously, is how much power we need to produce. The other is how much pressure of water there is in the river. That depends very much on the season. You can guess that when the Spring melt is in full flow, the water-pressure is so high that even if we wished to generate at full capacity, we would have a lot of the sluices open, in order to prevent too much water going through the turbines." He smiled. "As I said upstairs, it's a well-built dam. We can control flows perfectly. Even in the heaviest flood period, there is no danger of too much water building up behind the dam because we have enough straight-through flow possibility to keep control. This is very important, because the level of this river varies enormously according to season."

"How does it affect it if the river is frozen, in mid-winter?"

"Not too much, because although the surface is frozen, even to a depth of many metres, the river above the dam is very deep, so there is always a flow of water below the ice. Clearly the engineers have to monitor the weight of ice building against the dam, and if it becomes too much, they need to break it up. They do this with small explosive devices, enough to shatter the ice, but too small to harm the dam. And downstream," he gestured down the river in front of them, "you can see the ice begins to form again after a few hundred metres. This is no problem, because obviously the flow of the river is taking it away from the dam. I think the lowest temperature they have recorded here, since the dam was built, was around minus thirty degrees. Even for this part of Siberia, that is exceptional; but it caused no problems to the functioning of the dam and generators. So we are confident in our machinery."

Lansky just nodded, without saying anything. The curious split personality of Oleg was emerging again. He was, clearly, a gangster – everybody knew it. And his brother was a particularly nasty, violent one. Yet, to listen to his pride in the dam and its construction was to see the other side, the would-be industrialist developer of Siberia's resources. Uncomfortable though he had felt while inside the dam, Lansky was impressed. This was not a fly-by-night game. There was a serious, major industrial project here, and one which would have the major bonus of spinning off a huge amount of cash, almost from day one. It was time to make his decision.

The minibus was waiting for them as they stepped back on to the roadway alongside the bottom of the dam. "So, Victor," said Oleg. "Let us take you to see the countryside. The river valley is very beautiful. We shall take a detour on the way back to the plant to show you the forest down there." He pointed down the river valley, back in the direction of the city. "Let's go. If you have any more questions about the dam, we can try and answer them as we drive. We have a small picnic prepared, that we can eat at the lookout point on the river bank. It is very beautiful."

Fifteen minutes later, standing on a brick observation platform at the top of the hill overlooking the river, Lansky struggled to agree with him. It wasn't beautiful – it was grey; sky, river bank, trees, icy water – all the same monotone dull grey. And it was cold. An aching, numbing cold, with the dampness of the drizzling snow in the air making it thoroughly miserable. The picnic consisted of some stale cheese and fatty ham filled rolls, and a bottle of Georgian brandy. The latter was clearly the way the Siberians coped with the cold, judging from the speed with which they swigged it back. Once again, Lansky was hit by the incongruity of it. A London property dealer, here he was in the middle the Siberian wastes, having a brandy-based picnic on a riverbank in minus God knew how many degrees. Oleg pulled out a camera. "Move over there, and you, Leonid, so I can have the river in the background. This picture can become famous, I hope. Maybe we can say it marks the beginning of a world-beating aluminium company. We can put it on the cover of our first western-standard company brochure. The grit and determination of the Siberian people, and the financial skills of the west, united in a great venture!" Lansky couldn't help smiling, just as Oleg triggered the shutter.

Gangster or not, the more he saw of Oleg, the more he couldn't help liking the more personable of the brothers.

"OK", he said, "we will need to work out the legal requirements, but I can say now I am ready to get involved in this deal, and get the business up and running." He lifted his glass, half-full of the Georgian brandy, and said "Gentlemen: to the success of our venture." Solemnly, they all drained their glasses. Lansky knew he was taking a big risk, particularly with his reputation, by getting involved with the Malenkovs, but he also knew how he'd feel if he passed up the opportunity, only to see someone else step into the frame. He was clear in his own mind that he would not get involved in how the Russian end of the enterprise worked; he was very definitely only responsible for the reputable, western part of the venture.

Oleg beamed. "That's fantastic! I knew you would be impressed when you got to see the operation we have here. I'm sure it's the right decision." His brother, also smiling, spoke in Russian. "Little brother, you had better tell our friend in the Kremlin that we are now ready to go." Oleg acknowledged him, also in Russian.

Chapter Eleven

Mayfair, London

December 1994

Victor Lansky was a rich man, but he still had work to do to raise $40 million in cash, at short notice. Fortunately, he was seen by his banks as something of a golden boy, and his good judgement in the property world had stored up a lot of bonus points for him over the years. He needed to call in a few favours, but between asset disposals and securitisation of some of his projects, he was pretty sure he could get himself in position within the four-week timespan he had agreed with the Malenkovs. In the end, the final negotiation and agreement in Krayanovsk had been disturbingly simple. Lansky had committed himself to subscribing forty million dollars in return for a holding of fifty percent in a British Virgin Islands company called Russo-European Metals Ltd. That company had a long-term deal to act as the sole sales agent for the Russian Joint Stock Company Krayanovsk Aluminium, whose major asset was the aluminium smelter. The dam and power plant were separately held by the Malenkovs, and Lansky had seen the equally long-term contractual agreement which made provision for the supply of power from the generator to the smelter. All the paperwork was beautifully written in English, by a firm of Road Town, Tortola, lawyers, and the stamps and seals and signatures were all shiny and pretty. But Lansky knew that it all, lawyers included, afforded him absolutely no protection. The agreement which gave him his partial ownership of the smelter was purely a verbal one. If things went wrong, and he tried to enforce that part ownership in Russia, he would be laughed out of Court. The simple fact of Russian law was that foreigners could not own Russian assets. More than once since he had signed the Heads of Agreement in Krayanovsk, and got back to London, he had awakened in the cold grey dawn, hit by the reality that he was handing over a substantial part of his hard-earned wealth to a pair of Russian gangsters, whom he had known for no more than a few months. And why? Because he was a gambler at heart, and he was sure the odds were stacked on his side. But lying in his bed, unable to go back to sleep, the demons in his mind kept taunting him with the bleak view of failure. Then back in his office, making calls, raising money, feeling part of the game, he was full of confidence. There was, though, one clause in the articles of Russo-European which had given him some pause for thought. That clause stated that in the event of the death of a shareholder, the remaining shareholders had the first option to buy out the share of the deceased at the issue price. Lansky had no dependents at the moment, but he did file away in the back of his mind the need to change that should he ever marry or have children, so that they could inherit. The Malenkovs had brushed any concerns aside, pointing out that it applied to them as well, and was simply in place to ensure that the company would continue to function. As they said, anyway, any heirs he might have would still have the forty million they would have to pay to buy him out, so they wouldn't be too disadvantaged. Anyway, it was time he started to get the business moving.

His first call was to Rory Davis, at Commet. He needed help with getting to grips with the logistics of moving sixty-odd thousand tonnes a month of aluminium from the Russian port of St Petersburg to a safe, secure destination in the west, where other people would pay them money for it. Commet's parent company owned port and warehouse facilities in Hamburg; as long as they had the space, Lansky envisaged regular shipments making the relatively short voyage across the Baltic, through the Skagerrak round the top of Denmark and down into the German port. Davis was enthusiastic. Still finding his top role at Commet somewhat daunting, he latched on to Lansky's proposal as a way of beginning to stamp his own authority on the company.

Vienna, Austria

All was not sweetness and light in the city of Mozart. Rumours to the effect that the Krayanovsk smelter was close to agreeing a marketing deal with a new western partner were beginning to seep out through some of Metalex's contacts in the Kremlin, and behind the bronze-tinted windows of the discreet office block on the Inner Ring, tempers were getting frayed. Roger Erlsfeldt was the German-American head of the company, and his anger was clear to the two traders sitting uncomfortably round the table with him.

"How is this happening? I thought we had the Kremlin privatisations tied up. Krayanovsk is the best aluminium asset in the country; we can't just let it go. Alex, I thought you had the President in the palm of your hand. For Christ's sake, we've paid him enough. What's going on?"

Alex Koch was an Austrian in his late thirties, responsible for running the Metalex operations in the Former Soviet Union. That meant, largely, ensuring that the right person got the money, the girls, the offshore properties at the right time, and in return, making sure that Metalex got the right access to the mineral wealth it wanted. He knew his head was on the block when things went wrong on his territory. The other trader in the room was Max Eisenstadt, a Swiss who ran the worldwide Metalex aluminium trading book.

"Roger," began Koch, "I think we've been stiffed. Somehow, I think through Yuri Ansonov, a pair of Siberian ex-KGB gangsters seem to have got into pole position on the Krayanovsk deal. How they've got to the President, I don't know, but I'm sure Ansonov must be the key. He's been more and more high profile inside the Kremlin; even though he's officially only the "advisor" to the President, he appears to hold more and more influence, especially over the last couple of months. Even so, I'm surprised he's been able to turn this one." Koch took a deep breath. "Look, Roger, I know it's my failure to produce on this, but frankly we have lost the Kremlin edge on it. We will have to get in another way. Max has been hearing some strange rumours in the aluminium market; we think there's a way to get to it from the other end."

Erlsfeldt looked enquiringly at Eisenstadt. "Max?"

Eisenstadt was in his late forties. Ten years with Metalex, after running the US end of a major European aluminium producer for ten years before that, he was the most well-connected man in the aluminium industry. Tall, stooped and balding, he spoke English with a pronounced American accent.

"Yeah, Roger, there's something odd I just picked up from a guy in London. Story is, these Siberian hoods, the Malenkov brothers, have done a deal with a guy called Victor Lansky to handle the western end of their operation. He's a half-Polish, half-British property dealer. Before that, he ran a pretty successful domestic UK scrap operation. Mostly copper. Used to be close to Mack McKee before he died."

Erlsfeldt just looked at his two colleagues for a moment.

"So you're telling me that we, the biggest metals trader in the world, have been beaten to a deal we really wanted by a pair of Russian Mafiosi and some Polish UK scrap dealer? You really sit here and tell me that?" His voice was rising. "With no shame? That's just the way it is? 'Sorry, Roger, but better luck next time.' You guys are fucking unbelievable. You better have a way still to get in there. And it had better work. We can't just let it drop." He paused, and drew breath. More calmly, he went on, "OK, so what do you suggest? How do we get our hands on that metal?"

Max Eisenstadt spoke. "I think we have to go through Lansky. I hear he's trying to tie up with Commet to take the metal into their Hamburg warehouses; that means he's either going to sell it directly on to the LME, or he's arranging a storage deal with them, to keep the metal and distribute it from Hamburg to the end users."

Erlsfeldt interrupted. "Yeah, so he's intending to do just what we would do. Or anybody else who knew how the metals business worked. So tell me something I *don't* know."

"Keep calm, Roger. This will work. The problem they've all got in this is money. The only reason Lansky gets to be involved is because we think he is fronting up some cash to help them buy out the smelter. But once they've done that, they still have to finance the raw materials and manufacturing and shipping time. We get to Lansky, arrange all that for him, and once it's all running, we slowly ease him out. He can keep a stake in the smelter if it makes him happy, but we still get the metal. Since we have to have a Russian partner, frankly do we care if it's the Malenkovs or somebody else? We'll always have the upper hand, because we have the money."

Erlsfeldt looked sceptical. "In an ideal world, that would be great. Sadly, the world isn't ideal. What do you think, Alex?"

"Worth a try. At the same time, I think I have to work on Ansonov. I don't know what he's planning, but looks like he's the coming man in the Kremlin. May not be finally the time to ditch the President, but its getting close."

"OK. I can't pretend I like it, but we have to be realistic about where we are. Contact Lansky, and let's see if we can persuade him to see reason."

Mayfair, London

Lansky knew word of his involvement in Krayanovsk would leak out, but frankly it didn't bother him. Since he would have to sell the metal anyway, the market would have to know who he was. So he was pretty sanguine when his secretary announced that Mr Koch of Metalex was on the phone for him. It was mid-December by now, the financing was in place, and Russo-European Metals was gearing up to begin making shipments from the plant within the next month or so. That meant the risk of ice at St Petersburg, but they would handle that when it arose.

"Mr Koch, this is Victor Lansky. What can I do for you?"

"Good morning, Mr Lansky. I am a representative of a company called Metalex. I don't know if you are aware of us?"

"Of course I'm aware of you. You are the biggest player in the metals market. Anybody who is involved is aware of you."

"OK, that makes it easier. You see, I wasn't sure if you were still in the metals business. I had heard rumours, but you can never be sure."

"I'm not sure that 'still' in the metals business is right. It's more 'again'. I used to be a copper scrap trader, but I sold out of that and for some years now I've been a property dealer. I am now, though, reactivating some interest in metals. What rumours have you heard?"

"Come on, Mr Lansky. You know what I've heard. That you are going into partnership with the Malenkovs to control the output of the Krayanovsk aluminium smelter. That they will be responsible for producing the metal and getting it out to St Petersburg, and you will be responsible for shipping it from there and selling it into the western market."

"Some of that may be true, but why should it concern you?"

"That's what I'd like to discuss with you. We have some ideas that may be of assistance to you. Do you think we could meet? I'm in Moscow at the moment, until after Christmas, but then over the Orthodox Christmas I shall be back in Europe, principally in Vienna, but I could meet you elsewhere, if it suited you."

Lansky thought quickly. What could Metalex possibly be able to do to help him? And why would they? Still, it never did any harm to talk to people – after all, that's how this whole affair had started.

"Well," he said, "I shall have to be in Hamburg in the second week in January, so that may be better for you than coming to London."

"Perfect. Say the 12th?"

"Yes, that will be fine. I shall be staying at the Vier Jahreszeiten. Dinner around 8:30?"

"I look forward to it."

Lansky was puzzled by the contact. He knew Metalex would have an interest in what they were doing, but why make such a heavy-handed approach? Surely it would have made more sense to engineer a low-key, seemingly accidental meeting, rather than potentially compromising their position by being so obvious. He had no doubt that Koch was going to try to muscle Metalex into the deal in some way. Ah well, he'd have to wait until early January to find out how. In the meantime, just to be on the safe side, he reported the call back to Oleg, who in turn mentioned it to Yuri Ansonov, a few days later in a call to the Kremlin.

The Kremlin, Moscow, Russia

Yuri Ansonov was not so relaxed to hear about Metalex's interest in the new deal in Krayanovsk. He knew the influence the trader had cultivated with the President, and in order to get to where he wanted to be, it was a link he had to break. The old man had been taking money from them for years, going back to the Soviet times when he was a senior official in the Ministry of Foreign Trade. They had almost run Russia's external trade in metals at that time; some would argue that the way so much of the profits from that trade had found their way to Vienna was at least partially responsible for the parlous state of the economy now. Ansonov smiled to himself. Well, that and the military spending, of course. It was early morning, and he was sitting in his office in the Kremlin, looking out over a central courtyard, still gloomy in the pre-dawn light. Flakes of snow were drifting down, caught seemingly motionless in the harsh spotlights at regular intervals round the building. Ansonov liked to start working well before dawn. It was one time of the day when he could be sure he would not have to nursemaid the President – the effect of the previous day's vodka and brandy would always ensure that the old man did not wake too early. Once he did appear, Ansonov concentrated on stopping him saying anything unplanned – unplanned by Ansonov, obviously. Anyway, that morning in mid-December, he had to decide how to resolve the Metalex issue.

His first call was across town to the Lubyanka, formerly the headquarters of the KGB, now, in the brave new democratic world, headquarters of the FSB. Comforting, how some things don't change, at least it is if you are on the right side of them. Although he was one of the real movers and shakers of Russian politics, Ansonov didn't ask for the Director of the Service. Instead, he asked to be put through to Denis Menkov, a former protégé of his from the old days. Menkov was an officer with lots of experience of Western Europe. After completing his training, he'd been posted to the Russian embassy in London, for unspecified duties. He'd carried them out well, and back in Moscow, Ansonov had taken the younger man under his wing, within the economic section, which he ran at that time. As Ansonov had risen in the hierarchy, Menkov had gone with him, and now that the boss was sitting at the very highest table over in the Kremlin, his task was to protect his back in the bear-pit of FSB politics. Without his former service solidly behind him, Ansonov would be vulnerable.

"Denis, good to speak to you. I have a small issue I need to discuss with you. Perhaps we could meet this morning?"

"Of course. A coffee at the usual place?" Menkov understood from Ansonov's tone that it wasn't something to be discussed in an official building – walls in Russian governmental departments very definitely do have ears.

"Yes, let's say at nine o'clock."

The usual place was a coffee house on Tret'yakovskiy Proyezd, sandwiched between elegant boutiques. As he walked through the snowy city, Ansonov reflected that if his plans came to fruition, he wouldn't be able to wander unrecognized through the streets of Moscow for much longer. Menkov was already sitting with his back to the wall as Ansonov came in with snow falling off his coat as he crossed the room. He stood up to welcome his boss – to all the world, they were just another two hustling Russian businessmen trying to put a deal together. "Yuri, it's good to see you. You're looking well. Power must be suiting you."

Ansonov smiled. Menkov was one of the few people in the FSB who were not frightened of the former Director. He shook Menkov's hand with genuine warmth. "You too, Denis. It's too long since we met. Power is good, but one has to be very careful. Have I ever told you, the higher you get, the fewer people you can trust?"

It was Menkov's turn to smile. "You have. And since there's now - for now – only one person higher than you, I guess you haven't got many left to trust."

A waitress came over to the table; Menkov ordered two coffees, which came back almost immediately.

Ansonov looked serious. "Yes, one man. And we're getting close to the endgame there as well, Denis. Things are falling into place. But I have a small issue. You are aware of the part our Siberian ex-colleagues, the Malenkovs, have to play." Menkov nodded "It is crucial that they secure the industries of Siberia – that gives us a huge power-base. They have the electricity generation, which is of course vital, but there may be a small headache with the aluminium smelter in Krayanovsk. You know, of course, that our dear leader has been in the pay of Metalex for years." Menkov nodded again. "Well Metalex are seemingly trying to muscle into the deal we have constructed for the Malenkovs. I don't know what they exactly intend to do, but they are showing too much interest in what is after all our business. Do you think you could investigate what they want to do, and see if you can't persuade them it would be best not to do it?"

Between old security service colleagues, it wasn't necessary to spell everything out. Menkov understood the boundaries of his orders. "How urgent?" was all he said.

"Not ultra. There will be a meeting in Hamburg on the 12th of January that I think maybe you should watch. If you talk to Oleg Malenkov, he will be able to give you the details." Business dealt with, he smiled again. "Now, tell me, what news of your family?"

Kempinski Hotel, Moscow

31st December 1994

Metalex had a tradition, dating back to the old Soviet times, of a New Year's Eve reception for the big names of the Russian resources industry. This was a respectable function, an early evening cocktail party, with a clear understanding that it finished promptly at 9pm, ostensibly so that the participants could all go on to their family or friends parties for the *real* New Year celebration. In fact, it was so correct only because of the year back in the 1980s when some of the KGB heavyweights had got so drunk and brought in so many prostitutes that the place resembled a brothel – it was too much, even for the freewheeling management of Metalex. It wasn't a function Yuri Ansonov would normally have attended, but this year he pulled a few strings to ensure that he and Denis Menkov were both invited. He wanted to see Alex Koch, who seemed to be the point man for Metalex.

Standing on the fringes of the heaving crowd in the ballroom of the hotel, Ansonov was amused to see how most of the people he knew who saw him there quickly looked away and avoided meeting his eye. He was under no illusion; he knew he was feared by the majority of the governmental apparatchiks, in fact it was a deliberate posture. If they didn't fear him, how could he hope to rule them? Hadn't it always been the Russian way? He was musing on this when Denis Menkov walked across the room towards him.

"OK, I've met him. He's that guy over there, with those two from the Trade Ministry. The one with the gold-rimmed glasses. I introduced myself as a member of the Mining Council of Siberia. He tried to arrange lunch with me, then I squeezed his arm and whispered I was only joking, I'm really FSB. He couldn't get rid of me fast enough." Menkov burst into laughter at Ansonov's shocked expression. "Don't worry, Yuri, I'm pulling your leg. I just said hello, and moved on to the next group. But now I know who he is. I'll be able to keep an eye on him in Hamburg. Oleg told me he would be meeting an Englishman in Hamburg. Oleg will be there, but not at that meeting. Do you want it to be Koch's last meeting?"

"I'm not sure yet, Denis. I know he's coming to see the President in the next few days, so I will have a better idea of what we need to do after that meeting. I guess you will be with the family for the next few days?"

Menkov nodded, as Ansonov continued, "I'll call you around the 4th, and by then I should be in a position to give you definite instructions. So, I think we've finished here. Let's go for one quick New Year drink, then I'll let you go home to your family."

But as they walked towards the big double-doors of the ballroom, Koch detached himself from the group he was with, and came across to them. He smiled as he introduced himself. "Mr Ansonov, my name is Alex Koch, from Metalex Moscow office. I don't think we've met before. It's a pleasure to see you at our little party."

As he replied, Ansonov signalled to Menkov to keep walking, and leave them. No point in Koch becoming too curious about the man he would next see in Hamburg.

"Mr Koch, thank you for a great evening. It's the first time I've come here; I thought it was about time I got to meet some of the people of Metalex who have been so influential in helping our President make sense of the Russian resources industry. Unfortunately, he could not make it himself this evening; he had some family business to attend to." In fact, the President had cried off because he had no intention of allowing Koch to question him over his preference for the Malenkovs. "But I know he is grateful for all the assistance you and your company have given him over the years, and keen to see that co-operation continue." Or at least, keen for you to keep paying him off, Ansonov thought to himself. "But you must excuse me, Mr Koch, I have to leave for another engagement. It's been a pleasure to meet you."

"Likewise, Mr. Ansonov. Perhaps we could meet again after your Christmas celebrations. Maybe we can get to know each other a little."

"Of course," replied Ansonov smoothly, "please contact the Secretariat at the Kremlin and let us arrange something. Now, if you will excuse me..........." They shook hands and Ansonov turned on his heel and left.

Chapter 12

Hamburg, Germany

January 1995

Commet's group office in Hamburg fronted Neuer Wall, but the windows of the boardroom on the second floor looked out across the Jungfernstieg to the Binnenalster, the smaller of the two lakes that form the centrepiece of the city. Lansky and Davis had arrived the previous evening for a meeting with Oleg Malenkov, to be followed by a tour of the company's warehouse complex down in the port area. It was a cold winter, and the lake in front of them was frozen solid. Davis pointed through the window.

"Look at those guys there, walking on the ice. They must be crazy. How do they know it's thick enough?" Sure enough, two figures were stepping out from the Jungfernstieg onto the snow-covered ice.

"Obviously some sort of macho game," grinned Lansky. "Bit like chicken. Walk as far as you can before the ice cracks, then run like hell before it actually breaks."

"You wouldn't catch me doing it. Still, it might appeal to your Russian gangster."

"Please, Rory, that's not a word we use. He's a businessman developing the resources of Siberia. Seriously, ignore what he looks like and concentrate on the deal. You're going to get a lot of LME selling, and your colleagues over here are going to get some serious warehousing business. There's going to be fifty to sixty thousand tonnes a month, and even if it doesn't all stay too long in the warehouse, they're still going to earn some big numbers in rent and storage charges."

"Yeah, I know. They're quite excited about it. They're laying on the full warehouse tour this afternoon. Got to be finished by six, though. I definitely have to catch my plane – I need to be back in London for a meeting tomorrow morning. Didn't you say you had dinner with Metalex this evening?"

"Yes, with Alex Koch. D'you know him?"

"I've met him. Their man in Moscow. I think he's Czech, or Austrian, or something like that."

"That sounds perilously close to 'all you central Europeans look the same'", Lansky said with a laugh. He looked at his watch. "Oleg should be here in a couple of minutes." He looked seriously at the younger man. "Rory, you know I'm trusting you on this. You'll hear a few things about our operation that you really don't need to know. I wouldn't want things to start leaking out."

Davis shook his head. "Don't worry, Victor. I'm only interested in the bit that affects my own company. I know you're being very open about everything, but you have my word I'll never use any of it. The only way this will work is if we trust each other."

"OK, I'm happy with that."

As he said it, there was a knock and the door opened; a secretary showed Oleg Malenkov into the room. Visiting warehouses obviously did not in his eyes warrant the smart look; Davis immediately understood why Lansky had warned him to ignore Oleg's appearance.

When the car dropped them off at the warehouse, though, Davis had to admit to himself that Oleg's heavy woollen trousers and shapeless parka were more suited to the temperature than his own city suit and overcoat. The sky was blue, the sun low above the horizon in the northern winter, and a sharp, bitterly cold wind blew from the east. Across the dock from the warehouse complex, the Blohm und Voss shipyard was clear in the diamond-bright air, with Hamburg's Altstadt visible behind it across on the far bank of the Elbe. Even here, deep in the port area, ice floes were floating on the river's surface. Davis was grateful when their guide ushered them through the door into the warehouse's office complex. The guide – the head of Commet's warehousing operations – was clearly enamoured of his company's facilities. The tour took them the best part of two hours; two hours of looking at piles of metal and then computer screens showing how it was all recorded, some of it to conform to the LME's warehousing regulations, and some of it in general storage, without being part of the LME system. Frankly, Lansky and Malenkov were bored, and simply feigned interest out of politeness. As far as they were concerned, as long as they were paid for their aluminium, they really couldn't care how it was stored. Davis tried manfully to support his colleague by keeping a dialogue of questions going, but he could sense the lack of interest in the other two.

A little later that afternoon, Austrian Airlines flight 272 from Vienna touched down at Hamburg's Fuhlsbuettel airport. Alex Koch had only hand baggage, and the formalities were swift for arrivals from fellow-EU countries, so within twenty minutes he was in a cab. He smiled to himself as he saw the name of the street they took out of the airport. Only in Germany could the road past the terminal building be called Zeppelinstrasse. He wouldn't have smiled had he known that he had a secret follower. Denis Menkov, who had been sitting behind a copy of Handelsblatt in the arrivals hall, had gently strolled out of the airport behind him and overheard him giving his destination to the cab driver. Stepping up to the next cab in line, Menkov repeated "Atlantic Hotel".

Three days earlier, in Moscow, Menkov had met Ansonov, at another anonymous meeting-place, to receive his final instructions before leaving for Hamburg. Using the FSB's computer systems, it hadn't been too difficult to establish Koch's travel plans, nor the fact that he would be staying at the Atlantic. Following him from the airport was just a kind of belt and braces operation, on the off chance he had changed his mind. Menkov was nothing if not thorough.

Hamburg's mercantile past, from the days of the Hanseatic League, to nineteenth century shipbuilding and ironworks, to its modern-day place as one of Northern Europe's great port cities, has left a legacy of not just one but two of the *grandes dames* of European hotels, staring at each other from opposite sides of the expanse of the Binnenalster. The Atlantic is on the eastern bank, just past the Kennedy Bruecke, the Vier Jahreszeiten nearer the centre of the city on the western bank. Koch knew Lansky was staying at the latter, and preferred not to use the same place as his quarry. Quarry, because he too felt he was playing Lansky, finally to land him in the enveloping folds of the Metalex net. Denis Menkov saw Koch going into the hotel, and redirected his cab to towards the centre of town. He had a few hours to kill before he had to take any action. He knew from Oleg Malenkov where Lansky and Koch would be later, so, getting the cab to drop him near the Rathausplatz, he found his way to one of the many small bars in that part of town and settled down to wait. His rented car was parked in a multi-story off Neuer Wall, ready to be collected later. He had not flown into Hamburg, and had no intention of staying there overnight.

Davis left from the warehouse direct to the airport for his flight back to London, leaving Lansky and Malenkov to make their way back to the Vier Jahreszeiten.

"You know this Koch is becoming very interested in our activities in Siberia," said Malenkov as they sat in the hotel bar in the early evening. "He doesn't seem to realise that Siberia's wealth is now for Siberians; his company's time was in the old days, when we could not control our own destiny."

"Yes, but even so, you do need outside investment. That's why I'm here, after all," replied Lansky.

Malenkov looked hard at him. "True, Victor, but you know you are here only as part of our consortium. You are not an outsider trying to own what is legitimately ours."

"No, but we will export the product, put it into the warehouse we saw today, and sell it. The proceeds of those sales will be paid into Russo-European Metals, which is after all a BVIs company. That's not really keeping the benefit in Siberia."

Malenkov laughed. "You're being very literal, Victor. My brother and I, and our co-investors, are all Russian. You are the only non-Russian, and you are there, as we know, because we have to raise some capital from the west. Control remains with us, in the interests of Siberia. The actual detail of the flows of cash is secondary. With Metalex, outsiders would control the resource. Do you not see the difference?"

Lansky nodded, but actually he thought the distinction a tad Jesuitical. Sure, control was Russian, but the money was being sucked out of the smelter into the pockets of a few individuals. Just because all but he were Russian didn't change that. A sudden shiver went down his spine. All but he were Russian............was that a long-term prospect? Or would he become expendable, as soon as the money started rolling in, and he was no longer essential. Well, he'd always been aware of who the Malenkovs were. He knew he needed to be careful.

Going in to the hotel's main restaurant was like stepping back in time, perhaps into a Thomas Mann novel. It was furnished in heavy buergerlich style, with big, gilt-framed portraits on the walls. As he was led across to his table by the tail-coated maitre d', Lansky speculated that they were perhaps likenesses of some of the great figures of Hamburg's past. Shipowners, maybe, or traders and industrialists, looking down with benign indulgence on the tables of their successors. Well, he mused as he saw what was obviously Alex Koch already seated, the Austrian certainly fell into the category of trader. Metalex had its tentacles in every corner of the metal producing and trading world. It was the most powerful, and also the most secretive. If nothing else, he was in for an interesting dinner, seeing how the big battalions worked.

"Mr Lansky, good to meet you. Please, take a seat."

"Thank you, it's good to meet you too. But please, call me Victor. No need to be too formal."

"OK, that's cool." Koch's mid-Atlantic English chimed with his sharp suit and brash tie. "I'm just having a gin and tonic here. What can I offer you?"

"The same, thanks." Koch signalled to the waiter, who was hovering, as Lansky went on. "I understand your main beat is in Moscow. That must be an interesting life these days."

Koch laughed. "It is. I really only came in just right at the end of the Soviet era, but it's certainly the hot place to be in the metals business right now. I guess you know we used to have quite an involvement with the old regime." Lansky nodded. "Well, the main part of my job is to make sure we carry that relationship forward with the asset privatisations that are going on right now. It's a fascinating time. Our real function has to be to help the miners and producers of metal to operate in a world where they have to think about commercial matters – in the past, the State took care of all that for them. Now, we try to make long-term agreements to smooth the changes."

Lansky decided to play innocent to start with. "So do you actually take ownership of plants, or just agree to take their production?" It didn't work. Koch looked hard at him.

"Victor, you know the answer to that. It's why you're getting interested in Russia, as well. The official rules are clear, and we play by the rules, of course, just like I'm sure you and your friends do. But hey, let's get some food ordered, and some wine. After that we can get to the serious discussions."

Unlike the room, the menu was light and modern. Koch was generous with the wines, too, with a beautiful Mersault, followed by a 1982 Chateau Margaux. As they finished the main course, Koch brought the conversation back round to what was in both their minds.

"OK, Victor, I guess you are curious as to why the Metalex Moscow man wanted to meet you. Or in fact, I don't think you're curious at all about why, I think you're more interested in what I might think we have to discuss." He held his hand up to stop Lansky interrupting. "We both know you have done a deal with the Malenkov brothers, and that deal covers the output of the Krayanovsk smelter. We also both know that it's exactly the kind of deal that Metalex would like to have done. So there are two things I want to say to you. First, think very hard about the Malenkovs; do you really want to be tied in with one of central Russia's premier bunch of gangsters? And when you've thought about that, perhaps you'd like to think about selling your position out to Metalex. Let us suffer the Malenkov headache, not you. You just take some money and run."

Lansky leaned back in his chair, his glass of wine in his hand. He looked at the beautiful deep red colour, and inhaled the powerful perfume. "Alex, this has been a delightful dinner. For this glorious wine alone, it would have been worth coming here. So don't spoil it. Yes, I have some association with the Malenkovs. Yes, I know what their reputation is. No, I don't have any involvement with their activities within Russia. And no, I don't want to sell out to Metalex. And, by the way, I don't think they would want a relationship with Metalex. They are very clear that they regard this as a Russian, even a Siberian, deal. We've had a pleasant dinner, a good conversation, let's leave it at that."

"You realise you are the only one in your consortium who isn't Russian, don't you? So if they are really so keen on the Russian aspect of all this, don't you think that may leave you a bit exposed? They're not nice people. You know that. I'm offering you a safe, comfortable way out. Anyway, you've just been telling me about your Polish ancestry. Given that, how can you want to work with Russians?"

Both of which, Lansky had to admit to himself, were issues he had had to force himself to consider. He had, and weighed them against his share of fifty-odd million dollars a month. He knew which won.

"Alex, I'm a big boy. I do know what reputation the Malenkovs have, and I do recognise that creates certain issues for me, issues which nobody but I can resolve. I appreciate your concern, even if my well-being may not be your primary motivation, but I repeat: I do not have any desire to do a deal over this with Metalex."

"Ok, so you want to stay with your Russian friends. Suppose we offer to buy all the metal from you? I know you've been with Commet and their warehouse today. I could show you a better offer for the metal than they will. We'll even prepay you, before it leaves Russia, if you give us an exclusivity."

"That's a suggestion I will consider. I have a verbal agreement with Commet, but that's all so far. We could think about that. But no way am I giving you an answer now."

"All right. Let's leave it there for this evening. You know where to get hold of me."

A few minutes more small talk, and they left the restaurant, Koch to look for a cab back to the Atlantic, and Lansky back to the bar, where he found Malenkov still sitting. Slightly nervously, fearing the Russian may be drunk if he'd been sitting there for the last two hours, he sat down opposite him. "So, Victor, you have had a good dinner?" The words weren't slurred, which was a good sign. "I have been upstairs, speaking to Leonid on the phone. It seems this Koch has been making a nuisance of himself in Moscow, trying to upset some of our associates. But it seems he may have bitten off more than he can chew. He has upset some very important people. That is not wise, in Russia."

"Well, he was quite keen to talk me out of our deal, but I made him understand that that won't happen. He did make one interesting suggestion, though. He indicated that Metalex may be a more competitive buyer of the metal than using the route we have been intending, through Commet and the LME. I think he will come back with a concrete proposal quite soon."

Malenkov looked at him for a moment. Then, very deliberately, he said, "No, Victor, we will not sell the metal to Metalex. I don't care if they claim to be more competitive. We will not deal with them."

Lansky looked blankly at him. "Why not, if it makes sense? Anyway, I thought I was responsible for selling the metal into the west? I may think Metalex is the best way to go."

"Victor, you **are** responsible for selling the metal in the west. But not to Metalex. There are reasons why we cannot do this. You don't need to know why. Just accept that it is so."

"But that's ridiculous. It's in all our interests to sell at the best price. If that comes from Metalex, so what? Their money is just the same as anybody else's. Why rule them out completely?"

"There are reasons," Malenkov repeated carefully, "why we cannot do this. Please, Victor, we do not want to fall out over this, but you must believe me. There are some Russian things you do not understand. And for your own sake, do not mention this idea to Leonid. It would annoy him very much, and that would not be a good idea. We do not deal with these people."

Lansky shrugged his shoulders. He thought back to Koch's comment about the Malenkovs not being nice people. Clearly some bad history there; still, he could live without knowing the details. "OK," he said, "so no deal with Metalex."

"Thank you, Victor."

The subject of their disagreement was not at that moment feeling too bright. As he had walked out of the hotel to find a cab, a man had approached him. "Mr Koch, I believe," he said. And shielding it from the hotel doorman with his overcoat, he had let Koch see a silenced pistol trained on his stomach. "Please accompany me this way." At the side of the Vier Jahreszeiten is a quiet, narrow street, with parking on both sides of it. Walking Koch up to a black Mercedes SL, the man said "Hold out your hands," and when Koch did as he was told, a pair of handcuffs were snapped on him. "That's good. Now, gently and easily, get into the car." And he opened the door, and pushed down on Koch's head as he ducked into the low seat. Shutting the passenger door quietly, he stepped quickly round to the driver's side and got in.

"Who are you?" said Koch, "and what do you want from me." But Denis Menkov was a professional. He said nothing, just pushed the central locking button and started the car. Putting it into drive, and easing away from the pavement, he then spoke. "Mr Koch, we are going for a short drive across town, then we are going to get out of the car and take a short walk. That's it. We have nothing to discuss, you and I. You just do what I say and all will be well." By now, Koch had picked up the Russian accent, and began to get worried. Metalex didn't really do seriously wrong things in Russia, but nevertheless there were people they had upset over the years. But in Hamburg? If it were the Russian mafia chasing him, why come to Hamburg? Surely if they wanted him, it would be easier for them in Moscow. It wasn't as though he had a raft of bodyguards or anything. Meanwhile, Menkov had made a big circuit round the Gaensemarkt and was approaching Neuer Wall. As they drove across the street, he pulled up on the edge of the Adolphusbruecke, and switched off the engine. In the silence, the click as he released the central locking sounded to Koch like a gunshot. Desperately, he looked around. But it was a January night, the weather was bitterly cold, and anyway they were on the edge of the business district. There was nobody around at this time of night. He took a breath to shout, but before he could get any sound out, Menkov hit him savagely across the mouth with the barrel of his pistol.

"Keep quiet," he spat. Getting out of the car, he stepped around the back of it and pulled Koch roughly out through the passenger door. He twisted the chain between the two handcuffs until they bit viciously into Koch's wrists and dragged the Austrian into the middle of the little bridge. With a cursory glance around to make sure they were not being observed, he brought the gun up behind Koch's head and blew away the back of his skull. He pushed the body over the low parapet into the river below. The thin sheet of ice gave way as Koch plunged through it. Menkov waited patiently until he saw the body rise again and lodge under the ice. As he turned to walk back to his car, he noted with satisfaction that it was starting to snow again. His overcoat was spattered with Koch's blood and brains, so he took it off and carefully rolled it up. He put it in the boot of the car. Unscrewing the silencer from the barrel of the pistol, he carefully put both parts into the pocket of his jacket. He got back into the car, and pulled away across the bridge. Fifteen minutes later, he was at the Horster Autobahndreieck, picking up the autobahn for Bremen, Muenster, the Ruhr and eventually Düsseldorf, where he would board his flight back to Moscow. As he put his foot down and eased into the outside lane, he felt a quiet satisfaction that he had made Hertz give him the SL500, not the 350. The extra horsepower would be good on a long journey.

After a couple of hours, well past Bremen, he pulled into a service area. He checked that the gun and silencer were out of sight in his pocket, got out of the car and went into the toilets. In one of the cubicles, he wrenched the lid off the cistern. He took the pistol and silencer out of his pocket, wiped them carefully all over with his handkerchief and dropped them into the water. The staff at these places had a reputation for being thorough, but he was willing to bet that thoroughness didn't stretch to cleaning the inside of the cistern. Hopefully, the pistol would have rotted away before anybody looked in there. Anyway, tying the pistol to the body of Alex Koch in Hamburg and Denis Menkov in Moscow would be beyond the abilities of any policeman. Seeing that the car park was empty when he got back to his car, he thought to combine the two stops he needed to make. The rolled up overcoat went over the fence into the woods behind the service area. He knew somebody would find that in a few days, but so what. As an FSB illegal, he certainly knew enough to make sure his coat was unidentifiable. He got back into the car. Not bad, he mused, accelerating back onto the carriageway, maybe I should buy one of these back in Moscow. As he hit 180 kilometres an hour, the radio station he was listening to started playing Chris Rea's "Road to Hell". Inappropriate, he thought. Quite inappropriate.

Chapter 13

Mayfair, London

Late January 1995

Lansky had been back from his trip to Hamburg for a few days. Although he'd been surprised by Oleg's vehemence in refusing even to discuss a deal with Metalex, he wasn't really concerned. He would obviously find it easier to work with Davis and Commet, whom he knew, than Metalex, whom he didn't, but he did expect Koch to make an approach with a concrete proposal to take the metal off them. He would listen to it, and then reject it. The alternative would be to get into areas with the Malenkovs that he thought would best be avoided. He guessed that Metalex had somehow outwitted the brothers in another business they had been trying to do, and they had reacted forcefully. Not his affair.

The direct line on his desk rang. "Hullo?"

"Victor, its Rory. I've just heard something very odd – shocking, in fact. Our aluminium dealer just got a call from Max Eisenstadt at Metalex. They found Alex Koch's body in a river in Hamburg yesterday. He'd been shot."

"What?"

"Yeah, they think he'd been in the water for about a week or so – apparently the river was frozen and snow-covered, so nobody saw him until the weather got a bit warmer and it thawed a bit. So it must have been within a day or so of when you saw him."

"But why? Was he mugged, or what?" As he said it, he couldn't help thinking of the real animosity for Metalex he'd seen in Oleg. But they couldn't have, surely? Those days were behind them. They were businessmen now.

"They say not. Apparently, he had his wallet in his pocket, and all that sort of thing. Anyway, I don't know any more. I just thought I should tell you, specially as you'd only just seen him."

"Yeah, thanks, Rory. Let's speak a bit later." And he hung up.

Lansky was shocked – seriously shocked. It was no use pretending to himself, he thought the Malenkovs were behind Koch's death. But why would they? It didn't make sense. He and Oleg had agreed there was to be no deal with Metalex, so what did they have to gain from killing

Koch? But if it wasn't them, that was surely too much of a coincidence? On the other hand, just as Metalex had clearly upset the brothers, there was no reason for him to think they hadn't also upset other Russians. And not only Russians. Metalex often had a heavy-handed way of getting what they wanted. It could have been anybody. Lansky sighed, and told himself to grow up. He could make up any number of stories about who had killed Koch, but there was only one he believed right now. There was a call he had to make. He couldn't avoid it.

"Hi Oleg, its Victor. You remember Alex Koch, whom I had dinner with in Hamburg? Metalex man?"

"Of course I know Alex Koch. What about him? I hope you are not going to suggest a deal again. That would be unwise."

"No, Oleg, we can't do a deal. Koch is dead. Shot and dumped in a river in Hamburg. They just found the body."

"But that is awful news. I cannot pretend that we liked the man, or his company, but that he's dead.............do they know when?"

"I don't know. I only heard the broad facts. Oleg, I have to ask. Do you think this is connected with our business?"

"Victor, my friend, you do not have to be so tactful. I know you want to ask if we are responsible for this. And the answer is no. Leonid and I did not have Koch killed. He was an irritant, no more. His company's time has come and gone, even if they do not realise it yet. Russia is for the Russians now, not for his company. He was a fleabite, nothing more. Victor, this is not our doing. But let me know if you hear any more."

Lansky was reassured, but not completely. True, as Oleg said, there was seemingly nothing to gain for the Malenkovs by ordering the killing. And, paradoxically, if, like the Malenkovs, murder had been part of your armoury, you probably wouldn't use it unnecessarily. It was a weapon you would use coldly and dispassionately – not to be wasted where it wasn't needed. Well, maybe. He could tell himself that until he was blue in the face – would he ever know? Maybe the German police would have an idea. That thought brought him up short. He was conceivably one of the last people to see Koch alive. Plenty of people in the restaurant could confirm the two of them had had dinner. He should expect a call from the Hamburg detectives.

It was not in fact the Hamburg police, but a Scotland Yard Detective Inspector and his Sergeant who came calling at Lansky's office later that day. After making introductions and showing warrant cards, the Inspector began to explain their visit.

"We've been asked to come and see you by the Hamburg police department. I understand you were in that city last week."

"Yes, I arrived for some business on the 12th, had a dinner meeting that evening and flew back to London around mid day on the 13th."

"Yes, it's the dinner meeting we need to concentrate on."

Lansky thought he might as well come clean. "Before you say anything else, I've just been told by an associate that my host that evening, Alex Koch, has been found dead in Hamburg. I was shocked to hear it."

"I can understand that, sir, nobody is untouched by a murder. Do you mind telling me what you did that evening? Just a timeline for the moment, to help us get a picture of what happened?"

"Certainly. I returned from my meetings in the Hamburg port late afternoon, together with a Russian associate called Oleg Malenkov. We'd been discussing warehousing business. When we got back to the hotel, the Vier Jahreszeiten, I went up to my room to freshen up and change, then I met Oleg again for a drink in the bar sometime after half past six. We stayed there talking about various things until I went into the hotel restaurant around eight thirty to meet Koch. He was already there, sitting at the table when I went in. Oleg stayed at the bar. I don't know for how long. Koch and I had dinner; we had a discussion about some business he wanted to do with me, and he left, I don't know exactly, I guess around half past ten. I went back to the bar, where I found Oleg again. He said he'd been in his room on the phone for most of the time I'd been at dinner. We had a few more things to talk about, then called it a night at something around midnight."

"OK. Did you actually see Mr Koch leaving the hotel?"

"Not really. As we came out of the restaurant, we shook hands, then he went off to the right, to the entrance, and I went diagonally left across the lobby to the bar. I was looking where I was going, so I didn't see him after we shook hands. I had my back to him."

"What was he going to do when he left the hotel? Do you know?"

"I assume he was going to get a cab. He was staying at the Atlantic – that's over the other side of the lake – so I presume that's where he was going."

"You didn't see if he met somebody else as he left the hotel?"

"No, as I said, I was looking in the opposite direction."

"Right, sir. And how was Mr Koch during your dinner? Did he seem normal? Or maybe agitated?"

Lansky smiled. "Inspector, it was the first time I'd met him. I have no idea if he was normal – I've got nothing to compare with. He called me up a few weeks ago and suggested a meeting, as he had a business proposition for me. We agreed meet in Hamburg as I had to be there anyway, and he could get there easily from Vienna, which was his home town, although he lived a lot of the time in Moscow. We met; he made his proposal, which I rejected. He then suggested a different approach, about which I was non-committal. I expected him to come back to me with a concrete version of his new suggestion within this week, or soon afterwards. And that was really it. We had a pleasant dinner, he was a good host – good food, very good wine and so on. I can't really tell you any more."

"I understand that, Mr Lansky. We're just trying to get background information to help out our colleagues in Hamburg. There is one other area, though. Your friend, sorry, your *associate* I think you called him, Mr Oleg Malenkov. Are you aware that he has a bit of an interesting reputation, back home in Russia?"

Lansky pursed his lips, and then spoke very carefully. "I am aware that Oleg and his brother Leonid have a colourful history in Central Siberia, which I frankly find rather distasteful. My association with them is strictly a business one, involving the operation of an aluminium smelter in a town called Krayanovsk. They own the manufacturing plant, and I am responsible for raw material purchases and finished metal sales in the west. I don't pry into what happened in the past – Russia has been a country in turmoil since the collapse of the Soviet Union. Our companies are all correctly established, and our activities are as you would expect of an industrial group."

The Inspector smiled for a moment. "Of course, sir, nobody would suggest anything to the contrary. Can you think of any reason why there should be any animosity between Mr Koch and the Malenkovs?"

That was the question Lansky himself really wanted a truthful answer to. But best to try and stop the hare running right now, if possible. "Nothing I'm aware of. They knew each other, of course. Koch was the Moscow head of a company called Metalex. They're big in metals, and it would be inevitable that they came across each other from time to time. Russia may have huge resources, but they're in a very few hands, so of course they all tend to know each other." So far, he'd told nothing but the truth. He wished they'd finish, though.

"Did you and Mr Malenkov talk about Koch and your discussions after your dinner, in the bar?"

"We did. I mentioned Mr Koch's proposal, and, although it directly concerned me, and only indirectly Oleg, he was broadly in agreement with my rejection of it. Other than that, we were really discussing other things."

The Inspector nodded to the Sergeant, who closed the notebook where he had been diligently recording the conversation. "All right, Mr Lansky, I think that covers it. I doubt if we'll have to bother you again, although I suppose it's possible the Germans may want you to appear at the coroner's post-mortem. I must be honest, I'm not really sure how their law in that area works. So just let me know on the number on my card if you're leaving the country, but otherwise, thank you for your time and for being so clear in your answers."

Outside in the street, he turned to the Sergeant. "Well, I don't think he had anything to do with it, but I wouldn't be so sure about his Russian friends. Why would you get involved with people like that?"

"Money," said the Sergeant, succinctly.

The Inspector laughed sourly. "Yeah, I think you're right. Oh well, I'll write up a report for the Germans, and that should be the last we hear of it."

The Kremlin, Moscow

Yuri Ansonov, sitting in his lair in the Kremlin, was quietly satisfied. Denis Menkov had carried out his orders efficiently and anonymously, and in doing so had helped his boss enormously. With Metalex now effectively a busted flush in Siberia, his central power base was secure in the hands of the Malenkovs. He was under no illusions; maybe one day he would have to deal with the brothers, but for the moment, and it was the moment that mattered, he could rely on them to be right behind him. The President was truly living on borrowed time. He picked up the phone and called the FSB headquarters.

"Denis, we need to talk again. I'll see you in half an hour, usual place."

So again they sat in the little coffee shop, anonymous and unremarkable.

"First of all," began Ansonov, "you did a good job on Koch. Thank you. I think that has resolved all of our issues with Metalex."

"Should mean everything is now clear for the Malenkovs at Krayanovsk."

"Yes, it all would seem to be falling into place. However, there is a potential issue which may become a problem in the future. At the moment, it suits me to allow the Malenkovs to have an association with the Englishman, Lansky. He brings money into the venture, and that is money that Russia needs, as we know. This will not always be the case, and we may need to ensure that Leonid and Oleg drop their new friend when it suits us for them to do so. This will not be probably for some years, but you know I always like to be prepared for events. I need you to go to England and have a look at this man; what is his background, what secrets does he have. You know the sort of things we need."

Menkov grinned. "Like the old days, then. Surveillance, information-gathering, set the target up, and then........." And he drew his finger across his throat, as though cutting it.

"Yes, maybe. Or maybe that won't be necessary. Maybe his involvement in our country will have run its course by then. You'd better take a few weeks leave of absence to give you the freedom operate. None of your FSB colleagues need to know where you are going."

Not for the first time, Menkov reflected on how far down the tubes his career and indeed life might go if Ansonov failed in what he was trying to do. Still, no point dwelling on that. He'd made his choice of master years ago, and the rewards were clear, as shown by the glossy Mercedes brochure sticking out of his overcoat pocket. Black, definitely. But the SL500, or should he stretch himself for the extra cost of the AMG? For sure he'd be well looked after if he did a good job in London. He could almost hear the roar of the AMG's exhaust pipes as he sat drinking his coffee.

Getting back to the Kremlin, Ansonov did not go back to his own office. Instead, he went through the secret, hidden door between his ante-room and that of the President. The secretary on duty there nodded him through into the President's private office; the man knew better than to question why Yuri Ansonov needed to see the leader. Closing the door quietly behind him, Ansonov greeted the old man, who was seated at his desk, slumped over his papers.

"Mr President, you look tired."

"Yuri, I am very tired. But you're the only one I can show it to. The people expect me to be strong, to show leadership. But it's hard to keep up the pretence. The country is suffering enormously, I feel I am carrying everything on my back. You have heard of the death of Alex Koch in Hamburg?"

Ansonov nodded, but kept silent.

"Russia has lost a true friend. He and his company were trying hard to help us realise our mineral wealth. He will be sadly missed."

Like hell, thought Ansonov to himself; he and his company were your paymasters. He couldn't give tuppence for the development of Russia; all they wanted was to rape the land and take the money.

More temperately, he said, "It's always sad when someone dies violently and unexpectedly. But actually, as we have discussed before, in many ways the era of Metalex and its like is over in Russia. We must begin to rely more on ourselves, and to have confidence in the ability of Russian companies, like that of the Malenkovs, to develop our natural wealth."

"Yuri, I know that's how you think, but after we finally cast off the yoke of the Soviets, do we really want still to be dominated by the KGB and its acolytes? I know you began your career in that organisation, but in the time you have worked for me, I have seen you change. You truly believe in the self-determination of the Russian people."

Ansonov struggled to stop himself laughing. Deluded old man, my KGB tentacles still reach out and control this nation, and that's how it will stay. It may be called democracy, but what's in a name? All it takes is to make the people think you are what they want. And to do that, you have to make them believe you are giving their country back to them.

Again, his spoken words were different. "I'm glad you have seen that change. But I want you to think of yourself. You have carried the burdens of state ever since you stepped in after the overthrow of the Soviets. It's been a heavy burden, and you have borne it like a true Russian hero. The people revere you, despite all the difficulties of their lives. But you cannot carry the weight for ever. You must begin to think of yourself. You are not such an old man, and yet you are running yourself into the ground. You are not well," he held up his hand as the older man tried to speak, "I have spoken with your doctor. He confirms you are exhausting yourself. You should begin to think of retirement."

He kept his eyes closely fixed on the older man. It was a big play he was making, sooner than he had intended. Yuri Ansonov was not a gambler, until he had all the cards rigged in his favour. This time, though, at the biggest moment of his life, he was playing his hand from instinct, rather than preparation. The president looked at him, holding his gaze firm. "Yuri, there is nothing I would rather do. But how can I? The Duma struggles to hold a debate without fisticuffs breaking out, they can barely agree on what day it is. How can we ask them to elect a new leader? It would be chaos."

"There is another way, Aleksey Andreivich." It was the first time Ansonov had ever called the old man by his name and patronymic, and he kept looking into his eyes, unblinking.

The President realised what he was being asked to do. "You," he breathed. "You want me to step aside and install you as leader. But that would be tantamount to a coup. After all I've said over the years about democracy, you want me to turn my back on it? I'm shocked, Yuri, truly I'm shocked."

"I know about your views on democracy. Just as I know about the money you've been taking for years from Metalex and others like them. One day, and it may be sooner than you think, somebody is going to look at how a man whose life has peaked as President of the Russian Federation can afford the properties and the investments that you have. You're a rich man; do you think the Russian people would be impressed with how you got there? Aleksey, if you cling on for ever, these questions will be asked. You are tired, you have kept the balls aloft for longer than anyone could have asked, this is the chance to get out, and maintain credibility."

Colour drained from the President's face as Ansonov was speaking. When he replied, it was almost in a whisper.

"Well, Yuri, what a viper I've been nursing all these years. Get out of my room. I need to think. I will sleep on it. We will meet again tomorrow morning."

Without a word, Ansonov turned on his heel and left the room. He was confident. He knew the President couldn't stand up to an investigation of his finances. Ever since he'd moved across from the Lubyanka to the Kremlin, Ansonov had watched his leader like a hawk. He had details of the payments, the hospitality, all the benefits secretly lavished on the leader by a raft of interested parties in pursuit of contracts and influence on the country's wealth. The populace at large might be able to stomach internal bribery – after all, it had always been that way – but the amount that had flowed in from abroad would sicken them. The President must know he was finished; the only question was, how did he want to bow out? Ansonov could offer him the cleanest, least personally damaging way. He was sure the man would take it.

Chapter 14

4 a.m. The President was slumped in a chair in his private sitting-room. On the low table in front of him was a two-thirds empty bottle of Hennessy XO and a tumbler. He shook his head as he looked at them. The rich, expensive spirit few of his countrymen could afford, but drunk out of the peasant vessel, not a delicate crystal balloon. Summed up his life, really. Pretending to be a man of the people, but enjoying the fruits of his corruption.

He knew Ansonov had him over a barrel; the dilemma was how to preserve his own dignity without simply rolling over in front of the younger man. The brandy was taking effect. His mind was playing tricks, rolling back the years. He saw himself as a young soldier in the hell of Stalingrad, truly the turning point for his nation. Then his recollection jumped to the 1950s, as a political commissar, leading him into the higher echelons of power in the Kremlin. That was when his doubts about the system had begun to surface and later, during the years in the Ministry of Trade when the financial squeeze Reagan put on was beginning to bite, slowly he'd been suborned by the material wealth dangled in front of him by the likes of Metalex. Eventually, he'd taken the bull by the horns and declared his position as the system went into its death spiral. Almost by default, he'd reached the top office. But to the people outside, far from being a venal, money-grubbing opportunist, he still stood as the emblem of the new order. And now Ansonov was threatening to destroy that legacy if he wasn't anointed as the successor. Ansonov, whom he'd relied on as his eyes and ears ever since taking the Presidency. He couldn't hand the reins of power back into the hands of the ex-KGB hierarchy. But equally, he couldn't stand to be exposed for his own shortcomings. He swigged another tumblerful of the spirit.

He knew what he had to do. Standing up, with some difficulty, he staggered across the room to the bureau. Opening the middle drawer, he took out a pistol.

His valet, sleeping down the corridor, was awakened by the sound of a pistol-shot. As he stumbled out of bed and through the door of his room, two soldiers were already standing, irresolute, in front of the President's door. Pushing past them, the valet opened the door, then quickly shut it again. He knew what had to be done. "You," he barked to one of the soldiers, "guard this door. Don't let anybody through it. And you, go and fetch Yuri Ansonov." He knew instinctively Ansonov was the man to call. After all, he'd been the old man's right hand, hadn't he? He'd know what to do.

British Embassy, Moscow

"Yes, I know it's early, but I need to speak to the Foreign Secretary. If he's not in the office yet, patch me through to his home line. Yes, it's important, or I wouldn't be calling personally at this time of day. Thanks." The Ambassador rolled his eyes at the Head of Chancery (in British embassies, always the head spook), sitting across the desk from him, in the grand Ambassador's office in the old building on Smolenskaya Naberezhnaya. "Why ask me if it's important? If the Moscow Ambassador calls for the foreign secretary at this time in the morning, it's probably not just going to be to say hello." He spoke into the telephone again. "Yes, James, good morning. Sorry to call you so early, but you better know this sooner rather then later. In fact, you better put the TV on as well, the BBC and Sky will soon have it. There's been a bit of an event here. The President is dead. They're not saying anything more than that – and that comes hot from our own Kremlin sources – so we don't know how, or what the implications are. Hold on a sec, there's a newsflash on the Russian TV." He paused, and listened to the Russian newsreader. In one of its smarter moves, the Foreign Office had sent a Russian-speaking Ambassador, for the first time in a long while. "OK," he said, "no indication of cause of death, but Yuri Ansonov has stepped into the breach and announced he will take over the reins on a caretaker basis while the situation clarifies itself. Oh, God, James, they've switched to funeral mode. There's a picture of the Pres on the screen, taken a few years ago, from the look of it, and solemn music. Christ. Nick," – to the Head of Chancery – "turn the sound off. I can't sit listening to their dirges. Sorry, James, back with you. That's an interesting move by Ansonov. We don't know him that well, but he's definitely hard-line KGB, sorry, FSB. What we do know is that he's been involved with some of the asset privatisations, very much of the Russia for the Russians school of thought. It's a big step for him. He's never been elected to anything, and I don't know what the Duma will have to say about it. Mmm? Yes, we'll do that. OK, I'll call you later, or as soon as we get any news. All the best." And he put the phone down.

"OK, Nick, we need to get on top of what's happening. Can you get a couple of your guys down to the Duma? See if they can pick up the feeling. That's going to be the key. If they're prepared to back Ansonov, then I don't think he'll just be a caretaker for too long. This could just be an FSB-backed coup. But the real interesting question is, how did the old man die?"

The Kremlin, Moscow

Yuri Ansonov was addressing his mind to that point at the same moment. Secure in the President's office, he wondered. Was suicide the best way? Clearly, there was no way it could be made to look like murder; that would involve too many people, and anyway there was no real time to concoct a plausible plot. A bullet in the head could be a stumbling block to a heart seizure, but on the other hand he could get an FSB doctor to certify any cause of death he wanted. The Russian people, though, to say nothing of the world's press, would expect to see the body lying in state, so they would have to be sure they could cover up the wounds. Having seen the mess the .45 bullet had made, Ansonov was doubtful of that one. Suicide wouldn't be too bad. Worn out in the service of the motherland, constant pressure from international creditors, after all the man had given his life to the country, all that kind of rubbish. Best keep the brandy bottle well hidden, though. Ansonov chuckled to himself. Power was amazing. He had been expecting to push his predecessor out of the way. Now, though, he had effectively the absolute power to decide how the man had died. *After it had happened!*

On to more serious things. He wasn't particularly worried about the Duma's reaction; they were so indisciplined they wouldn't be able to act, even if they wanted to. But other things needed doing. Siberia clearly was secure. Anyone who doubted the legitimacy of the new regime would simply run into a bullet from one of the Malenkovs' enforcers. But in the Urals, and in Moscow itself? Better get some FSB troops on the streets, just to ensure order. St Petersburg? They were all so wrapped up in their businesses with the west that they probably wouldn't even notice there had been a change in the leadership. And a suitably sombre TV appearance, where he could stress his desire to keep Russia's interests at heart, to keep Russia's resources for the benefit of her people, that would soon get the factories and plants in the Urals on his side. One of the benefits of the role he'd filled for the last few years was that most of the Cabinet had seen him as the mouthpiece of the President. They were used to taking instructions from him: all that was going to change was that now they would be *his* instructions. He didn't foresee any serious problems. Yesterday, Yuri Ansonov had taken a gamble. Today, already, he knew it was paying off, in spades.

Most citizens of Moscow were shocked at the death of their leader, sympathetic to the enormous pressures that had driven him to take his own life. But over the next few days, they noticed little change. True, the FSB soldiers were more in evidence than they had been before, but it was a background presence. At the Duma, voices were raised in support of the new order, and in opposition to it. The agents of the British embassy, trying to gauge how the feeling of the Members was running, in the end had little to report back. Ansonov had played his hand well. The handover of power, as he liked to describe his blatant seizure of it, was seamless. Troops had to beat up the workers at one factory in Yekaterinburg, when they demonstrated in favour of democracy, but that was about it. Pretty quickly, life got back to normal.

The body of the former president did lie in state, for all who wanted to see; the doctors had managed skilfully to reconstruct most of the bits of the head that had been blasted across the room. The State Funeral was ten days later, attended by all the world's significant leaders – and a fair few insignificant ones as well – including the British Prime Minister and Foreign Secretary. Along with the Americans and most of the Europeans, they were granted a one-on-one private audience with the new (still technically acting) President in the Kremlin. Ansonov welcomed them to the Head of State's reception room, impressed to be addressed by the Ambassador (who was accompanying them) in his own language, until the latter reverted to English for the sake of his two bosses.

"Gentlemen," began Ansonov, "I am pleased to welcome you here, although obviously I am sorry it is in such sad circumstances. The President was a great man, and a true Russian patriot. And yet, I think he was able to embrace positively our most important western friends, amongst whom we are pleased to count the United Kingdom." Well, he certainly embraced the west when it paid him off, he thought to himself. "Our two countries have a shared history going back many years, encompassing the way we stood shoulder-to-shoulder with each other against fascism during the Great Patriotic War. Going back further, of course, although my country no longer has a royal family, we are warmly aware of the family relationship between our last Czar, Nicholas, and your own Royal family. And of course, let us not forget the part played by English merchant adventurers in bringing the Russian fur trade to the international world many hundreds of years ago. So it is with more than a nod to the past that I welcome you here today as one of our most important friends."

"Thank you, Mr Acting President. May I from my side say, despite the sad circumstances, that it is a pleasure to be here. As you know, this is my first official visit to Russia, but I can assure you that my Government holds the country and its people in the highest regard. We are aware of the great sacrifices made by that people earlier in this century, and we are very pleased to see Russia beginning again to be a positive force for good amongst the world's nations. We strongly believe that Russia is one of the key, the vital, members of the international community, and we are grateful to your predecessor for the progress he made in bringing his country back to the top table of international affairs. We look forward to an ever closer, ever warmer relationship between our two countries, each contributing what it can to help the other."

They continued their conversation, mostly diplomatic niceties, for an hour or so. In the car back to the Embassy, the Prime Minister said, "James, he didn't seem the secret service hood you suggested. I actually quite liked him. He's obviously heavily into the Mother Russia thing, but I suspect we probably come across a bit Rule Britannia as well. That's what diplomat speak does to you." He pointed at the Ambassador. "It's all your fault, Crispin, you make us sound like we're trying to be Palmerston."

The Ambassador grinned. "I know, I know. It would all be so much easier if you could all say just what you wanted. Then all we'd have to do would be sort out the wars."

The Prime Minister laughed. "You know, if you'd spoken to Palmerston like that you'd be out of a job in disgrace by now. In fact, if you'd spoken to Mrs T like that, you would too. But seriously, what do we think of this guy?"

The Ambassador spoke again, no laughter this time. "He's OK, but be careful. We've been doing a bit of digging. The Mother Russia thing isn't a joke. He is genuinely opposed to letting foreigners get their hands on Russian resources. He's backed some pretty unpleasant guys to keep the westerners out. For example, down in Krayanovsk, in Siberia, we believe he is the invisible hand that stopped Metalex, the conglomerate, getting its hands on an aluminium smelter. Instead, he backed a pair of gangsters, as I say, to keep the foreign company out. That may not be too serious. Incidentally, we think there's a Brit, guy called Lansky, involved as well. But what may be serious is how they behave over oil and gas. So we'd advise being friendly with him, but be very careful. Incidentally, we don't think the 'Acting' title will be there much longer. There's no coherent opposition."

February 1995

London

London in mid-winter was better than Moscow, mused Denis Menkov as he sat in the bar of Brown's Hotel in Dover Street enjoying a pre-dinner drink. He hadn't actually made too much progress with the task

Ansonov had given him but it wasn't from lack of trying. Although bits of Lansky's past had been slightly questionable, Menkov had not been able to uncover anything which he felt they would be able to use as leverage, if necessary. The property business was completely clean, and so far the old scrap days looked equally unpromising. Tax dodging, paying bribes to some of the scrap consumers, but things like that were hardly going to cause Lansky anything more than a fleeting embarrassment. Maybe this evening's dinner would give him some pointers. Posing as a Russian businessman with funds to invest, and a liking for the high-intensity world of commodities, Menkov had arranged to meet Rory Davis; he hoped that a better understanding of the market where Lansky had made his first fortune might reveal some skeletons. Finishing his drink, he shrugged into his overcoat and headed for the door. It was a short walk to the restaurant Davis had suggested in Bruton Street.

"Mr Davis, thank you so much for agreeing to see me. And at such short notice."

"No problem," smiled Davis as they were shown to a discreet table in a corner of the room. "It's always a pleasure to meet potential new clients. But I wasn't sure from your phone call exactly what is your interest in the market. Are you an investor, or are you involved in the physical metals business, or what?"

The waiter interrupted the flow of conversation briefly to take their order. Then Menkov pulled out a business card he had had printed earlier in the day, with a genuine pay-as-you-go mobile phone number on it, together with a fictitious Moscow number and address.

"As you will see from my card, I fall into that unspecific group of "Business Consultants". In my case, I represent a number of rich, but discreet, Russian businessmen, for whom I undertake certain investments. We have been considering the commodity markets recently, particularly the metal market, which is, I think, understandable since Russia has such a wealth of mineral resources. My clients are considering expanding their portfolio in both mining company equities and in commodity futures, as a linked investment. I have spoken with many people in the resource area, and almost universally they end by recommending me to your company, as about the most influential in the metal brokerage business. I understand that there are other companies, such as Metalex, for example, who may have a stronger position in the physical metal market, but my clients initially anyway are most interested in looking at London Metal Exchange futures rather than at holding physical metal."

"Well, yes, the futures would be the obvious investment; it's much easier to buy and sell futures on the LME than it is to trade real metal. And anyway, you would have the logistical problems of handling bulk metals if you went the physical route. But what are you actually thinking of? Although this doesn't necessarily help my company, have you considered putting money into one – or several – of the commodity hedge funds? They've been quite successful in bringing new money into the market over the last few years. That way, you get the benefit of professional money management, and, of course, because they are large pools of money, you get access to a wider spread of commodities. If it were helpful, we could certainly introduce you to one or two of them, with whom we have good relationships."

Menkov leaned his elbows on the table. "Mr Davis, let me be frank. Some of my associates have interests in the Russian metal industry. You know, of course, that many assets in Russia are being privatised. Well, let's just say that my investment group has an involvement with some of those privatised assets. The new owners naturally want to explore how they can use the knowledge of markets they will gain through those assets in other investment areas."

Davis was wise enough to the ways of the world to understand what the man opposite him was hinting at. His people had acquired mines, smelters, whatever, and on the back of the legitimate business those companies would be doing, they wanted to trade in the market. It was legal, broadly, but if the CEO of a major western miner or smelter were caught doing it, that would be the end of his career, very quickly. Still, Davis wasn't a moral policeman; if this guy wanted to open an account and trade through Commet, Davis wasn't responsible for where he got his trading information.

"Yes, I see," he said. "So you would in a way be pooling these people's funds, and buying and selling in the market on the basis of the background information they had about supply and demand out of Russia."

"Effectively, yes, it would work something like that." As he was discussing it, it struck Menkov that the fiction he was creating to try and get information was actually not a bad idea. No, he told himself, stick to the brief. Don't get seduced by the prospect of easy money.

"Well," began Davis again, "I do understand their point of view. No point in having information if you can't use it. And in a way it fits with what we're trying to do currently. We have begun to increase our business in Russia, and the privatisations are certainly changing the landscape. We were never very close to the old State metal export agency – they had strong relationships with some of our competitors – so we are making a concerted effort to get to know the new owners of Russian resources." It was an exaggeration to describe the new business with Lansky quite in these terms, but he might as well put a bit of a gloss on it. "So we'd certainly be interested in trying to do something with you."

"That's good, but tell me some more about your moves into Russia. Maybe we have some contacts in common."

"Well, we don't actually have a Moscow office yet, so generally what we are doing is working with those players who have good partners in the west; so far, we have not started direct business with Russian companies, because we are constrained by our parent company in offering credit facilities to companies whose balance sheets do not support them. And obviously, since these Russian metal groups are effectively new entities, it's difficult for them to satisfy our credit requirements. But we're making progress. One example I'm thinking of is a good old friend of the company who is getting involved in some aluminium business in Russia. So in that case, precisely because he is a good old corporate friend, we are able to be a little more flexible."

"I see. Well, firstly, you would not have to worry about credit facilities for my associates. The company would be western, of course in a beneficial tax regime, like the BVIs or Cayman Islands, and would be well supported with cash. That cash would then be available for meeting margin requirements for trading with you."

Davis grinned. "We always prefer clients who put up cash to those who want credit. Much cleaner for everybody."

"Of course, Mr Davis, we understand that. But I'm intrigued about how your business works. It's an area which is obviously new to us all in my country. I have read textbooks about futures markets, but I must confess that it is something of a privilege to be able to talk to an expert like yourself. The technicalities of the market, yes, I can understand those from the books. But the contacts, the personal touch: how does this build up? For example, you mentioned a "good old friend" who you were working with in Russia. How does one become a "good old friend" when the business is new?" He smiled self-deprecatingly. "Please excuse me if I am being naïve, but I find the workings of your business fascinating."

Davis smiled back, twirling his wine glass stem in his fingers. "That's OK. I understand it's a confusing business to outsiders. We don't make anything, we don't really sell anything, we just shuffle huge amounts of money around, and try and keep a tiny margin for ourselves. Of course, because the numbers are so big, that tiny margin adds up to quite a lot. But because of that, the contacts we have, the people we know, are very important. In order to make the right decisions for ourselves and our clients, we need access to information, and that information comes from our contacts in the business. Commet is more successful than most of its competitors for one principal reason: we have a wider range of contacts, so we get to know more information. We then have to take the opportunity to turn that information into money. Take the guy we're talking about; he started trading with our company over twenty years ago, and became a good personal friend of my predecessor as MD. He ran a very successful copper scrap gathering and trading company. Over the years, we got to trust his opinions of the market – in other words, he had a good feel for how prices would move. So when he gives us tips or information, we tend to take notice. It's a two-way street, of course, and we reciprocate by giving clients like that information that we think will help them as well. It takes a while to build up this kind of trust, obviously. So anyway, our friend dropped out of the business for a while, and concentrated on his interests in property, until he called me last year to say he was getting involved with a Russian aluminium group. Although it's a slightly different business than before, we respect his instinct for a good business, so we're prepared to go along with most of what he asked us to do. Obviously, I can't be too specific about that, as it's confidential between us and a client."

Menkov was sure he was on the right track – the client in question had to be Lansky. He needed to try to probe Davis a bit about how things had happened in the past. "Of course, I understand your rules about confidentiality. But in the past, that sort of thing was much more lax, I think. So maybe what you're describing about how you get to know clients like this so well, would be different now. Would it not now be called insider dealing?"

Davis looked hard at him for a moment. "No, I don't think so. Or course, I was not around at the time, but I doubt very much if the company would have got involved in anything like that, even in those laxer times. You have to bear in mind that insider dealing in the commodity markets is anyway much more difficult to define than it is in equity, or stock, markets. For example, if I got a phone call now from my office in Chile, and they told me that a smelter over there had blown up, and I bought some copper on the back of that information, clearly that wouldn't be insider trading. Everybody within range of the smelter would have heard it; it would just be that my people were quicker to react, and I bought the copper before the market as a whole had absorbed the news. So in what is essentially an event-driven market, it's a difficult concept to apply. It's not the same as getting a preview of a company's annual profit statement and trading its equity on the back of it. No, the kind of information we're talking about is more subjective. For example, a scrap trader, like the guy we've been discussing, is always aware of the availability of scrap. If he finds he can't get material to buy, the likelihood is that the price will go up. So if he mentions to us that that is the case, it suggests to us that we should buy the market, because that's where the overall lack of availability will become apparent. So it's not so much inside information, as trusting the other's instinct. And you only get to that position when you have developed a strong relationship."

This wasn't really what Menkov wanted. He had hoped to chisel out evidence of insider trading, or some other dubious business practices that Lansky had been involved in. All Davis was telling him was that the man was well-known and respected for his market knowledge and opinions. That was not what Ansonov needed. Sensing he was not going to get what he wanted, Menkov let the conversation switch back to a discussion of what business his mythical group of investors might like to do with Commet. At the end of the evening he had a good handle on how to open an LME account, but no dirt on Lansky. That was a disappointment.

The next morning he was on the phone to Ansonov. "It's no good, Yuri, he's obviously no angel, but there's nothing I can find that is going to give us any serious leverage on him. I think we're going to have to set something up ourselves."

"You may be right. You'd better come back to Moscow, and then you can go and have a talk with Leonid and Oleg and see what you can come up with. You should have enough experience between the three of you." Ansonov smiled mirthlessly to himself. Anything his hit-man and the brothers Malenkov constructed would almost certainly discredit Lansky more than any real events in his past. But it had to be. The Englishman was necessary at the moment, but there would come a time when he became surplus to requirements, and Ansonov had to be sure he had a sufficient lever to remove him totally when he felt the time was right. These tactics had always served him well in the past, and he knew they would again in the future.

Menkov headed back to Moscow the next morning, after first taking an early morning stroll down to the Embankment to throw the pay as you go phone far out towards the middle of the Thames. Too bad that whenever Rory Davis tried to call his new client - either on his mobile or the Moscow number – he would get no connection.

Chapter 15

Summer 1995

London

Lansky was busy, that spring and early summer. He had a serious job to do, first ensuring the smelter had sufficient raw material feedstock to be able to function, and then to sell the resultant product to release cash back to the partners. Raw materials were pretty straightforward, but nevertheless time-consuming. The producers of alumina, the basic feedstock of an aluminium smelter, were headquartered around the world, and although Russo-European Metals was a western company, it was BVI-registered. Lansky had to tour his potential suppliers to explain to them how the structure worked, and that they should not be concerned by the slightly grey-looking entity they were to deal with. Russo-European was cash-rich (full of the money the partners had originally invested) and in the end the argument that all material would be paid for before it was shipped into Russia and that the Russian resource sector was one they could not ignore swayed pretty much all of them. Lansky metaphorically tipped his hat to the Malenkovs, though; without the intermediary of Russo-European, none of the alumina companies would have touched the deal with a bargepole. Metalex sat fuming on the sidelines as their confident expectation that the funding gap would prove too difficult for their opponents to bridge was demonstrated to be wide of the mark. The deaths of the former President and Alex Koch had robbed them of their eyes, ears and influence in Moscow, and they were on the back foot, trying hard to regroup and reposition themselves.

Selling the production absorbed more of his energy. The amount of metal they produced in the first few months was constrained by the raw material availability, but once Lansky's raw material purchases started flowing, they rapidly ramped up to something approaching full production. Although Victor Lansky had vowed to himself that he would not get involved in the Russian end of the business, he was drawn into agreeing to make a journey with a trainload of aluminium from the plant to the port of St Petersburg. Oleg was insistent that he do this, in order to see "the efficiency of the whole transport system." As Lansky was the one who would take the flak from the western customers should any shipments be delayed, he reluctantly agreed that it made some sort of sense for him to have first-hand knowledge of how the logistics worked.

Krayanovsk, Siberia

And so he flew into Krayanovsk again, in late July. This time, instead of grimy grey, the skies were bright cobalt blue, marred only by the plumes of smoke billowing out of the tall chimneys of the smelter. As the car took him towards the centre of town, he marvelled at the change summer had brought to the landscape. Instead of the grey dusty snow of winter, the ground was a riot of flowers amongst the bright green leaves of the silver birches. He was lucky; it had been a dry summer so far and the pestilential midges had retreated for the time being, infesting the boggy land further north where pools of rain still sat on the semi-frozen tundra. A rain shower would bring them back instantly, though, hungry for blood. The Malenkovs greeted him like another long-lost brother, and the afternoon passed in a blur of lunch, vodka, toasts to the success of the venture and for Lansky, eventually falling exhausted and fuzzy-headed into bed.

The next day, they again toured the plant and the hydro dam. Both were now blasting along at full capacity, although the level of water in the river was far lower than it had been earlier in the year. Oleg explained that the peak flow was at the height of the spring melt, during the second half of April, and the low water period started in late summer, where they were now, and lasted through until the first snowfalls of autumn started to fill the river again, before it iced over for the winter. "Our seasons are not entirely like yours," he said, "summer is actually very short here in Siberia, and winter far longer than in Europe. It's around twenty-two to twenty-five degrees here most days now, for another week or so. Then it will start to cool again, as autumn starts. The leaves on the birches will fall, and you will only see green on the fir trees, until the snow covers everything. But you will see, as you go westwards towards St Petersburg with the train, the weather will get warmer. In the Moscow area, it will be hot and airless." He gestured around him with an arcing movement of his hand. "Not like this big open sky of Siberia." In truth, although he had serious reservations about travelling on the freight train, Lansky was actually looking forward to his trip halfway across Russia. There may be a lot of monotony, but he'd see far more of the country than he ever could from an aeroplane. And his mobile phone, wherever there was a service, would surely keep him in touch with the world.

"So, tomorrow morning," Oleg continued, "we must be ready to leave the plant at around 9 a.m." Seeing Lansky's look of surprise, he added,

"Of course, I will also be coming. We cannot leave you alone on the train. The only company will be the three train drivers and our Chechen guards. None of them speak English, so we think the fairest thing is if I accompany you." He laughed. "It will be the first time for me, as well."

"How active are the guards? I mean, do you really expect someone to attempt to rob the train?"

Oleg looked seriously at him. "Expect? No. But need to take precautions? Yes. We ourselves have not lost any cargo, but we know of other enterprises who did not have sufficient guards who have been robbed. On the whole, people, especially here in Siberia but also around Moscow and St Petersburg, know that to steal from the Malenkovs is not a clever idea." He gave a great guffaw of laughter. "Do not forget, Victor, that when you first met us, before you knew us and became our partner, you too believed we were just a pair of gangsters. Who would dare to steal from such people!"

Inwardly, Lansky winced. He was still trying to convince himself that it wasn't true. The concept of Chechen rail wagon guards didn't help.

Punctually at eight the following morning, the pale blue Mercedes picked him up again from the hotel, to take him across town to the smelter. This time, though, instead of stopping outside the administration office block, the car carried on, skirting the edge of the factory buildings until they drove into the freight yard and stopped in the shadow of the massive rail wagons queuing to be loaded by scurrying fork-lift trucks. Oleg was standing chatting to a group of men wearing what looked like military fatigues. Seeing Lansky step out of the car, he hurried across to greet him.

"Good morning, my friend. Are you ready for the great Russian railway adventure?" And he laughed uproariously. "So, you see they are just finishing loading the final railcars. Each car takes sixty tonnes of aluminium, and on this train we have sixty cars. There is a locomotive front and middle, and an accommodation car also in the middle. The guards will be based in there. There are ten of them, and they take turns in some of the aluminium cars, to protect the whole train. We have several teams, obviously, as there will normally be several trains under way at the same time. This team is made up of Chechens." He smiled thinly. "We also have Afghan war veterans, but we try not to mix them with the Chechens." Seeing Lansky's quizzical look, he continued, "Chechens are Islamic, and some of them still have a strong feeling for the mujahideen. That makes for potential........let's say disagreements, with the war vets, who spent ten years fighting those people in Afghanistan. But as long as we keep them apart, they are all happy to take our money and do their job. We shall ride in the front engine, where there is the train crew accommodation section. It is quite comfortable, although we may get very tired of each other's company." He laughed again. "As you know, we expect this journey to take just over a week. If we are too bored, we can stop in Moscow, and leave the train for the final stage to St Petersburg. So, the car will drive us up to the front of the train in a moment, but first of all, come and see how they stack the metal in the railcars." Oleg led the way over to the gaping door of the wagon that was currently being filled, and, climbing up on the step, Lansky was able to see the shiny blocks of aluminium ingots being stacked up to just over head height. "From the point of view of space, we could get more in, but we have to be very careful about weight. Although the railcars are effectively ours, they will have to go over a weighbridge in the area of Novosibirsk, and the Russian railway authorities are very strict. Even if we tried, we could not bribe them. They are aware that an accident involving an overloaded train would be a major setback to Siberian development, so they are very careful." Idly, Lansky thought to himself that if that were true, they must be the only unbribable people in the entire country. "Anyway," Oleg went on, "let's get in the car and go down to the front of the train. We're virtually at the end here, so it's about a kilometre to the engine." Seeing Lansky's look of surprise, he said, "Work it out. Sixty wagons of almost twenty metres length. This is not your London commuter passenger train." He was right. The car drove alongside the railway siding for almost exactly a kilometre until they reached the huge diesel engine at the front. They swung up a ladder to the back cab, and, once inside, were in a high-tech control room. "Of course, all these controls are duplicated in the front and back cab of this engine, and in the one in the middle of the train as well. Just through here," – he opened a door in the wall of the cab leading towards the middle of the locomotive – "through here we get to the accommodation section. There should be six sleeping berths, a bathroom and a kitchen. But no windows, so we will mainly travel here in this cab. We can of course go through to the front of the engine once we get going, and see the drivers at work"

"Are there really only three drivers? For potentially almost two weeks?"

"Yes. It is actually a problem. There is so much freight now being shipped out of Siberia which used to stay in the region and just go to the military factories. So there is now a shortage of train crews, as well as rail cars. My friend, there is a shortage of everything! We have to make do with what we can get. These three train drivers earn more than anybody in the smelter at the moment. It is their opportunity, so they will drive on/off shifts of eight hours until we reach St Petersburg. Then they have a week off, and come back to Krayanovsk to reload."

"But isn't that potentially as dangerous as overloading the train? I mean, they must be seriously overtired at the end of each trip."

Oleg shrugged. "It's not so bad. They are warm, air-conditioned, they have enough good food. I think the worst thing must be lack of exercise

– I believe most of the drivers do some gym practice en route. And then whenever they have to make a stop – which definitely happens a few times each trip – they will get out of the cab and wander around for a while. So, anyway, let's sit down and we should be starting very soon."

In the cab there were the two drivers' seats facing down the length of the train – Lansky assumed that at the other end of the double-ended locomotive two of the drivers would presently be sitting in the equivalent forward-facing seats. Between them and the door to the sleeping area were two twin-seater benches facing each other across the width of the cab. Climbing into one of the driver's seats, Lansky could see the train stretching away from him into the distance. It was an impressive sight. A kilometre of train sounds a lot, but it's only up close that it can truly be comprehended. Following the curve of the wagons, he could just see the tiny figures and trucks putting, he assumed, the final bundles of ingots into the last few wagons. It was just a few minutes before nine o'clock. "Seeing it like this, Oleg, I don't really understand how you could rob it. Even if you stopped it, you can't just walk away with a handful of aluminium ingots. How would they do it?"

"It's more complicated than that. They would bribe the drivers to stop, or bribe a signalman to change a signal to make the train stop, and then they uncouple one or two or three wagons, and let the rest of the train go. Then they have time to discharge the metal and take it away to store out of sight somewhere. Then there are many potential buyers. Maybe local Russian factories, or I have even heard of western companies buying from them. They must know that such small quantities are stolen, but if the price is right, they can close their eyes to that. In the end, this is why it is so difficult to insure these cargoes. Many people just resort to the armed guards. We of course do both – we have armed guards, and the insurance company charge us less because of that. It also helps that the rail cars are effectively ours, and all are listed by serial number with the insurers. Of course, in truth the guards are a better protection than the insurance."

"What sort of arms do your guys have?"

"Remember where you are. They have Kalashnikovs. That factory was geared up to produce millions of AK47s, for the Soviet army, for the eastern European bloc and for all the client states. Now the regime has changed here and in the east bloc, poor Kalashnikov have no market. So they have diversified – terrorists and private armies, mainly. And then responsible companies like ours, who just want to protect their goods." Seeing Lansky's face, he grinned. "Victor, I told you early on, the first time you came to Krayanovsk, that you should not involve yourself with these details. I say it again. Just see this week how smoothly the system works, but don't dig too deeply into it. Here, I think we will be moving soon. Sit back and enjoy the Russian countryside."

Sure enough, the noise and vibration from the massive diesel engine just behind their backs increased as the driver slowly pushed the throttle lever forward. The huge train began slowly, at first imperceptibly, to roll forward.

Oleg reached down into the briefcase he had been carrying, and pulled out a map, which he placed, open, on the flat space of the console between the two seats. "So, Victor, we will start with a history and geography lesson. We are here" – he jabbed his finger on the map – "and as you see, Krayanovsk is some way south of the main route of the Trans-Siberian railway, which goes along here." Again, he gestured with his finger on the map. "If we went direct, at full speed all the way to St Petersburg, then the journey would take only three and a bit days. There are two reasons why we can't do that, which I'll explain in a moment. First, though, consider the railway. It was built at the end of the nineteenth and beginning of the twentieth century, mainly to allow goods from Siberia, at that time principally wheat, to be transported to European Russia. They used slave labour to construct most of it, with some help from the army. The slaves came from all parts of Russia, dissidents, criminals, people who were simply in the wrong place at the wrong time. Also, people from the wider Russian Empire – Ukrainians, for example, or Poles. Maybe even some of your ancestors, my friend. The Czars were not too fussy in how they recruited their labour force. Anyway, it was a massive undertaking." Outside the windows, the outskirts of Krayanovsk were just beginning to give way to flat, open countryside. "Ultimately, when finished, it linked St Petersburg with Vladivostock, on the Pacific coast. Although it was built for trade, it found military uses early on. Before it was even finished, it was used to send troops to the Far East to fight in the war against the Japanese, in 1907. And then in the Civil War, it was largely under the control of Kolchak and the Whites, and the Czech Legion. Kolchak was based in Omsk, where we'll pass through later, and the Czechs eventually used their armoured trains to get themselves to Vladivostock, to get out of Russia when the Reds finally won. But now, back to the original purpose – taking exports from Siberia to Europe." As he was speaking, the brakes screeched, and the train ground slowly to a halt. "Ah yes, this is why our journey takes longer than you would expect. As I said, we are south of the main rail line, so we have to go up this side line until we reach it. But before we can join the main track, we have to wait for a space in the regular flow of trains. There are still some trains ahead of us on this track, so they have to get into the traffic flow first. This first few hundred kilometres will be slow, will be stop-start all the way to the main junction. Then when we get on the real railway, because it's only one track in each direction, we will also have stops if a train in front stops, like at a station or something. Sometimes we will be lucky, because there are some passing places, so if we can use those we can leapfrog trains in front." He looked seriously at his companion. "This railway is a very big operation. Passengers are really of secondary importance, although it's the passenger trains that dictate the speed of the whole line; but the amount of freight that is moved is enormous."

"This may be a naïve question, but are there signals all the way along the line, so that the trains are always under control?"

"Yes, each sector is guarded by a signal; so when a passenger train is stopped up ahead of us, the signal will prevent us from closing up on it. There is also an emergency system if a train breaks down. Then they have to act quickly and plant magnesium flares in the track behind the broken train. Of course, they must be very far behind, because it takes a long distance to stop a train as heavy as this one. Where there is a signal, of course, they can have mobile phone contact. But out here, away from the cities, the signal is very poor; they really have to rely on the old systems."

Lansky nodded his understanding as the train rumbled into life again, and this time kept going – albeit slowly, it seemed– for an hour or so, before grinding to a halt again. A couple of minutes later, there was a sharp knock at the door, and what he assumed was one of the drivers came into their cab and addressed Oleg in Russian. While the two were talking, Lansky stood up and walked through into the living quarters. Opening the door at the far end of that compartment, he looked along the walkway through to the other end of the locomotive. The lighting was dim, but he could make out the giant diesel engine filling the cavernous space of the locomotive. As he was looking through the open door, the driver revved the engine again and once more the train started rolling forward. The noise generated by the engine was deafening and Lansky quickly closed the door, blanking out the bulk of the sound. He made his way back to the rear cabin, where the off-duty driver and Oleg were still chatting. A few drops of rain spattered the windscreen; through it, all he could see was an endless expanse of flat land rolling off towards the horizon. The shower was over almost as soon as it had begun as they trundled forward.

So the day rolled on; Oleg started brightly enough, pointing out bits of landscape to Lansky, but after a while, as it was all the same, mile after mile, he said less and less. Lansky was dulled into a semi-comatose state, only awakening fully when the train lurched and jolted as it alternately stopped and restarted at frequent intervals during the day. The drivers stepped into the rear cab from time to time, at one point one of them bringing with him a selection of sandwiches – and no vodka, Lansky was relieved to see. Eventually, the sky started to darken as night approached.

"Come on Victor," said Oleg. "We'll go through into the living area. The drivers should have prepared some hot food this time. We can sit out there and eat, it will be a change. Lansky roused himself, thinking 'Christ, another six or seven days. I don't know if I can take it'. Oleg watched him, guessing what he was thinking. "Yes," he said, "it's dull, isn't it? And we have days still to go." He laughed. "But look at it this way – we will make a lot of money out of this business. What's a little boredom compared with that?"

Lansky smiled back. "I guess that's a fair way of putting it. I'll never begrudge train drivers their money again. They must be superhuman to manage to stay awake. Have we joined the main line yet?

"No, the last time they told me, they estimated sometime between two and three o'clock tonight. We won't really notice any difference, except that there will be a track next to us for trains going the other way. This first night when we are still on the branch line is the time of the highest risk of being attacked – so let's hope the guards are all fully awake. There have been some attacks on trains on the main line, but they're much rarer. Obviously on this branch line there is not going to be any traffic going the other way to distract them, and until we reach the main line we really are in the middle of nowhere. But we've always been OK so far, and our men are well-armed. Come, let's go and eat. And in your honour, I have brought some red wine and cognac with us. Normally, the train is dry, for obvious reasons."

Chapter 16

Krayanovsk Rail Spur, Central Siberia

One a.m. Lansky was shaken awake by a sudden lurch as the train's brakes were applied heavily. The wheels screeched in protest as they locked. The din lasted some minutes; emergency stopping a full freight train takes a while. Eventually, the noise dropped enough for Lansky and Oleg to be able to hear each other speak.

"That feels like an emergency stop," said Oleg. "Let's go into the drivers' cab and see what's happening."

They walked forward through the rest of the accommodation area, and stepped into the forward cab, which was a mirror-image of the one they had been in during the day. Two drivers were sitting in the seats, the third one standing in the gap between them. All three were peering forward into the dark. Oleg said something to them in Russian, and they replied, pointing forward through the cab windscreen. Lansky looked into the darkness, and then saw what they were pointing at. Way out in front, beyond the cone of light projected by their headlamps, he could see the bright flame of a magnesium flare. Oleg spoke again to one of the drivers, who replied animatedly. "He says that's the third one; we went over the first two, as we were trying to stop. They don't know what's ahead, or why the flares have been put out." One of the drivers picked up a walkie-talkie handset and rattled off a burst of Russian into it. "He's asking the guards to go and investigate," said Oleg. "It may be an accident up ahead, or a broken-down train. Apparently, normally the person who put the flares out would wait by the third one, because they assume by then any following train will have been able to stop." The walkie-talkie burst into life again. "Four of the guards are going to go forward and have a look and see if there's anyone around. We'll just keep our heads down up here, until they give us the all clear."

"Well, I suppose it's all more exciting that just sitting staring at the landscape rolling past. Let's hope it's not gangsters who want to take hostages."

Oleg laughed. "No, that won't happen. There may be some gangsters stupid enough to attack Malenkov property, but certainly none who would harm us or our colleagues. That would be very silly." Lansky wasn't sure whether he found that concept reassuring or not.

They watched through the window, and then, in response to another bit of Russian on the radio, the driver extinguished the lights, plunging the whole scene into blackness. "They don't think there's anything to worry about, but to be on the safe side the guards wanted the lights off to preserve their night vision, just in case," Oleg explained. Lansky and the others peered forward, trying to see what was going on.

Outside, in the darkness, four of the Chechen guards crept forward, moving silently on rubber-shod feet. The others ranged themselves along the sides of the train, Kalashnikovs gripped tightly in their hands, eyes searching through the night-vision sights. The only sound was the dull throb of the train's diesels turning slowly at tick-over. Lansky and his companions in the driving cab tried to pick out any movement out in the darkness. The seconds ticked away, then the walkie-talkie crackled again. As one of the drivers replied, Oleg looked across at Lansky. For the first time, his air of total command slipped, and Lansky saw a glimmer of uncertainty on his face. "They say there is nobody at the flare. That's quite odd. It may be that this really is a hi-jack attempt."

As he spoke, they suddenly heard the rattle of automatic gunfire from behind them, from down the train. One of the train crew pushed passed and they followed him through the cavern of the engine room into the cab at the other end of the locomotive. The firing was getting more intense and through the windows they could see down the length of the train. Bright orange spurts of flame flashed out in the darkness from the muzzles of the guns. They could pinpoint the position of the attackers out to their left facing backwards down the train. The answering fire came from close by the side of the train, where the Chechens were prone on the ground next to the track.

It seemed to be a stand-off; the firing kept coming out of the darkness, followed by the shorter staccato bursts back from the Chechens. Lansky was just about to ask what happened next, when suddenly four lights flashed on in the distance. They seemed to be moving fast towards the train, and then he realised the attackers were in two trucks, heading straight for them, firing over the roofs of the cabs as they approached. They had made a fatal mistake; the disciplined firing of the Chechens reached a crescendo as they poured bullets into the trucks. The muzzle flashes now were almost constant, the whole scene reminding Lansky of Guy Fawkes Night. Then when it was about a hundred metres from the train the leading truck rolled – obviously one of the guards had hit a tyre and flung the whole vehicle onto its side. The other one, about fifty metres further behind, seemed to pause for a second, then made a U-turn to the right and roared away, the Chechens pouring fire after it. After a few seconds, they stopped firing and silence descended.

Lansky didn't immediately say anything. He was shaken. It was one thing to joke about hijacks and hostages, but he'd never expected this journey to include a fire fight. Oleg looked pale; he hadn't seriously thought this would happen either. He regained his sang-froid first, relaxing as he realised they were safe. "We will have to wait a bit longer, while they check the truck over there for life." As he spoke, they heard the muted bark of a handgun from the direction of the wreck, and then another.

"Are they just killing them?" Lansky asked.

Oleg shrugged. "What else? They tried to kill us."

The walkie-talkie came to life again, and one of the train drivers listened intently then replied briefly.

"They say its all clear," said Oleg. "Shall we go down and see what they found?"

Lansky wasn't keen to go and inspect the bodies, but he knew he had really no choice. Reluctantly, he followed Oleg down the ladder to the ground. The train had all its lights blazing now, and they could clearly see the little knot of figures standing by the overturned truck. As they approached, Oleg called out to the men, who responded instantly. Reaching them, Lansky looked on the ground in front of them, and then quickly looked away. He had no wish to see six bodies after they had been chewed up by short-range automatic fire. One of the Chechens casually flicked at the pile on the floor with his boot. He said, something, at which the others all laughed. Oleg turned to Lansky. "Our men don't think much of the opposition. They say they were just amateurs, not in the top league."

"What happens now?"

"We go on our way."

"What about the bodies? What do we do with them?"

Oleg looked surprised by the question. "We leave them here. What else? You want to take dead bodies with us?" He laughed.

"No," said Lansky. "I just thought we'd bury them, or hide them, or something."

"No point. Between the vultures and the wolves, there are enough scavengers. There won't be much left in a day or so. And if their friends or families come looking for them, well, maybe they'll think twice about trying to steal from us again." Seeing the look of shock on Lansky's face, he went on: "Look, Victor, they chose to come out here with guns to try and steal. I'm not going to pretend I care what happens to them. They should have kept out of our way. It's a tough world in Russia at the moment. They knew what they were risking. It's not white-collar crime. It's dog eat dog. I told you before, let us take care of all this kind of stuff; you concentrate on the commercial side." As he spoke, there were bright flashes as one of the Chechens photographed the scene.

"What I don't get, though, is what they expected to do? How were they going to get away with any cargo in those two trucks? What they could get in there wouldn't be worth dying for."

Oleg looked seriously at him. "Well, these people have a tough life; they'll take that risk for almost anything. But this time, they're actually not so stupid. The train drivers say that just ahead of us is a small siding which leads to a sawmill. The hi-jackers never know how well defended the trains will be, and they would have hoped to have inflicted some casualties on the guards. Then, they would have offered a bribe to the guards and train crew, and detached maybe one or two wagons from the rear of the train. The main train would have continued, and the shortage would not have been found until it reached the port for discharge. The train crew and guards would then swear blind it had been complete on arrival; two railcars in the chaos of St Petersburg would be impossible to prove. Meantime, the thieves would have taken the wagons up the siding and unloaded them at their leisure. They could then sell the cargo, probably to a foundry of some sort quite locally." He laughed. "There is a black market for everything in Russia. The mistake was to attack a Malenkov train. Our guards do not give up easily." He shrugged his shoulders. "But if we hadn't been here, who knows? Maybe our men would have been venal, too. But I doubt it. Crossing the Malenkovs is not smart."

Lansky turned away and started back towards the train, digesting what Oleg had said. In principal, he agreed. It was their own fault the thieves had died. It was just that he wasn't used to seeing the reality of gun law laid out in front of him. And then, on top of Alex Koch's death in Hamburg, he did ask himself how deep he was getting in.

They all piled back onto the train; Lansky didn't feel like sleeping, and sat back in the cab, watching the dark landscape roll by. After one final stop at around three o'clock, the train finally picked up speed, and he could see through his side window the lines of a track running parallel to theirs. Clearly, they'd now joined the main line. The regular beating of the wheels on the rails, the dull thrumming of the diesel engine, the warmth of the cab, all were soporific. Lansky sat, half dozing, half thinking. He felt uncomfortable with what was happening. Sure, in the past his scrap dealing had not always been totally above board, but now he was implicated in murder. There may not have been any evidence proving guilt in the death of Koch, but he was sure. He knew, as well as if he'd seen it, that the Malenkovs were responsible for it. This time, though, he had seen it, had sat in a front-row seat while six men were gunned down on the orders of his business partner. Back in London, he'd rationalised to himself that, although he knew the brothers were murky, he could stay at a healthy remove from their actions. But now….and he suddenly realised the implications of the photographs the Chechen heavy had taken. That was evidence that he had been there, that he had stood by while murder was committed. Sure, there had been guns used on both sides, but that wouldn't show on the pictures. He shook his head to clear it. He was being paranoid. The men had been hijackers, had been trying to steal. They had got what they deserved. He would put his suspicions out of his mind, and get on with the business. Anyway, they were Russians. Revenge for his ancestors. Let them die. Deciding there was no point in going back to his bunk, he settled down in the seat and dozed off.

Once established on the main line, the train made good progress and the days passed. Slowly, because in the end, sitting on a train for days with nothing really to do except chat to Oleg or watch the countryside go by was an extremely dull occupation. Lansky wished he had brought more books with him. The signal he had hoped for on his mobile phone was sporadic, good when they were near a town, non-existent away from the settlements.

As they approached the Moscow area, the train started to experience hold-ups again. "Near the capital, there are more trains," explained Oleg. "We will be routed round the east and north of the city and then on to the St Petersburg line. That's the busiest line in the country – tourists, businessmen, as well as all the freight headed for the port." He laughed. "With that sort of traffic, it's almost like being in Western Europe. And, of course, let's not forget all the politicians dashing back and forth between the two cities. Let them. Soon enough, they'll understand that the true powerhouse of Russia lies out to the east, in Siberia. Minerals, oil, electricity. That's where the wealth to rebuild the state will come from, not their property deals, or money trading. And you're part of it, Victor, you're part of the rebirth of a nation. Don't you feel that this trip across Russia has bound you more into our enterprise? That you truly are one of us?"

Lansky wasn't sure if he was being over-sensitive, but that talk of being more closely bound to the enterprise, was that a veiled reference to the existence of the incriminating photographs? He smiled. "Sure, Oleg, I understand far better now how the business functions, in reality, not just in the papers and numbers I see back in London. So once we get round Moscow, I guess it's not so far to go?"

"That's right. Past Moscow, and we're talking hours, not days."

The horizon was no longer clear and sharp as it had been crossing the wide open spaces. The smog of Moscow and the fumes from its factories were beginning to smudge the view. As they approached, there were more frequent groups of houses visible. The vast, wide open wheat fields they had been crossing began to be broken up into smaller pieces, with more varied crops on them. The whole landscape was becoming more domesticated. The railway was getting busier, too. They could see local commuter trains on the lines branching off towards the city, and once again the stop-start progress began.

"Hours only to St Petersburg when we have gone around Moscow," said Oleg, "but also hours still to go around Moscow. I guess we shall not arrive finally until late tomorrow. When we get round Moscow, I'll give the freight guys a call. This metal for sure will be going into warehouse to await shipment, but if there's a vessel in loading at the moment, we may as well stay and watch it. That way, you will have seen the whole transport process, from Krayanovsk to the deck of a container ship in St Petersburg. From there, my friend, the responsibility passes to you and your arrangements for selling the metal and getting it to the customer or the LME warehouse."

Lansky laughed. "Yup. And having seen it all once, I can happily never have to do it again. Don't get me wrong, it's been a worthwhile exercise, but I've seen enough of the inside of a locomotive cab to last me the rest of my life. Incidentally, when we …umm……dealt with the hijackers, one of the Chechens took some photographs. What was that for?"

Oleg shrugged. "Just what they do. No particular reason. They're not civilised people like us. He probably wants to show it to his friends. They like to keep score."

"So it was just for him? Not a kind of record of what was done?"

Oleg shook his head. "Yes," he said blandly, "just for him. I guess he'll keep it safe."

That didn't fill Lansky with confidence. He really would rather have been reassured that the photos had been destroyed. It wasn't that he didn't trust the Malenkovs, but he would have felt far more comfortable if he didn't think they could have that kind of hold on him.

The Kremlin, Moscow

He would have been even more disturbed had he been able to overhear the conversation between Ansonov and Denis Menkov a few days later. Ansonov was holding a large photograph in his hands. "This is good, Denis. Lansky and Oleg are both quite clear, standing just to the side of the men with guns, the dead bodies right in front of them. The soft westerner, though, is clearly averting his eyes. I don't really care how you go about your business, but how did you get this done?"

Menkov smiled. "Simple, really. What's the best way to win a war?" He answered his own question. "Be on both sides. I paid the hijackers to stop the train, and they thought I would arrange things with the guards to make sure they would not react too violently. Then I told the guards I had heard there might be an attack and that they should be on full alert while they were on the rail spur. I also told them to make sure I got nice clear pictures. I think this should give us what we may need on Lansky, or possibly Oleg, in the future."

"Absolutely, Denis. Who knows when, or indeed if, we will ever have to use it? But as we both know, it's always best to have these kind of things on file, just in case. You've done well." He tossed a full envelope across the desk. "Buy yourself something. But make sure you keep close to Leonid and Oleg. This is not over yet. While the foreigners are still involved, we're only halfway there. Incidentally, will the friends and relatives of the hijackers keep quiet, in case anybody should find them?"

Menkov glanced into the envelope before he answered. US dollars – good, they were still the best. "Of course; I have taken care of that. They have also been paid off, and the bodies returned to them for burial. That's important to these peasants in Siberia. They won't say anything; anyway, there's no trace to see at the ambush site, so it won't even arise."

He got up to leave, as Ansonov spoke again: "By the way, implication in murder is good, but potentially terminal. Just to make sure we will have exactly all the kinds of leverage we may need, try to get something with sex or drugs; or both. That can always play well."

Menkov nodded. "OK. I'm sure I can think of something." He left the room, carefully tucking the envelope in his inside pocket.

Chapter 17

London

December 1995

R usso-European Metals was a cash machine the like of which Lansky had never seen before. All through the second half of that year, the money poured in and he could barely believe how successful the business was. The LME aluminium price, which ultimately dictated how much money they could make, held up firmly throughout the year. On the whole, Lansky eschewed selling the metal to real consumers, those factories who actually used it. Instead, he sold on the LME through Commet, and simply had his metal delivered into their warehouse in Hamburg and put onto LME warrants, thus turning it into deliverable material which could be used to satisfy his LME short positions. It was a win-win for everybody; under LME rules, Russo-European got paid within two days for its deliveries of metal, Commet earned substantial commissions for executing the LME trades, and the warehousing company were happy because their sheds were nice and full, earning them consistent rental income.

Cash-cow it may have been, but it was also pretty involving and time-consuming for Lansky. Since the train ride, he'd barely left London, with the need constantly to be on top of the pricing of the metal and ensuring the physical movements ran smoothly. He had come to respect the efficiency of the logistics department at the smelter, and they were a big enough user of St Petersburg port to ensure satisfactory service. Apart from one fleeting visit to London by Oleg in October for the annual LME Dinner, neither had he seen anything of the Malenkovs. He was surprised in early December to get a phone call from Oleg.

"Victor, hi. I've just arrived in London with an associate of ours. Can we meet this evening? We're staying at Browns, so perhaps we could meet for dinner at the Mirabelle?" Lansky smiled to himself. It was amazing how quickly the nouveau riche Russians were becoming familiar with London's upmarket hotels and restaurants. A few years ago, in the old days, they wouldn't have had a clue where to go. Ah well, such was the liberating effect of the end of the Soviets.

"Sure, Oleg, I'll see you there around seven thirty. Is the associate somebody I met in Krayanovsk?"

"No, he's from Moscow. He's not directly involved in the smelter business, but he has very good connections and can probably be of quite a lot of help to us. Anyway, I think it might be useful for you to know him." He laughed. "Let's face it, you are our man in London; we rely on you here, so why wouldn't we want you to get to know as many of our associates as possible? We're all one happy family now." And he hung up.

Lansky winced as he put his phone down. He still didn't like to be reminded of how closely he was tied in with the brothers. Any associate of theirs was likely to be suspect. But then, he reflected ruefully, what did that say about him?

Promptly at half past seven, he stepped into the Mirabelle, and was shown to the table, amongst the shimmering mirrors and glass of the elaborate interior. Sitting with Oleg at the table was a nondescript-looking man, a bit younger than his host, dressed very stylishly, in what were clearly expensive clothes. As Lansky approached, the two of them stood to greet him.

"Victor, my friend, it's good to see you again. Let me introduce you to one of our Moscow friends, Denis Menkov. Denis, this is Victor Lansky, whom we have told you so much about." The two shook hands and exchanged pleasantries in greeting.

"Denis is part of an investment group in Moscow that we have had some dealings with before, and he is interested in knowing more about our aluminium operation. He has been down to Krayanovsk a few times to see how the manufacturing side works, but of course to get a full picture of the whole business it is essential to understand how integral to the whole is your piece of the operation in London."

"Ah, I see. So are you looking to invest in the company, Mr Menkov?"

"Please, call me Denis. No, we are not necessarily looking to invest in the aluminium business, but we are interested to see how the model Oleg and Leonid have created down in Krayanovsk might be applicable elsewhere in Russia. You know, of course, that Krayanovsk Aluminium Smelter is not the only natural resource facility which is being privatised by our Government." Lansky nodded. "Well, we are interested to see if the way this deal has been structured could be used elsewhere, for example in the oil industry. So far, Russo-European Metals is the only company which has asserted its total independence from outside participants. Mostly, in Russia the privatised companies rely on foreigners like the oil majors or Metalex to handle the marketing of their products to the West. But you and Oleg and Leonid have created an environment where you have sole control over your own product. This is an area that many Russian companies look at with envy, and my group would like to see if we can turn that envy into something more positive. In other words, can we replicate what you are doing?"

Lansky gestured with his hands. "I don't know. What we have is appropriate for our business, where we have a very clearly defined product which can be sold not only to consumers but also to the terminal market. That is a big advantage, because it enables us to control our cash flow by always having the possibility to sell to the terminal market, even, although we have not yet experienced this, in times of slack economic performance and therefore poor consumer demand. Without that luxury, Russo-European would not be as stable and secure. We are also fortunate that in global terms, the plant is right down at the low end of the cost curve. Add to that the fact that the quality produced by our smelter is amongst the best, and you can begin to understand why our business is successful."

"Bravo, Victor," interjected Oleg. "You have really become part of the team. You are as proud of our business as I am myself."

"I'm not sure about 'proud' of it. I am pleased with the positives that allow us to be a highly profitable operation. But you see, Denis, that our model would maybe only work if all those propitious circumstances could be replicated. In oil, for example, I understand Russia is not necessarily a particularly low-cost producer, at least once you have taken freight costs into account. So that would probably mean less flexibility to continue producing even if the world price dropped substantially. You see, we can continue to do that. Many others would have to close before us. Again, we are fortunate that we control our own power supply, which, as I'm sure you know, is a vital part of aluminium production." As he spoke, Lansky could hear the enthusiasm for the project in his own voice. Oleg was right, he was becoming brainwashed.

Menkov's true interest was not in the development of Russo-European's business; he was more concerned with how he could obtain the kind of stuff Ansonov wanted. Nevertheless, he listened as Oleg and Lansky rattled on about how they ran their operation. A lot of it he knew anyway, close as he was to the Russian leader, but it was interesting for him to see how Lansky had been drawn into the inner circle. Clearly, he was still an essential part of the operation, so whatever leverage they got on him was going to have to have a long shelf life; they needed dirt that would stand the test of time, and be usable at that indeterminate date in the future when Lansky was no longer of any use. He had been intending to suggest finding some willing girls in a club and taking them back to the hotel, where he had been sure he would have been able to engineer a damning tableau to photograph. However, as the evening progressed, he became convinced that such a simple ploy was not going to work. He would need something a little more refined than crude pictures with hookers. He spoke in Russian to Oleg, who replied immediately, in English.

"Of course, that's an excellent idea. Let's ask him now. Victor, Denis has just made an invitation. Every year, for the Russian Christmas celebration, he takes a chalet in Courchevel, for the ski-ing. He is normally joined by business associates from Russia, and occasionally from the west. I will be there this January, and Denis is asking if you would like to join us. We will be a party of about ten or fifteen, for around five days. You can enjoy some ski-ing, some good food and some excellent company from many different Russian backgrounds. What do you say?"

"First of all, thank you for such a kind invitation. Provided the dates do not clash with anything in my diary, I should love to come. I can check tomorrow morning, and confirm definitely then, but I don't believe I will have any problem. I'm looking forward to it already! I love ski-ing, and Courchevel is one of my favourite resorts." To himself, he thought, even if being there with a bunch of Russian gangsters will be a new experience. Denis Menkov seemed straightforward enough, but Lansky had no illusions. He was sure he was another man on the make in the confusion of post-Soviet Russia, just like the Malenkovs. What he didn't realise was that they would not just be gangsters, but state-supported ones.

Later that evening, after Lansky had left them, the two Russians sat chatting in a bar.

"You know, some of that stuff about seeing if your model could work elsewhere in Russia is true", said Menkov. "Yuri is very keen to try and use your concept in other industries. You know we're getting what we want in the oil business, even though in something that size we have to work with the western majors. But even there, the joint venture deals are structured to favour us – the westerners are so greedy for our resource that they are almost blinded to what they are giving away to us. In some of the other metal industries, though, we may be able to replicate what you've done. That seems to be what Yuri is working towards. His power is growing all the time."

"And by using you and other private agents to help policy along, he can circumvent the so-called democratic processes," interjected Oleg. "But, just to make sure you fully understand, Lansky is still essential to our progress."

"Don't worry, Oleg. We know that. You can rest assured that for the moment he is still protected at the highest levels. Yuri Ansonov is not stupid enough to cut off his nose to spite his face. Lansky will be fine as long as we need him. And then.......... well, if we don't need him, who knows what may happen."

It wasn't only the Russian government who were aware of Lansky. He was on the radar of the British, as well. Since the Prime Minister's visit to Moscow, when he had first heard the name, he'd made sure both the Moscow Embassy in Russia and MI5 in London had kept their ear to the ground where Lansky's activities were concerned. There were two reasons for the PM's interest; one, of course, was that it was always good to see an example of a British businessman enjoying success. The other reason followed on from that; if he was successful, and making so much money, could he be tapped for a donation to the Party? Perhaps a knighthood, or if the numbers added up, a peerage would in due time be the fitting reward for a major industrial coup, which is how Lansky's involvement in Russo-European increasingly appeared to the outside world. As far as the UK end were concerned, that was precisely it. Lansky had taken a risk in investing in Russian resources, and it appeared to be paying off in spades. Obviously, they claused their reports to the PM with suitable cautions, about it being early days, about potential tax-related issues stemming from the BVIs domicile of the company, and general Civil Service bet-hedging, but broadly they found no real problems.

In Moscow, however, they were not quite so sanguine. The Head of Chancery, who had been tasked with overseeing the collation of the information they could gather about Lansky's Russian involvement, was beginning to find the relationships out in Siberia quite disturbing. Obviously, Denis Menkov was known as an FSB operative, rather than one of Ansonov's main fixers, but nevertheless just the clearly visible link between him and the Malenkovs rang bells.

The Head of Chancery sat in a chair in front of the Ambassador's desk. "It's all very well London telling us to keep an eye on Lansky's activities as a good news story of British success in Russia, but the fact remains that the guy is tied up with some very nasty people. Not only is he in business, as a partner, with the Malenkovs, but they themselves seem to be getting closer and closer to an FSB hood called Denis Menkov. He's in and out of Krayanovsk all the time at the moment. The Malenkovs obviously still have some kind of link with the security services, even though they branched out years ago. I can't imagine he's down there on a personal basis."

"Mmm. The PM seems very keen to use Lansky as some kind of example. The trouble is, although we have our doubts, everything we give London is just rumour and speculation. We need to get some detail, some concrete evidence that they are still just the same old gangsters. I mean, look, they parade themselves as businessmen. They don't hide the past, but they imply it's all changed now. Presumably nobody down in Krayanovsk will say anything about them?"

"No, they're all very tight-lipped. Which in itself is suspicious. There was one thing, though, that we could never really get to the bottom of. Something happened on one of the aluminium trains. I don't exactly know what, but one of our agents reported rumours that a few people had been killed in slightly odd circumstances. Probably clutching at straws, but we do know Lansky and Oleg Malenkov took a ride on one of those trains back in the summer."

"Yes," said the Ambassador, "but to be honest, a few people being killed is not really news. We know all these guys, not just the Malenkovs, but all the industrialists using the railway have armed guards on the trains. So it wouldn't really be a surprise if one of them had killed some of his rivals who were trying a hijack." He grinned. "Wild East, out there, you know. It would only be news if you could definitely show Lansky was involved, or even knew about it."

"Yeah, and that's the difficult bit. The rumour is that there was a very inept hijack attempt, and that the train involved had some VIPs on it. But that's as far as our informants can get. No specific time, or place, and no evidence as to who the VIPs were, if they actually existed. Still, we'll keep digging."

"I think you should. I don't want to be thought of as opposing the PM's positive view of Lansky just for the hell of it, but I am seriously worried. I think this guy's business dealings could explode in our faces, if we're not careful. I think he's potentially political poison."

"OK, well, I'll keep my people working and my ear to the ground. Maybe we can flush something out."

"I had dinner with the Austrian Ambassador a couple of nights ago. Although Metalex is more international than Austrian, they still see them as a national champion, since their HQ is in Vienna, and they're still smarting over losing out on that Krayanovsk deal. They get good information in that company; maybe it's worth putting some feelers into their Moscow office. For sure they won't be interested in protecting the Malenkovs.

"Good thought. I'll get someone in there to feel out the lie of the land."

Chapter 18

January 1996

France

It was still dark as Lansky carefully drove the Ferrari off the Shuttle train at Calais. The Ferrari was a new toy, delivered only a few days before Christmas. Sleek, black with tan leather upholstery, it was a brand-new 355. It was the first time for years that he wasn't driving a Porsche and he was looking forward to the long run down the autoroute to the Alps, undecided as yet whether to make it in one hop or to stop overnight en route. He'd left London late the previous evening, and stayed just outside Folkestone to get an early train under the Channel. Hopefully, this way he would be ahead of the bulk of the traffic, giving him a reasonably clear run. As he eased out of the Shuttle terminal area and accelerated away, he was grateful for the French toll-road system, which at least kept the local traffic off the autoroutes. The engine behind his head was singing away as the little car sat rock-steady on the road at 130 miles per hour. Next to him on the passenger seat was the bag holding his ski-boots – bulky luggage like that doesn't fit in the front boot of a Ferrari. The dawn came up, the sun rising in the clear cold winter sky as he passed the signs pointing to the site of the Field of the Cloth of Gold, shortly after he'd turned on to the A26 to take him southwards. On the horizon, he could see the huge slag heaps towering above the old coal mines. He'd made this journey many times before, every time promising himself he would stop on his way and visit the First World War battle sites and cemeteries; he'd never done it yet, and as he flashed by the monumental memorial to the Canadians at Vimy Ridge, he knew this was another year when he would just put that trip in the box for the future. The names were evocative, though: Arras, St Quentin, Cambrai, and then further south he would come into the French sector, at Chemin des Dames and the Argonne in Champagne. He was still holding the car steady at 130mph, trusting to fortune that he would spot any gendarmes crouching behind their radar guns in time to slow down. The traffic remained light; the French had returned to work after their Christmas and New Year holidays, and the English school holidays were over, so this Autoroute des Anglais was clear. Lansky smiled to himself; clear roads were a bonus to be gained for celebrating the Orthodox not the Western Christmas. As he crossed the

115

gently rolling hills of the Somme valley and breasted the rise out onto the great plain of Champagne, he began to think this might be a record time for the journey. So far, the Ferrari was everything he had hoped, fast, comfortable, solid. He reached forward and turned up the CD player.

Some hours later, Lansky was just taking the A40 out of Chambery. The only stops he'd made had been to refuel, and by now, mid-afternoon, the sun was dropping rapidly in the winter twilight. The outside thermometer on his dashboard was indicating only just above zero. At this rate, he was going to be climbing the hill up to the village of Courchevel, perched on its ledge at 1850 metres altitude, in the last knockings of daylight. Snow chains being an impossibility in a car with so little clearance between tyre and wheel-arch, he hoped the road was completely clear. Now his mind began to focus on the week ahead, which until now he hadn't really thought too much about. He knew he wouldn't embarrass himself with his ski-ing, being a pretty good recreational skier, but he did have some misgivings about what the company might be. He'd only had a quick briefing over the phone from Oleg, but he understood that the group would include both Malenkovs and, obviously, the host, Denis Menkov, whom he had met in London. Apart from that, Oleg had reeled off some other names which meant nothing to him, but who were clearly well-known to a Russian. "Don't worry," Oleg had exhorted him, "you will have fun. Some ski-ing, some eating, some drinking….and anything else you want. Russians know how to enjoy themselves, and this is a big holiday for us. You know, Christmas is a big religious festival still in Russia, but when we are on holiday in the Alps, we tend to treat it more like festivities than a religious fete."

Lansky rather assumed the company would consist of nouveau riche fixers cum industrialists, rather like the Malenkovs, with presumably a few other European hangers-on like himself. The car phone rang just as he was on the road round Brides-les-Bains, leading him to the entrance to the valley he had to climb. It was Oleg. "Victor, are you on your way?"

"Yes, I'm just at the bottom of the hill, so I shouldn't be too long. I've just reached the snow line, but I guess the road is cleared all the way up."

"Yes, the road is clear, but there is some ice in the village, so be careful with your beautiful new car! You have the directions I gave you, to find the chalet?"

"I do, and I know roughly where it is, anyway."

"Good. I will have them open the garage doors. There is a space in there for you. So, we look forward to having a drink very soon." The phone went dead, as he hung up.

Lansky concentrated on his driving. It was a pretty easy road, meandering its way up through La Tania and then the various different Courchevel levels, until eventually he came out of 1650 on the long, curving road round to the top of the valley and his destination, 1850. The car twitched a couple of times as he found some ice, and he changed down and dropped his speed a bit as he saw the road surface glinting in the cold light of the rising moon. Gingerly, he tiptoed into the village. His destination was on the left of the centre, up on the Bellecote side. Following the directions he had, the car sliding quite a bit now, he slowly climbed to the turning indicated. He could see the gates to the property about a hundred metres down the road, but he could also see a solid sheen of ice. Ah well, in for a penny, in for a pound. He put the car in second gear and eased forward. Slithering and sliding, just managing to keep going in the right direction, he reached the gateway. The ramp into the driveway of the chalet proved too much, though. Try as he might, revving the engine, trying to start up in third, he couldn't get the spinning wheels of the car over the bump. Embarrassing, or what? There was nothing else for it. He rang the doorbell, and, when it was answered by a member of the chalet staff, asked for Oleg and explained the problem.

Oleg burst into laughter, and called out in Russian. In response, half a dozen men appeared, and Oleg marshalled them to push the car over the obstacle. That done, Lansky rolled it slowly forwards into the garage. "Victor, give the key to the butler and he will get your luggage brought in." He laughed again. "That must be the richest party of car pushers ever. Still, it is a Ferrari, so nothing but the best." Still chuckling, he led Lansky indoors. "Come and meet everybody. We are just about to have a drink. After your journey, I'm sure you would like to join us." A staircase led directly from the front door, up to a double-height hall. From there, Oleg led him into a sitting room, again double height, with floor-to-ceiling windows on one side, through which he could see across the darkened piste outside the twinkling lights of Courchevel centre below. A huge fire blazed behind a glass screen on one of the other walls. The car-pushing party were gathered to welcome him, Denis Menkov in the middle of them.

Apart from Menkov and Leonid, whom obviously he knew, there were three other men. They stepped forward in turn to introduce themselves. Two were Russians, who just grunted their names and shook his hand, the third bowed stiffly from the waist and said, "Hi, I'm Ludo, from Zurich. How was your journey down here in your beautiful little car? I guess you made pretty good time. The roads must be clear at this time of year."

"Yes, it was a very easy journey, until the last few metres, as you saw. Thank you all for your help. Obviously, Ferraris don't do slippery roads too well."

Leonid stepped forward and embraced him in a bear hug. "Victor, my friend. It is a long time since we met. Since the summer, in Krayanovsk, things have been going well, no?" He spoke briefly in Russian, then

117

continued. "Forgive our friends, their English is not so good, but they are very old friends from Siberia. Denis, here, you know; he is not a Siberian. He is a soft Muscovite." Menkov laughed, as Leonid continued, "Ludo is our friend from Switzerland. He looks after some matters there for us. But he has another, more important task. He is the man who has arranged the visas for everybody, including the girls who will be joining us tomorrow. This is a vital task, to make the party go well. So we are all very grateful to Ludo. But Victor, we are forgetting our manners. We are just having a glass of champagne." He gestured to the butler, who had been hovering in the background, and now stepped forward, with a tall, elegant flute of straw-coloured wine. Lansky raised it to the others.

"Gentlemen," he said, "Thank you for your assistance in enabling me to finish my journey. I look forward to some good ski-ing and some good company over the next few days. Your health." And they all solemnly raised their glasses in a toast. Leonid turned back to the Russian-speakers, leaving Lansky standing between Oleg and Ludo, from Zurich. Time for some small talk, he thought.

"So, have you all been ski-ing today?"

Ludo answered. "Yes, we had a good day. We have two groups, or two standards, I should say. Oleg and I have been up at the top of the Saulire, and down the back, where there are some black runs, and the others have been more here around the village."

"Leonid can ski as well as I can," interjected Oleg, "and so can Denis, but he only arrived earlier today. The other two are not so good, so Leonid has been accompanying them for the last couple of days. I think finally though he has managed to persuade them to take an instructor tomorrow." He smiled. "I think you can already guess that for Russian men, it is perhaps difficult to admit that they need a teacher, especially when they can see so many people who ski so easily. So Leonid should be with us tomorrow, and I guess you will be, too. I understand you are quite a good skier."

"I'd certainly like to join you. I'm an experienced skier; I wouldn't say good. Style gives way to expediency, once it gets technical. But before all that, I'm going to need to hire some skis. I didn't bring any with me."

"That's easy. I'll just tell the butler to call the ski shop and get them to come up here. They will bring a selection in the van with them, and you can choose what suits you."

"Sounds good. Look, I must go and take a shower and so on, after sitting in the car all day. What time do we have dinner?"

"Around eight. Let me show you to your room. Excuse us, Ludo."

As they stepped into the hall, Oleg said quietly, "Victor, I'm glad you have come. Ski-ing just with Ludo is tough. He is Swiss, it is second nature to him. I was exhausted by lunchtime today. I hope when you and Leonid and Denis join us, the pace may drop a little." He led the way up the staircase and along a corridor. "Here, this is your room. I hope it's OK. If you need anything, just call the butler. Otherwise, we'll see you in time for dinner. Your luggage will already have been brought up and unpacked." With that, he left Lansky in the doorway to the room. Looking around him at his accommodation, Lansky was impressed. He'd been a rich man before his involvement with Russo-European, and he'd stayed in some pretty luxurious ski lodges, but this was in a different league. The room was on the same side of the building as the sitting-room, with the same view across the piste down to the village; it was big, beautifully furnished, with a dressing room and bathroom off to the side. There was a large TV, a fax machine and a full-size desk, with even a Reuters terminal on it. As a nice touch, the Reuters was showing a page of LME prices. Lansky chuckled. A hint from Malenkov of how this was all paid for? Unable to stop himself, he checked the aluminium price. Still firm, still good for Russo-European.

The butler knocked on his door just after he had finished showering and changing to tell him the ski shop staff had arrived, so he could sort out his hire skis. Impressive again, everything he was shown was high-quality and brand new. He chose himself a pair of Salomon intermediate piste skis, with the assurance from the shop that if they weren't quite what he wanted, he could change them any time. So, he was fully equipped for tomorrow.

He went into the sitting room, where the group was sitting around the fire. The champagne earlier had obviously been an aperitif to the aperitif; now, they were holding what looked like some form of vodka cocktail. Denis Menkov beckoned him over. He and Leonid were studying a piste map. "So, Victor, you will ski with us tomorrow? Leonid and I are just thinking of where we shall go. The weather forecast is perfect. Bright sunshine, maximum temperature just above freezing in the village, colder obviously at altitude. Oleg tells us the slopes behind Saulire, down toward the Suisses, were good today, and not crowded. Maybe we go up there in the morning. We have a lunch table reserved at le Chalet de Pierres at one thirty, so we can have a good morning's ski. Ludo and Oleg will also join us. Our two other friends have a lesson with an instructor which will finish at one, so that will give them perfect time to reach the restaurant. Probably we will not all ski in the afternoon, because some of us at least should be here to welcome the rest of our party. There are three girls Leonid and Oleg know from Krayanovsk, and two other associates of mine from Moscow. But look," he pointed to the piste map, "this is where we will go in the morning."

"Yeah, that should be good on a sunny morning. I've skied here quite a few times before, so I'm reasonably familiar with the layout of the resort. But where did all you guys learn to ski? In Russia? Or always here in Europe?"

"Well, I worked for some years in western Europe, so I learned here during that time. I know Oleg and Leonid used to ski in the Caucasus, but they too have been many times to the Alps as well. Right, Leonid?"

"Yes, although I learned originally during my military service. Oleg of course managed to avoid that, because he was studying when he should have been a soldier. But military service was not too bad. That's where I learned to be a businessman, and the techniques I learned there have been good for me."

Yes, thought Lansky to himself, I could see you as a Russian King Rat. Out loud, he said "Well, it will be interesting to see how everybody gets on, ski-ing together. Certainly looks like great conditions. The snow was just about all the way down to Brides-les-Bains as I drove up. As long as the sky stays clear, we should have a great few days. But Denis, what did you do when you were working in Europe? Were you managing investments then as well?"

"Actually, I was in Government service. I was at the Embassy, part of the time in London, and part in Berne. I was attached to the commercial section, so I was involved in helping Russian trade. I learned in the West how capitalist businesses work, and that gave me a lot of help when the Soviet system collapsed. I was able to apply my knowledge to developing Russian investment opportunities." In fact, he reflected to himself, that wasn't so far from the truth. Just because his involvement in investment opportunities sometimes included killing, and always was at the instigation of the President, it didn't mean he wasn't as keen as the next man to see Russian businesses thrive. It was all a question of emphasis. The butler came up and spoke to him.

"Gentlemen," announced Menkov, "our dinner is ready to serve. Let's go through."

The dining room was spectacular. Again with floor to ceiling windows, but this time facing directly down the valley, what drew the eye was not the lights twinkling in the distance far below, but the terrace outside, half of which was taken up by a swimming pool, illuminated from underneath, with the heat of the water rising as steam into the cold night air. Seeing the direction of Lansky's gaze, Oleg gestured to the window. "See, look down. The other half of the swimming pool is indoors, so you can get into the water in the warm, and then swim out into the outside. There's a bar and sitting area inside down there, and of course sauna and so on." He grinned. "We Russians always like to have a sauna or steam room, and after ski-ing it's a great way to relax the muscles."

"How do you stop all the heat escaping from the room, if the pool is indoor/outdoor?"

"There is a flexible plastic screen which goes right down to the water level. So when you want to go outside, you either swim under it, under the water, or you can push it aside as you go through; then it drops back into place after you. It's a good system, although of course the whole thing uses a lot of energy to keep warm in the snow. Not very green, but never mind."

They sat down to dinner: the food, served by two very cute French waitresses, was serious five-star standard, and the wines, served by the butler, of equal merit. In fact, Lansky glanced at the label on the red burgundy they had with the main course of succulent venison, and nearly made a double-take. It was a top-growth Richebourg, and they were downing major quantities of it. Again, as with the chalet, the sheer extravagance hit him. Somebody was spending serious money here. A lot of the conversation was in Russian, so he found himself more and more talking to the Swiss, Ludo. It transpired that the latter was a lawyer in Zurich, who handled various tasks for several groups of Russian businessmen. It was clear, from his references to Russo-European and its affairs, that he was pretty much an integral part of the Malenkovs operation. Probably made him a bent Swiss lawyer, thought Lansky to himself. Dinner swung on through the evening, the cognac was called for, and eventually Lansky made his excuses, pleading tiredness from the drive down, and headed upstairs to bed.

Chapter 19

January 1996

Courchevel, France.

The next morning was bright, crisp and clear. The extravagance of the Russians was again evident in the clothing they were wearing at breakfast and the equipment they put on for the day's sport. The outside door of the ski-room gave directly out onto the piste, where the instructor was waiting for his two pupils. Unsteadily, they set off behind him down the easy Bellecote slope to the centre of the village. Menkov prepared to lead the others off.

"Wait a minute," said Lansky. "What about Ludo? Aren't we going to wait for him? I know he hadn't appeared at breakfast, but shouldn't we tell him we're ready?"

Oleg answered. "It's OK. He has to go down to Geneva today. He has to pick up our young ladies. He arranged the visas, so he has to go and make sure there are no hitches. He'll be back mid-afternoon, and then ski-ing again with us tomorrow. Let's go!"

They also had to go down to the centre, to pick up the lift which would take them up towards the top of the valley. From their chalet to the lift station was just a straight schuss for them, and they overtook the other two dutifully following along behind their instructor after a couple of hundred metres. Bringing up the rear, Lansky saw Leonid alter his course to throw up a swirl of loose snow over the two of them as he passed, roaring with laughter as he did so. Aha, thought Lansky, it's going to be one of that sort of day.

By the time they had ridden the telecabine up to the mid station and then taken the bubble lift to the top of the Saulire, the Russians decided it was time for the hip-flasks to come out. Thereafter, they spent the morning in perfect conditions high up at the top end of the valley. In mid-January, the resort was not particularly busy, and they had a lot of the runs to themselves. Lansky was relieved to find he could keep up relatively easily. He skied with an elegant style, perfected over years, which was matched by Menkov. Leonid betrayed his military training in the aggressive way he skied, whereas Oleg was somewhat more cautious. All had a tremendous enthusiasm, and Lansky found the morning exhilarating. The only stops they made were to recharge themselves from

122

the hip-flasks. Lansky passed on that, mostly; swigging five-star cognac mid-morning was a tad too extreme for him. Eventually, the time came when they had to go back down towards the village to meet the others for lunch. From the top of the Saulire, the piste descends a steep-sided v-shaped valley, emerging back into the sunlight on the wider slope leading down to the mid-station. From there it's a relatively easy run down to the top of the village, where the Chalet de Pierres restaurant sits at the top of the Jardin Alpin.

"OK," said Leonid, standing on the edge of the lip of the valley. "It's a straight run from here. Everybody know where we're going?"

Getting nods of assent, he pushed off down the slope. One by one the others followed him, dropping off the lip, the speed building rapidly as they arced down the steep slope. It was lunchtime, and there was virtually no traffic on the snow to slow their progress. Leonid pulled out a lead on the others, daring to take a steeper line down the valley. Behind him, the rest were neck-and-neck, skis chattering over the packed snow. Carving their turns, they flashed down the side of the valley, finally bursting out of the narrow gorge onto the wider slope above the gondola mid-station. Leonid by now was a speck in front of them, until he caught the edge of his ski in a rut and went tumbling head over heels in a flurry of loose snow. Seeing him sit up and begin to dig his skis out of the pile of snow where they had landed, the others went straight past him, hell for leather, each determined to get to the restaurant first. As they arrived outside its protected terrace, gasping with exertion and laughter roaring out of their lungs, there was nothing to choose between them.

Bending over his ski poles, panting, Oleg said "Did you see Leonid? That was a great fall. Teach him to boast about army skiers being the best. Victor, coming down there like that, you're one of us. You have become an honorary Russian."

As they were standing laughing, Leonid coasted to a standstill next to them. There was snow in his hair and dusting his clothes, but he was grinning from ear to ear. "Ha, a small fall, when I caught an edge, but none of you could keep up with me!"

"Maybe, Leonid," said Menkov, "but we all still got here before you. Maybe if you went a bit slower, you wouldn't fall over. What's that English story, Victor? About the tortoise and something?"

"You mean the tortoise and the hare. Aesop's fables. But I don't think any of us came down there like a tortoise. I bet your army instructors wouldn't have been too impressed."

"Pah. We'll have another race, this afternoon or tomorrow. You'll see. If I can stay on my feet, none of you can stay with me."

They stacked their skis in the rack, and walked up the few steps onto the restaurant terrace. The sun was at its zenith in the bright blue sky, but without the gas space heaters it would have been too cold to sit out on the terrace. As it was, it was crowded with skiers sitting at lunch. Menkov led the way across to a table at the back, in the sun but sheltered by the restaurant building and the bank of snow protecting the side of the terrace. It was clearly the best-placed table there, and when they got closer, Lansky saw the 'Reserved – Menkov' label on it.

"This is our usual table," Leonid said to Lansky as they sat down. "You see from here we have the whole terrace in front of us, so we can look at all the girls. And then beyond that we can see the piste, so we can criticise all the skiers; perfect position, huh?" Lansky had to agree. They were definitely well-placed, and from the way the head waiter came bustling across to them, greeting Menkov by name and suggesting a champagne to start, they were well-known as well. The other two Russians arrived just as the champagne was poured; they looked as though they had had an exhausting morning, and gulped their drinks with relish.

The Chalet de Pierres is generally reckoned to be the best slopeside restaurant in Courchevel, if not in all the Alps, serving high-class food accompanied by a seriously good wine list. Menkov had pre-ordered for them all, rather than taking the a la carte food, and again Lansky did a double-take when he saw the red wine being opened for them. Chateau Lafite 1982 is something most people don't experience in their lives; and yet, he reflected, they weren't going to get the full flavour and body of that wine drinking it outside in an air temperature barely above freezing. Still, it was prominently displayed on their table, for all the other diners to see, and actually he was beginning to understand that that demonstration of wealth was the real important factor. But he'd enjoy it, wrong temperature or not; rude not to, really.

Lunch lasted until around three thirty, when the two Malenkovs decided it was time to return to the chalet, rather than ski any more. Menkov suggested to Lansky that perhaps they could have a couple more runs, while the sun was still visible up above the mountains on the horizon. As they got down to the Croisette, where the main lifts begin, Menkov proposed that they take a lift on the right, and then up over the top of the ridge to do the former Olympic ladies downhill run into Meribel, in the next valley.

"We won't have time, will we?" replied Lansky. "By the time we've got down, we will be too late for a lift to get us back up again to get down this side."

"Doesn't matter," said Menkov. "Once we get to Meribel, we can call the chalet and get then to send one of the cars over to pick us up."

Lansky shrugged his shoulders. "OK, if we can do that, I'm up for it. It's a nice run down there, it'll finish the afternoon off well."

The sun was low in the sky by the time they finished the pattern of lifts that took them to the top. The run was challenging, not excessively steep, but it bent and twisted over the contours of the mountainside, at times plunging them into narrow gullies, and then out onto wide open expanses of snowfield. With the dropping temperature, the surface was turning icy, and Lansky was grateful for the new skis, with their razor-sharp edges that enabled him to cut into the ice and hold himself across the slope on the traverses. They didn't push themselves at Leonid's kind of pace, but took the run steadily, enjoying the last run of the day and as the mid-winter sun finally dropped over the ridge of mountains to the west, they came out from amongst the trees that surrounded the last stage of their run into the big open space of the Rondpoint des Pistes above the village of Meribel. Signalling Lansky not to stop, but to follow him, Menkov led the way to the piste-side Hotel le Chalet, outside which he stopped.

"Looked like you were enjoying that," he said.

"Yeah, it was great. It's always satisfying to take a run like that in one shot, without stopping. Mind you, I don't think our time would challenge the Olympic women."

Menkov laughed. "True. But we kept a good style and rhythm all the way down. Let's go in here." He gestured towards the entrance to the hotel. "It's got a nice bar, and we can have a drink and then call the car to come and get us. It's too cold to sit outside."

They went in, and sat down at the bar. Thirsty after the long run down, they both ordered a cold beer; first swigs downed, Menkov said, "I've known Oleg and Leonid for quite a long time. You're relatively new to their business, aren't you?"

"Yes, they approached me with an idea about eighteen months ago. They had the possibility to acquire the smelter at an attractive price, but they wanted to get someone else involved in the West who had more experience of the international metals business. I'd actually been out of it for some years, since I sold my company and moved into property, but you don't really forget what you learned in your first career. I was quite dubious at first, but the economic logic of the deal finally convinced me. It's been a very successful partnership, as I'm sure you know."

"Yes, indeed, so I understand. But why were you dubious to start with? There was such a good deal on the table."

Lansky paused for a moment before answering. How much could he say to this man, who was obviously a close friend and associate of the Malenkovs? Well, why not be honest? Oleg particularly knew what his doubts had turned on.

"To be frank with you, Denis, I was concerned about their reputation. They seem to have been involved in some pretty rough things in the past, even if I only believe half what I've been told."

"Yes, there is some truth in that, and I can see that it might have been a problem. But, you know, you have to look at things in context. Soviet Russia was a hard place, if you wanted to improve your lot in life.

Don't get me wrong; at a basic level, the state provided. But for anyone who aspired to move away from that basic level, the odds were severely stacked against them. So when the shackles were removed, and people began to understand that they could do things they'd never even dreamt of, some went to excess. Look, I can't honestly say conditions are better for the mass of the people than they were under the Soviets; I really don't know – I suspect they're really no better off. But what I do know is that the window opened by the collapse of the Soviets enabled many to kick and fight and grab to get themselves up to a totally different level. It was their one shot; some took it, and succeeded; some ended up with bullets in them. Most stayed where they were. But don't judge them by the standards of the West that has had a more or less free society for hundreds of years. Leonid and Oleg did some bad things. Most of the stories you have heard are probably true. But that was then. Now, what they are trying to do is a legitimate business." And I'm the President's personal enforcer, to make sure it all goes how we want, so we can keep power for an elite as limited as it was under the Soviets, he could have added. But didn't, obviously.

"Ye-es. That's kind of how I've rationalised it to myself. But your life has also clearly changed. What was it you said? You were in Government service? How did that change to this life, where, if you'll excuse me saying it, you seem to be a lot richer than most Government servants I've met?"

Menkov smiled. "I suppose I could take offence at that. But I don't. I too was lucky. Amongst my contacts were a number of people who have emerged as industrialists. They – just like the Malenkovs – were unsure of how to advance internationally. How to invest, how to deal with corporations. I had some of that expertise to offer them, from my time in the West. In fact, we're not that different, you and I. We're both involved in helping Russia step away from the past and become an accepted part of the international community, not the bear to run away scared from. And about the wealth…well, people have to pay for expertise, and I've made sure they pay me well. Let's face it, you're also taking a big chunk of money in return for your knowledge."

"Partly for that," replied Lansky. "But I guess you also know that I'm a shareholder in Russo-European, and to get that share I actually put in quite a big investment. But in principle you're right; it would be naïve to deny that I have been making a lot out of this arrangement. It's gone better than I think any of us could have hoped. It looks like it's going to continue, as well. There's a clear demand for our metal, and unless there is a major economic slowdown, it looks set to keep on. In fact, if anything, demand is growing, what with the increasing use of aluminium. Car manufacturers are getting keener and keener on it as a much lighter, and therefore greener, material than steel. Of course, if they saw the filth belching out of the chimneys at Krayanovsk, maybe they wouldn't be so sanguine. But that's not our problem."

Menkov gestured at the by now empty beer glasses, and getting a nod from Lansky, signed to the barman for a refill. He took out his mobile phone. "Let me just call the chalet and get one of the drivers to come over for us. It'll take him about half an hour to get here, so that should be fine." He dialled and then spoke in Russian into the phone. He laughed at something said on the other end, and then hung up. "I told them where we'd been; Leonid swears he could beat you down that run, and wants to have a race tomorrow. He's taking this ski-ing very competitively."

"Yeah, he doesn't like being beaten, does he?"

Menkov had been photographing the group all day on the mountain, and sitting in the restaurant at lunch. Now, he pulled out his camera again, framing Lansky against the backdrop of the bar. "Sorry," he said, grinning, "it's an annoying habit of mine. I like to keep a record of what I've been doing all the time. I'll make sure you get copies of the good ones."

They chatted on, inconsequentially, until their driver stuck his head round the door of the bar. Menkov acknowledged him, and the two of them finished up their beers before leaving. Outside was a black Range Rover, with dark windows and a Swiss registration plate. The driver was already loading their skis onto the roof. They climbed in the back, and the car moved off smoothly.

"Everybody back from Geneva with no problems?" Menkov asked the driver.

"Yeah, we went down in both cars with Ludo this morning. No problems at all, except the flight was late. We actually only got back up to the chalet about an hour ago. But they're all in good form. The girls all went off shopping as soon as they arrived. Something about needing new ski gear. They took Oleg and Ludo with them to pay. Leonid's gone down to the Elephant bar, said I should drop you there with him and then wait and bring you all up together. Stefan is taking care of the girls and the others in the other car."

"I've got to say you have this very well organised, Denis. This beats getting a taxi back if you overshoot at the end of the day."

"We like to make sure everything runs as smoothly as we can. You know which is the Elephant bar, don't you?"

"Yes, it's that one under the central lift buildings and everything, on the downhill side of the Croisette. Everybody calls it the Elephant bar, but it's actually got a real name, which I've never known."

"Nor me. But if we join Leonid there, just for a quick beer, we can then go up to the chalet and get ready for dinner. Should be fun this evening, the girls are always excited when they first arrive so there'll be lots of noise and drinking."

Lansky's mobile phone rang. "Victor, hi, it's Rory Davies. Are you in Courchevel at the moment?"

"Yes, I drove down here yesterday. Why?"

"I've just arranged a long weekend there starting the day after tomorrow. I remember you had said that's where you were going, so I thought maybe we could meet up on Saturday, either to go ski-ing together, or for dinner or something."

"That'd be great, Rory; I'm staying with my Russian associates and some of their friends. I'm sure we could all get together. After all, we're effectively all partners in the same business. Where are you staying?"

"At the Annapurna."

"Oh, that's easy, then. It's just up the slope from us. Why don't you give me a call on Friday evening when you get here, and we can arrange something."

"Sure, I'll speak to you then." And they hung up.

"That'll be good," Lansky said to Menkov. "That was a guy called Rory Davies, who runs the LME broker we use. He'll be here for the weekend. Oleg met him before, when he and I went to look at the warehouse in Hamburg."

Menkov knew he would have to play the meeting with Davies carefully, after the previous one he had had. Still, at least his cover story about an investment group was broadly the same, even if he would have to explain why he had become uncontactable after his dinner with Davies.

"Maybe he'll be crazy enough to try and keep up with Leonid."

The drive back around the ridge between the two resorts took them about half an hour, and then the driver stopped outside the bar where they were to meet Leonid.

It was furnished like a traditional Pall Mall club, with deep, highly polished leather armchairs, and book-lined walls. Leonid was sitting in an alcove with a vodka in front of him. Surroundings might be like St James's, thought Lansky, but you couldn't accuse Leonid of looking like a Landon clubman. He was still wearing his ski gear, and there was a nasty weal on his forehead.

"Hi, Leonid. What have you done to yourself?" Lansky greeted him.

"Hah, its nothing. I went for another couple of runs after you left us, and I took a small fall. The ski hit me on the side of the head as it came off." He touched the mark. "Actually, it's quite painful. But the vodka will cure it! Let me order you one." And he snapped his fingers for the waiter.

Menkov laughed. "Well, Leonid, I make that two falls to you, and none to the rest of us today. Tomorrow, we can give you some tips. Victor and I took the Olympic run down into Meribel. No stops, no falls, just smooth, stylish ski-ing."

"If you don't fall over, you haven't been trying," Leonid growled, in mock anger. "And you give me tips? I don't think so. The only tips will be your ski tips, always failing to keep up with me. I don't need this nancy-boy western style; I ski like a true Russian – flat out all the time." The waiter arrived with the vodkas. "Here, a toast to a great few days to come, and to you trying to catch up with me!" They were all laughing as they knocked back their drinks.

"Leonid, I just had a call from Rory Davies – you know, he runs Commet." Leonid nodded. "He will be in Courchevel over the weekend, so I thought we might try to get together. You know his company is being very helpful to us with the storage of our metal, so it might be nice for you to meet him. Oleg already did, in Hamburg."

"Sure. Let's ski with him. Maybe he will present a challenge to me." And Leonid laughed again.

Mentioning Hamburg brought back thoughts of the death of Alex Koch, and Lansky's suspicions of who had been involved. But, as ever, in the company of either of the Malenkovs, he found them engaging and entertaining. Maybe what Menkov had said in the bar over in Meribel was true – the bad things were in the past, and should be left there. What he didn't of course realise was that the man who was really responsible for that death in Hamburg was indeed sitting in front of him, but it wasn't the one he thought.

Chapter 20

Courchevel, France

They got back up to the chalet in the early evening to find the rest of the party, already back from their shopping, in the sitting room drinking Krug. As well as Oleg, Ludo and the two other Russians, there were also now five girls sitting amongst them. They were all stunning, and dressed as if they had just stepped out of a fashion magazine. As Lansky took a glass of champagne, one of them stood up and came across to him.

"Hi, we meet before. In Krayanovsk. In sauna."

Lansky recalled the face – and indeed the body. "Of course. It's..............Olga, isn't it?" She nodded. "Well, it's a pleasure to see you again. Perhaps we will have a little more time to get to know each other than we did last time."

"Yes. We become good friends. Come, sit down." She drew her arm through his and led him over to a sofa by the roaring fire. "So, Victor," – she gave it a very long 'i' sound, drawn out, like 'Veektor' – "you have been ski-ing today. With Oleg and Leonid? Did you have fun?"

"Yes, we had great fun. We skied all morning, and then Leonid and Oleg came back, and Denis and I carried on and skied over into the next valley, to Meribel. You just arrived here this afternoon?"

"Yes, we got to Geneva late, our aeroplane was late. This bloody Russian airline! Then we drove up here with the Swiss man – Ludwig, or something? – and then we went shopping. We all had to get some new ski suits. We only had last season's. So Oleg bought us all new clothes, and then we came back here to bathe and change in time for you all to come back for dinner." She stroked the silk of the blouse she was wearing. "Oleg also bought me this – very pretty, no?" She pouted. "But he would not buy me the necklace I wanted to go with it, so I have to wear this old thing." This old thing, dangling against her tanned flesh, looked pretty good to Lansky.

"The blouse is very pretty," he said. "Oleg is a generous man. So do you live in Krayanovsk?"

"I come from there. But now we live sometimes in Moscow, sometimes in Krayanovsk. We have many friends we visit." I bet you do, thought Lansky. The girl went on, "She" – pointing at one of the others, equally blonde, equally stunning – "she is my cousin, Maria. We have been

130

friends with Oleg and Leonid for a long time. They often invite us on holiday, especially ski-ing. We love to ski." She gestured imperiously to the butler to come and refill their glasses. She giggled. "I love champagne. Tomorrow we will ski together. You will see how good I am. And you will love my new ski suit." She lowered her eyes, and looked at him under her lashes. "It's very sexy. Very tight here." She rubbed her hand across her hip and thigh. She raised her now replenished glass. "A toast. To my new English friend. We shall have much fun together!"

"I'll drink to that," said Lansky. "I'm afraid I can't claim my ski suit is very sexy. It's more designed for comfort. But I'm sure yours is splendid. Have you hired your skis and so on yet?"

"We have told the shop what to bring. They will be here by breakfast time."

The phrase 'Siberian princess' was floating around in Lansky's mind as he was chatting. Still, he thought, that's not my problem. And she was very attractive.

Denis Menkov strolled across and sat with them. It seemed to Lansky as though the girl became guarded in her speech, almost as if she were overawed or frightened by him. The conversation carried on, inconsequential, but with a distinct feeling that Olga was careful about what she said in front of Menkov. The latter had his little camera in his hand again, and they all soon stopped noticing the flashes it made as he recorded the evening.

They drank their way through a fair few bottles of Krug before the butler announced dinner. Menkov arranged the seating as they went through to the dining room. Lansky was slightly disappointed to be seated between Maria, Olga's cousin, and Ludo. He would have preferred to stay with Olga, but she was put down the other end of the table, with the two non-English speaking Russians. Lansky soon discovered that that was a problem with Maria. Her English was very basic, so she spent dinner speaking Russian to Leonid on her other side, leaving Lansky largely chatting to Ludo.

"Without wishing to appear naïve, Ludo, what exactly do these girls do?"

Ludo looked at him for a moment. "Well, they're not actually what you think, or not entirely. The three from Krayanovsk I have met before. Two are cousins, one is a close friend. Their fathers are long-term associates of the Malenkovs. What that means, I've never really wanted to know. So Leonid and Oleg have known them for many years, since they were children. They do nothing ....untoward with them. They are the children of friends. Whether they are otherwise available" – he looked sideways at Lansky – "I don't really know. Their families are now rich, but we don't ask how, they are very attractive, and they like to have a good time. The two from Moscow, well, you may find their sort in many clubs in Moscow. But I'm only really guessing. I'm a lawyer. I do what my clients ask, without judging them." He glanced down the other end of the table, and then back at Lansky. "But I would say, from the way she looks at you, that Olga is taken with you. Maybe you'll find out the answer to your question."

The food and wine was again splendid, and dinner went on. Off the subject of the Russian girls, where Lansky felt he was making certain assumptions, Ludo was good company. Almost unnoticed by now, Denis Menkov's camera flash was ever-present. As the coffee and the cognac appeared, Lansky glanced down the table and saw Menkov bending over Olga, saying something in her ear. She nodded nervously, and then her eyes flicked towards Lansky. Seeing him watching, she turned quickly away and nodded again to Menkov, more emphatically this time. Curious, Lansky thought, then dismissed it from his mind. The others may already be moving on to cognac, but he was still enjoying the Haut-Brion, and intended to finish the bottle which was still two thirds full in front of him.

They kept chatting and drinking, until Oleg suggested they move back into the sitting room, and then put some music on the sound system. Olga came across to Lansky. "Victor, this is like our own night-club. But even better, I think there is a swimming pool downstairs. Come, let's go and look for it."

"OK, it's down there, under the dining room. Why, do you want to go for a swim?"

"Let's go and see; maybe now, maybe tomorrow." And taking him by the hand, she led him down the stairs to the pool and bar area. Menkov watched them go, with a smile playing around his lips.

The pool room was lit with wall-mounted sconces, the bulbs flickering to give the effect of torchlight. Olga gestured to the bar, in the near corner of the room. "Get me a drink, please, Victor. I would like a cognac." Stepping round behind the bar, Lansky searched among the bottles until he found a bottle of Hennessy XO. He poured generous measures into two of the crystal balloons on the top of the bar and handed one to the girl. Nodding her thanks, she took it over to the sofa in the opposite corner and sat down, slipping off her shoes and curling her legs under her as she did so. "Come, Victor, sit down." Bringing his glass and the bottle with him, he followed her and dropped onto the seat next to her.

The pool stretched out in front of them, divided half way along by the heat-retaining plastic panels. Beyond was the darkness of the terrace. She rested her head against his shoulder, as she drank her brandy. "So, last time, at the sauna in Krayanovsk, the water was cold. Here, I think it will be warm. I'm going to take a swim." She drained her glass, and stood up. She smiled seductively as she stood in front of him and slowly unbuttoned her blouse. She dropped it to the floor, and her skirt followed.

She was wearing nothing underneath. With a giggle, she turned and dived into the pool. Surfacing, she swam powerfully forward, and then, ducking under the heat barrier, out into the dark night. Lansky swigged his brandy, and poured himself another. Outside, Olga raised her head into the air. Turning, she ducked under the water again and swam back into the warmth of the pool room, jumping up in the water in front of Lansky as she reached the other end. He was mesmerised by her body as she slipped back down into the water. "Come on, Victor, it's wonderful. Take your clothes off and have a swim with me."

Gulping back the rest of his brandy, Lansky needed no further invitation. Stripping off, he dived into the pool and followed Olga out, under the barrier into the night.

"Aaah!" he gasped, as the freezing cold hit him. "It's too cold."

"Pah. Not for a real man, surely." She turned on her back, and paddled to the end of the pool, tantalising him with flashes of flesh. Lansky stayed treading water, as the girl swum round and grabbed him from behind, squeezing him and whispering throatily into his ear. "Let's go back inside. I know how to warm you up."

They swam back and climbed out of the pool; the girl led Lansky over to the sofa, and, as she straddled him, the red light of the security camera blinked away in the corner of the room. When they had finished, Olga quietly slipped off him, put on one of the dressing gowns hanging on the wall, and left him. Out in the corridor, she met Menkov. "Well done," he said. "That was exactly what I needed. I think you'll find Oleg will buy you that necklace you want tomorrow." Smiling, she skipped off up the stairs to her room.

Lansky was actually too embarrassed to go back and join the others. He had heard rumours of Russian girls, and knew the new rich liked to keep their guests well entertained, but he couldn't be sure if that was what had happened, or if the girl was genuine. Maybe he'd find out the next day. Gathering his clothes, he dressed and slipped out and up the stairs to his room. In the back of his mind was the half hope that he might find Olga waiting for him there, as if he were James Bond. He didn't.

Back in the sitting room, to which Olga had returned, once she had dried her hair and dressed again, the others carried on with the party, scarcely missing Lansky or Menkov, who had also returned to his room after carefully taking the film out of the security camera above the swimming pool bar and hiding it at the bottom of his briefcase. He was the host, nobody would search his room, but old habits died hard.

The next morning, Menkov was up early, making a call to Moscow. Yuri Ansonov was pleased to be told Menkov had the pictures they needed.

"Very good, Denis", he said, "So now we have Lansky in our hands. For the moment, we don't need to do anything. The time is not yet right to turn up the heat on him. Leonid and Oleg still need him to look after the western part of their business. But the time will come when we can dispense with him, and you have made sure we have the weapons to use. Have you made sure the girl is taken care of? She has done her part for Russia."

Menkov laughed. "Actually, from the enthusiasm she gave her task, I would say she was pleased to be able to help Russia in this way. I suspect she will continue to do so for the rest of the time we are here. But that's private enterprise. Yes, I have made certain she has been well rewarded for her……..exertions."

Ansonov laughed as well. "Of course. Russian girls always take their work for the motherland seriously. Have a pleasant stay in Courchevel. We shall meet on your return to Moscow."

The day followed a similar pattern to the previous one. The non-skiers went off for their lesson, and the rest of the group went up to the top of the resort to find the more challenging runs. One bonus as far as Lansky was concerned was following Olga as she wiggled her way down the slopes; the ski suit flattered her figure, just as she had suggested it would. Lunch was again at the Chalet de Pierres, and today the whole group skied again in the afternoon. As the sun set over the ridge to the west, Leonid again challenged them all to a race down from the Saulire. This time he stayed on his feet, but was unable to keep up with Olga's cousin Maria, who turned out to be an expert skier, leaving Leonid with the others struggling in her wake. As they sat relaxing in the bar at the bottom of the run, prior to heading back to the chalet, Oleg forced his brother to drink a toast, as a forfeit, to "the pride of Russian womanhood." Menkov looked at Olga, and smiled.

After dinner, drinking, talking, laughing, this time Olga followed Lansky into his room at the end of the evening. Later, as they lay in front of the picture window looking out over the twinkling lights of Courchevel, she said seriously: "Victor, you should be careful of Denis Menkov."

"Denis? Why? I mean, I assume he's a gangster, like the others, but that doesn't really affect me. I know he has some dealings with the Malenkovs, but nothing to do with the business I have with them."

"It does. I don't know why, but you should be careful. Yes, the others are gangsters – in Russia today this is not so unusual. But Denis is more than that. He is a dangerous man. He is associated with politics, and I think he also has some links with Security. I don't know why, but he is interested in you."

"How do you know?"

"Victor, I like you. We have fun. Don't ask me how I know; I am Russian, I understand some of these things in my country. Take care when Denis Menkov is around." And she turned over, and pulled the duvet up over her head, refusing to say another word.

Lansky had had quite a lot to drink during the evening, but he now lay awake, worrying. Was this trip a bad idea? He had been determined to keep a long distance between himself and the Russian end of the business. And yet, if what the girl said was true, people involved in Russian politics were looking at him. That didn't really sound like keeping a low profile.

By the time he was awakened by the attentions of the girl next morning, he had made his decision. At breakfast, he took Oleg aside. "I'm really sorry, but I'm going to have to leave early. Something's come up – don't worry, it's nothing I can't resolve very easily – but I have to go back to London. Please accept my apologies. I know today is Christmas Eve, and I hope Denis will understand, but I really do have to go and fix something."

Denis Menkov, when told, feigned disappointment, but in reality he had what he wanted from the visit to Courchevel, so he didn't really care if the Englishman was there or not. Olga was genuinely sorry. Putting her arms round him, she pleaded with him to stay.

"We've had such fun. If you leave, I will be sad and it's not good to be sad at Christmas. Please stay." Eventually, he managed to convince her that he had to go.

Frankly, if it had just been Olga, he would willingly have stayed, but the idea of what Menkov was and why he might be interested in him was not something he wanted to get too close to. Maybe later, back in the safety of London, he would ask Oleg about his friend. But all the worries he had experienced after Hamburg flooded back into his mind, as he pointed the little Ferrari back down the hill. Just as he got onto the A430, he remembered Rory Davies, and the meeting they were supposed to have. Calling him from the car, he realised he couldn't confess to the younger man that he was frightened by one of his business partners guests, so he cooked up some pretty lame excuse about problems he had to sort out in London.

Part Two

Chapter 21

London

January 2000

T he next four years were very kind to Victor Lansky. A change in Russian corporate regulation to allow some limited foreign joint-venture ownership enabled Russo-European to become visible as the owner of the smelter, and not just a sales agent. The combination of the huge amounts of money spun off from the company and the relationship the Malenkovs had with Ansonov enabled them to buy into other smelters across Siberia, with the result that by late 1999, their share of the global aluminium market had grown to push them into the top league, alongside well-established Western companies as well as the newer producers of the Middle East. The Malenkovs were amongst the elite of Russia's oligarchs, all stories of gangsterism in the past forgotten. They were the darlings of Russian society, with all the trappings of the super-rich to go with it. Lansky sat outside Russia, controlling the flow of metal into the Western economies. The arrangement with Commet was still important, but they had outgrown it. Lansky now negotiated directly with the CEOs of aerospace and automotive companies to satisfy their need for his aluminium, and he mixed with the Chairmen and Presidents of the world's foremost mining companies. And he was courted by the politicians. Aside from investment banking in the City, the British economy lagged behind some of its European partners. For a Prime Minister desperate to look as if he still belonged at the top table, Lansky was a godsend. True, Russo-European was a privately-owned BVIs company, with its manufacturing base in Russia, but nevertheless Lansky could be portrayed as a British merchant, proof that the heritage of nineteenth century trading success had not gone away. It helped that he was personable, that he came from humble origins – the son of a Covent Garden porter. That chimed with the political times. Of course, the legend conveniently ignored the fact that he was half-Polish, and the son of an aristocrat, albeit an exiled one. Soundings were taken, words were exchanged, and mutterings began to be heard that it would not be long before Victor Lansky was honoured by his country. Actually, honoured by a grateful government, to whose party he had donated a large sum of money. But no matter; Lansky played up to it all. He loved the fame, the influence, the connections his wealth brought him. He first made the Sunday Times rich list in 1998, at a relatively low level, and then shot up it in 1999. In 2000, it looked like he would really hit the big-time, amongst Britain's super-wealthy. With all the money, he got the trappings of wealth as well. The little Ferrari had been joined by a garageful of stablemates, the Mayfair apartment had become a Chelsea house, and now, in January 2000, down in Poole his new 120 foot yacht was just undergoing its sea trials ahead of sailing for the Caribbean. The Russian girl, Olga, still featured in his life, but just as often he was photographed with the lissom younger generation of Eurotrash. Always careful, though, to maintain the dignity required of an industrialist, and a future knight of the realm.

One of his new best friends was Jacob Feinstein. Jacob was the up-and-coming generation of the family that owned one of Britain's foremost merchant banks, an institution that had been raising capital for British industry and providing investment advice for the wealthy and landed classes for the last two hundred-odd years. Jacob was the confidant of a couple of Government ministers and had been instrumental in guiding Lansky's political donations. He was also the head of international business at Feinstein's Bank. He could recognise an opportunity when it was staring him in the face. Russo-European Metals was a huge opportunity, with a little lateral thought. He entertained Lansky to dinner in the private dining room in the apartment above the bank's headquarters building in the heart of the City. Over the brandy, he brought the conversation round to his thoughts on the future of Russo-European.

"You've made a fortune, Victor. No point in pretending – we both know it, and there's only the two of us here. Russo-European has been a cash machine for you, and I guess for your Russian associates as well. The question is, do you want to carry on as you are, or do you want to take it to the next level, to maximise what you've already got out of it? Do you want to keep on with the day-to-day operations, or do you want to get on with the next project?"

Lansky laughed. "I'm not altogether like you, Jacob. I see this as my big project. I'm not sure what the next one would be."

Feinstein leant across the table. He was a tall man, well over six foot, with tightly-curled blonde hair. His face was full of enthusiasm. "That's easy. Between you and the Malenkovs, you are one of the biggest players in your industry. In aluminium, you are as significant as the world's major mining companies. What you don't have is anything other than aluminium, so in overall terms, you don't stack up against them. What you should be looking at is how you could leverage that position you have in the one industry to turn yourselves into a true resource conglomerate.

You guys could be amongst the world's biggest miners. Never forget, basic raw materials are the absolute bedrock of the industrial world. Look at all the retail and IT billionaires – without raw materials, they're nothing. Its all very well to talk about the digital age, the information era, but without the stuff that's mined out of the earth, none of those industries are going anywhere. You know Feinstein's has long been associated with the mining industry, obviously particularly in precious metals, like gold and silver. Well, I've had a few chats with some of our guys, and we think the time is right to ramp up Russo-European and get it on the takeover trail. There are a lot of interesting assets out there that could diversify the company substantially. And you and the Malenkovs own it all, don't you?"

"Yes, all but a couple of very small shareholdings that were given to some people at the outset, as thanks for their help. But they're insignificant. To all intents and purposes, Leonid, Oleg and I own it all. So why should we want to change that? It would take us lifetimes to spend the money we've already made. Yes, we keep a very tight rein on how we run it, but you know we've stepped away a bit, we do have quite a few people now to do the regular stuff. And, of course, don't forget how much of it is in Russia. Leonid and Oleg have to keep absolutely on top of that."

"Exactly. That's the point. You could loosen that dependence on Russia. I know you've all been focussed totally on Russia to develop your existing business, but this is the chance to break away from that. To become truly international. Potentially, that could put you three guys amongst the most powerful individuals in the mining industry. Doesn't that sound an attractive prospect?"

Lansky sipped his brandy reflectively. "It does, but I'm not sure its going to happen. To do it, we'd have to float the company, right? I assume that's what you're suggesting."

Feinstein nodded. "Yes, we'd float it to get the capital in. But you three would still be able to retain a fairly sizeable shareholding. And then, if we price it right, we can be pretty sure the share price will rise, so then we use that paper to buy some more assets. Frankly, your business operates so well, is so low-cost, that it will almost drive itself."

"It's interesting, but one immediate flaw I can see is that to be sure we remain low-cost, we have to keep hold of the dam and the hydro plant. That's not owned by Russo-European; that is still owned directly by Oleg and Leonid. And before you say the new vehicle would have to buy it, I'm not sure if the Russians would let a foreign-domiciled firm own the plant that powers the town of Krayanovsk, as well as our smelter."

"Mmm. But you have a long-term supply deal, don't you?"

"Of course, and it's at a very advantageous price. But again, I don't think the Russians would like details of that to become public. While it's our private company, we don't have to tell anybody about it. If we were public, we'd almost certainly have to disclose the details, and that would not be popular. It's a complex place to do business, Jacob, and it all works because nobody rocks the boat. Your idea is very tempting, frankly, but I'm not sure we could get it off the ground."

"Look, this is just a first thought. I'm sure we could structure it in such a way that we could get a flotation off, despite the power company issue. I assume you, or rather the Malenkovs, don't look to make too much profit on the electricity?"

"No, it's run effectively as a service to the smelter; we prefer to keep the input prices low, and that maximises the benefits in Russo-European, which is, after all, a BVIs company. But that's another reason why we couldn't open it up to scrutiny." Lansky paused. "Look, all this I'm telling you, it's purely as a friend. I wouldn't want it to go beyond these four walls."

"Of course not. You have my word on that. One of the reasons I suggested dining here rather than in a restaurant was precisely in order to avoid any risk of being overheard. I just see a deal which I think could be good for all of us. I realise there will be problems, but the end result, I believe, would make it worth expending some energy trying to get around them. Look, nothing formal, but suppose I produce a brief memo outlining what I think would be possible. Would that be helpful? Then you could talk about it to the Malenkovs, and see if it makes sense to you all."

"OK, I guess it can't do any harm to have a discussion, but I'm not massively optimistic. How long will it take you?"

"Not long. Give me a week or so, and I will get something done. Now, you up for moving on to Annabel's?"

Next morning, Lansky was as usual in early to the Russo-European office just off Grosvenor Square. Going through his regular morning business, he couldn't get Feinstein's suggestion out of his mind. What the banker said was true; they had become pretty much the most influential player amongst aluminium producers. Krayanovsk was the jewel in the crown, but the acquisitions of the other smelters they had made had boosted them right up the global league table. The prospect of turning that into a major mining conglomerate was mouth-watering. In the back of his mind, he knew that if he could use Russia like this, he'd be getting something back for his father's memory. Convincing the Malenkovs, though, could be difficult. They would see such a move as giving away control, letting someone else participate in what was theirs. And then there was the question of diluting the Russian-ness of the business. They would probably not take too kindly to that, either. Still, money definitely talked, and maybe there was a chance if he made them focus on how much money this could generate. He picked up the phone.

"Oleg, hi, it's me. I need to talk to you about something. Are you still coming to London next week?"

"Yes. I shall arrive Monday morning for three days. I shall be in the office all day Tuesday, for the meetings we already have planned. Is this for something else?"

"Yes, we need to schedule an hour or so, just you and me. It doesn't concern anybody else here."

"Well, I think the secretaries have already emailed you my schedule. For me, we could make it around 11:30 Tuesday morning, before the lunch meeting we have. Would that suit you?"

"Perfect. It's just thoughts I have been having about future developments and what we may be able to do over the next few years."

Oleg cackled. "I just hope we keep on making this much money for the next few years. That will keep me happy. I'll see you next week."

Feinstein was as good as his word and had an outline proposal on Lansky's desk by that Friday lunchtime. The latter shoved it in his briefcase to take with him as he walked out of the door. He had important things to do that weekend. He was off for a final look at his yacht before she left for the Caribbean. The next time he would be aboard would be in Jamaica, in the second half of March. He was excited about the yacht as he pointed the little Ferrari south westwards out of London.

It was already dusk as he got to the south coast town of Poole, and he drove round to the boatbuilders, against whose quay his beautiful yacht was proudly moored. At 120 feet, she dwarfed every other vessel around her, and he was pleased to see the skipper had ensured that the crew had her fully lit up in anticipation of the owner's arrival. Although he had been down in Poole earlier in the winter when she had been launched, this was really the first time he had seen her in the water, so he crawled all over her, from stem to stern, like a schoolboy with a new toy. Finally, as the chef would not join the ship until she reached the Caribbean, he took the skipper ashore for dinner in the town, where they celebrated with a couple of bottles of champagne.

He spent Saturday morning with the skipper, confirming his plans for the season, discussing where and when the yacht would need to be to pick up him and his guests for the cruises he had planned. After late spring and early summer in the Caribbean, he was intending the boat to be back in Europe, in the Mediterranean, for the summer. Tentatively, he was thinking of basing them in Corsica, but he'd also agreed to be in Greek waters around the end of August. It was a busy schedule, but it was his first season of ownership and he wanted to try and squeeze everything in. So it wasn't until lunch on Saturday that he got around to looking at Feinstein's proposal, sitting at the table in the main saloon with a beer and a sandwich that the crew had rustled up for him. He sat studying the two pages Feinstein had given him for a long time, deep in thought. He was roused by the ring of his mobile. "Hello. This is Victor Lansky."

"Victor, hi, it's Jacob. I just wondered if you had had a chance to look at what I sent across to you yet."

"Jacob, yeah, I'm just looking at it now. It seems very clever. Are you sure it would work?"

"Yes, we're quite happy that it all stacks up. The biggest problem, as you suggested, is getting around the mixed ownership of the hydro dam, because without security of supply from that, you potentially prejudice the overall low smelting cost you have. And that low cost is what investors will be interested in. But I think our way around it is pretty good. We spent a long time talking to Russian lawyers about it – without naming names, of course – and they are comfortable with it."

"Okay, well, look, I'm seeing Oleg on Tuesday, and this is one of the subjects we will be discussing. I'll let you know after that if we think it's worth pursuing."

"Fine. I'll look forward to hearing from you."

It was dark by the time Lansky made his farewells to the skipper and crew, wishing them a comfortable transatlantic passage, despite the winter cold, and confirming again that he would see them next in Jamaica in March Giving the boat one last, lingering look of satisfaction, he got back into the Ferrari and drove gently back up the motorway to London, his mind on the deal Feinstein was proposing, which pushed his pride in his new boat into second place.

Chapter 22

Mayfair, London

Oleg Malenkov was in great form the following Tuesday in the Russo-European office. He'd morphed from the scruffy thug Lansky had first met five years ago into a smoothly-presented international jet-setter. True, he couldn't do anything about the overall coarseness of his features, but it was amazing what grooming and clothing could do, when expense meant nothing.

He and Lansky had had discussions and meetings with a number of their employees, covering a variety of everyday topics, and then finally at around 11:30 they were alone in Lansky's private office.

"OK, Victor, so you had some thoughts you wanted to discuss. Let's do that now."

Lansky opened the draw under the top of his desk, took out a copy of Feinstein's proposal and handed it across. "Have a look at that. I think it might interest you." Oleg took the papers and started reading. As he read the introductory paragraph, he glanced up at Lansky in puzzlement. Then he looked down again, and continued reading before saying anything. When he reached the end, though, he looked across with a very serious expression. "Victor, why are you showing me this? This is not how our business is meant to go. We don't need to bring in outside shareholders, we make enough money as it is. Are you suggesting you support this idea?"

"I'm suggesting that it is a proposal to which we should give serious thought. I know we make lots of money as it is, but this would be a way of growing our business out of its reliance on Russia. We could become truly global players. I haven't made a decision as to whether we should do it or not; but I do think we should consider it and think about the implications."

"I'm glad you say you have not made a decision, because this is not your decision to make. This" – he waved the sheets of paper in his hand – "this is about power. It's about transferring the power centre of our business from Russia to a group of international shareholders. But Victor, surely you understand that we cannot do that? The whole purpose of our enterprise is to develop Russia's assets. You know that your involvement has always been to facilitate the flow of metal into the west, as well as helping with the initial funding. But this is about power, not money.

We've always been happy to share the money, but there's no question that the power could ever move outside Russia. This is not going to happen."

"Oleg, I'm not trying to usurp anybody's power. I know this is a Russian enterprise, but surely we can talk about how we can develop things further? Anyway, even if we did float the company, there's nothing to stop you keeping a controlling shareholding. You and Leonid would still be able to make sure you controlled the Board. It's just that we would have another pile of cash for expansion."

"It's lucky for you that you raised this with me and not Leonid. He would frankly be very annoyed that you would even want to discuss this, but I will try and explain. We have been called many things in the past – you have yourself even referred to us as gangsters. We know this, and we know that there are things in our past which are not very edifying. Things that need to be forgotten, traces of a different era, when life was lived differently in our country. These things should not be brought into the open, which would happen if we had outside shareholders crawling all over us. That is the first point. The next is that our intention in this business has always been to develop Russia's resources. It is not in our plan to dilute that by spreading ourselves outside Russia. The third point is more......" he hesitated for a moment, "delicate. There are people in powerful positions who have been extremely helpful to us. They have a clear agenda for the future which includes our business. They are also Russian patriots who would not wish to dilute the control vested in Russia of our enterprise. I don't really want to say any more about that, but maybe you can work out for yourself what I mean. Now, let's not discuss this further. It's not going to happen. I will take this" – he held up the document – "and show it to Leonid, but only to demonstrate the kind of things that are being said. I will not suggest to him that you wished to discuss it seriously."

"But actually, Oleg, I *do* think we should discuss it seriously. I understand all your comments, but nevertheless we all put money into this business and we should all be able to discuss its future rationally. This is not a bad plan; it warrants our consideration."

"Victor, we have a lunch meeting to attend. Let's do that. Seriously, my friend, do not go down this road. It will not be a good one for you to travel. Please, as a friend, I'm telling you to leave it alone."

The atmosphere between them over lunch was frosty, which was noted by their host, the major shareholder of a large physical metal merchant to whom they sold substantial quantities of metal for the Italian market; Lansky had always declined to deal directly with customers in that country, preferring the credit risk of the merchant to that of the end users.

Oleg returned to the subject once they had returned to their office, while he prepared himself to take the evening flight back to Moscow.

"Victor, I mean what I say. Do not have any further discussion about Russo-European with Feinstein. It will do you no good and it will cause waves in our relationship, which I really don't want to see happen. We have had a good four years and there is no need to start to change things which are successful."

Lansky was beginning to get irritated. Although he quite liked Feinstein's plan, as he had said earlier to Oleg, he had by no means made a decision. But now, the way the Russian was hectoring him, effectively telling him what he could and could not do, as if he were just an employee, was beginning to set his mind. A historian would have suggested that the Pole in him was beginning to resent being ordered around by a Russian again.

Oleg went on: "As I said, I will have to mention it to Leonid, and he may have to speak to some of our friends about it, just so that everybody who needs to be is aware that there are people out there who would like to get a piece of Russo-European. But I suggest you do not speak of it to him." He paused. "Forget it, Victor, be happy with the money and forget about the power. None of us are men who need the aggravation of running a public company. I must go. The car will be waiting. Until next time, Victor."

Lansky sat in his office, deep in thought after the Russian had left. Although he could see the points Oleg had made about not changing the status quo, nevertheless he was puzzled by the way he had reacted to what was after all no more than the first mention of an idea. Certainly the Malenkovs would not like their history exposed, but on the other hand the rumours had all been out there for years; they were actually in inverse proportion to the success of the business. Presumably, anything which could have been proven would have been already. Anyway, for sure they had ways of muzzling any stories which came out now. No, the problem must lie with the shadowy "friends" Oleg had mentioned, who would not have wanted to see outsiders get their hands on the company. Over the last few years, as success had built up, Lansky had more or less forgotten all his concerns about his business partners, which had made for a much easier life. But that conversation with Oleg brought all the doubts back again. He remembered how friendly the Malenkovs had been with Denis Menkov in Courchevel that time, and how Olga had warned him to be careful of Menkov, with her suggestion that he was involved with the security services. Could there be any truth in that? Could the Malenkovs have some link with the murky side of the Russian government? Oleg was clearly still touchy about the need to keep the business purely Russian – he smiled to himself, 'purely' seemingly in both senses of the word. The more he thought about it, the more attractive Feinstein's suggestion was. Just as the Malenkovs wanted to keep everything as closely held as possible, so Lansky was beginning to feel the opposite – let in as much scrutiny as possible; he knew the real underlying business they owned stood up on its own, and any reference to a dubious past could presumably be left there, in the past. Investors might be shocked, but the truth was that what would attract them would be the present and future earnings, not a lesson in Russian history. But that would be apparent to Oleg as well, so, he kept coming back to it, the issue must lie with the identity of the Malenkovs' associates. Maybe, in the end, if he couldn't get them to float the company, he should start thinking about getting out, taking the money and running. Certainly it did seem that after that conversation with Oleg he should perhaps be a bit more circumspect about his plans.

Moscow, Russia

Two Days Later

The Malenkovs had taken a penthouse office suite for Russo-European in Moscow's ritziest building. Apart from the almost ever-present smog, they had a wonderful view out of the windows of the office they shared across the city towards the Moscow Hills in the distance. Today was a sunny day, the air pollution was low and the crisp white blanket of snow lent a picture postcard air to the vista. Leonid's humour didn't match it. Oleg had shown him the proposal Feinstein had made, presenting it as something which had come unsolicited to Lansky, and carefully avoiding mentioning that the latter had shown some interest in discussing it further.

"Little brother, this shows how careful we must still be. We have made a huge success of this business; we have gone far beyond what we could ever have dreamed of, but that just means that the vultures keep looking at us with greed in their eyes. This Feinstein, why does he think he can run our business? What has he ever done? He comes from a rich family who have given him everything. He has never had to fight to create his own business, or his own wealth. And now he thinks with his big, rich friends he can walk in and take what is ours. We built this, and we built it here in Russia through our own efforts. I will not see it stolen from us." His voice was becoming louder and louder, as he worked himself into a fury. Oleg thought it time to try and calm him down.

"Relax, Leonid. They are not trying to take anything away from us. This is just a suggestion of how we could use western capital to expand our company and become more than an aluminium producer. It is the way in the West to use capital from investors to expand businesses. They are just looking at us as if we were no more than another opportunity for them to exploit. They would put money in to the company to enable us to buy other companies and grow that way."

"And in return they would expect us to give them control. That will never happen. We do not need their 'growth'. We make plenty of money, our government is happy with what we do, why do we need Feinstein? Anyway, we could buy his bank with our loose change. Who does he think he is?" In the midst of his ranting, another thought struck him. "Have you mentioned this to Denis Menkov, or Ansonov?"

"No, if we can kill it now, then I don't think we need to. But if we hear any more, then I think we shall have to. We cannot pretend Ansonov does not have a serious interest in what happens to Russo-European. But if it goes no further, then I think we can ignore it."

"Does Victor understand that there is to be no discussion of this? Because obviously it will be him to whom Feinstein tries to talk. It's clear from this paper that they don't really understand how the power in Russo-European functions."

Oleg walked across to the window, and stared out at the sunlit, snow-covered city for a moment before answering. In his mind he weighed the desire to protect Victor, who had after all become a good friend, against the need to avoid the explosion which would come if his brother found out that's what he had been doing. He chose the middle course of the diplomat. "Leave Victor to me. It is true he believes we should discuss this proposal between the three of us, but if you let me deal with it, I can persuade him he is wrong."

"Why persuade him? He is wrong. That's simple. Just tell him. And whatever the shareholdings in the company may suggest, he is here only for the money he brought at the beginning and for the access he has given us to the western market. In fact, we probably don't need him any more, if he's going to be awkward. His place is not to tell us how to run the company. He can concern himself with operating the business, but it is for us to decide what the underlying business is." Oleg had to hand it to his brother; for all his ranting, he had in fact summed up the relationship perfectly.

"OK, Leonid, I agree with you, but let me handle Victor. I am sure I can make him understand that this is not something he should be wasting any time on."

"OK, but make sure. I don't want to have to talk about this again, and I would rather that Ansonov never knew about it. It would not please him."

Oleg was confident that he had made the position absolutely clear to Lansky and that would be the end of it. Unfortunately for him, he had misjudged.

London

The more Lansky thought about it, the more he came to resent Oleg's attitude. Certainly, he understood that he had been brought in by the Malenkovs as an outsider, to take care of the issues that they could not easily handle, but he also felt that he had become a genuine partner over the years. The way Oleg had treated him, the suggestion that he was in some way less significant than the other two, in fact annoyed him more than the actual rejection of Feinstein's plan. Nevertheless, he felt the only way to assert his independence was to go ahead and discuss it further; he wasn't going to be slapped down like a naughty schoolboy. Ultimately, despite Oleg's warning, he knew he was going to have to have the conversation with Leonid as well as his brother and it would end up taking the form of a showdown about the structure and influence of the whole edifice they had created. He reasoned with himself that if he kept quiet this time, there would always be something else that came up and in the end the result would be the same – was he an equal partner, or actually just another employee of the Malenkovs? He decided that the only way to resolve the issue was to force the discussion. He arranged to see Feinstein again, to talk through his concept further.

They met a couple of days later, again in the privacy of Feinstein's dining room in the apartment perched on top of the bank's office building.

"Jacob," he began, "this is not to be taken as an indication that we definitely want to go ahead with any changes to the company, but I would like to continue the dialogue, to see where we can get to. I should tell you that my Russian partners are not particularly keen on bringing in outside capital, whereas I have a more open mind to it. As I think I said to you before, they very definitely believe the company needs to stay with its Russian roots, and, at the moment anyway, that seems to be more important than maximising the outright value of the potential we can see in the business." He grinned. "So what I am saying is that even if I decide I want to go ahead with some sort of flotation, there would still be a lot of work in convincing Oleg and Leonid that it's the right course to take. That may make a lot of work for you and your people ultimately with no reward."

Feinstein held up his hands. "Victor, that's understood. We know it's a big decision and therefore that it's not easy. There are two sides to everything and all we would like is the chance to put our proposal in front of the client and have a full discussion. Ultimately, obviously, it's up to the three of you to make the decision on the basis of all the considerations of your business. All I can do is show you what we believe could be achieved and how to do it if that's what you want. So don't worry about our time or anything. If the deal comes off, then we get our reward. If it doesn't, well, there'll always be another one coming up. That's how true investment banking works. Now, you'll recall from the original proposal that we intend to use a series of trusts to get around the fact that the smelter and the electricity supply are technically under different ownerships." Lansky nodded. "Well, I'd like to bring in one of our guys who has worked on similar structures before, who will hopefully be able to run through that in more detail, since it is really the key to the success of the whole scheme. Is that OK? He will be discreet about the issues we are discussing."

"Sure; as long as we all understand that, for the moment, these conversations stay within these walls."

"That goes without saying. Let me just call him up here." He picked up a phone and dialled an internal number.

It turned into a long meeting, and at the end of it, Feinstein's analyst was left with a lot of questions for which he had to find answers – and his boss wanted them quickly. Sighing as he got back down to his desk, having left Feinstein and Lansky debating where they should go for dinner that evening, he realised he was in for a long evening's work. It was particularly annoying as an old university friend of his was over from Vienna, where he worked, and they had been intending to meet up for a few drinks and to catch up. Sighing again, he picked up the phone and made his excuses, explaining that he had a lot of work to do on a big Russian deal in the aluminium business. As he put the phone down, it occurred to him to wonder if he should have said that. But it would be OK, Mike was an old friend; anyway, he hadn't mentioned any names or details.

Mike was an old friend, but he also worked at Metalex, and it had been second nature from his first days at that company to keep his ears open for anything which might concern their products. He himself worked in ship chartering, but he knew exactly who to call when the words 'aluminium' and 'Russia' came into the conversation. He rang the Metalex office and asked for Max Eisenstadt.

"Max, hi, it's Mike from the chartering department. I'm in London, and I just heard something which might be of interest to you. I have an old friend who is a pretty senior analyst at Feinstein's, the bank. Well, he and I were supposed to be meeting this evening, just socially, nothing special. He's just called me to cancel, and the reason he gave was that he was working on a big Russian aluminium deal, and wasn't going to be able to get out. I don't know if that means anything to you, but you're the aluminium guy so I thought I'd better pass it on."

"Thanks Mike. It doesn't immediately say anything to me, but we'll have a dig around. Appreciate the tip, anyway. Have a good time in London. We'll have a drink when you get back."

Eisenstadt was intrigued. Russia was a very big deal in the aluminium business, yet Metalex were still on the outside looking in, kept out by the ever-growing empire of Russo-European. Their access to the political influence had not really recovered from the death of Alex Koch and Ansonov's grab for power. It was difficult to imagine that any big Russian aluminium deal did not involve the Malenkovs. He needed to put out some feelers, to see if Feinstein's really had something significant to work on.

Over the course of the next few days, he spoke to a lot of his contacts, always trying to see if any of them had any knowledge of what might be happening. He got no significant response, but an idea was beginning to take shape in his mind. It was important to remember that Feinstein's was a bank, not a trader. He should not be looking for evidence of a big trade, but rather for some sort of financing deal. And when he thought about it, that could only really point to one thing – the Malenkovs were looking to raise capital through Russo-European. He went up a floor, to Roger Erlsfeldt's office.

"Roger, I've had some information that suggests that the Malenkovs might be looking to raise some new capital. It's very vague, but that's the only assumption I can make. Maybe it's time for us to have a talk with them, see if we can put anything together. We were kicked out of that business by them before, but that doesn't mean we shouldn't try again. Circumstances always change."

"By all means try it. You know I want that Russian aluminium business. But this is not just commercial, Max, as you know. Are we better talking immediately to the Malenkovs, or should we follow the political route? I don't believe they could be doing anything without that hood in the Kremlin knowing about it. Maybe we should talk there, and then approach the Malenkovs from above. But they can't need money, that business must be making them a fortune. They must want either to cash out themselves, or they want to expand, presumably outside Russia." He paused for a moment. "Or should we approach Lansky first off?"

"That's probably the easiest route, but actually I don't think it's the right one. We know he is the western face of the whole deal, but that's really about the sales of the stuff. This is the Russian end, who owns what. So I think we have to go either for the Malenkovs, or try to approach the politicians. I would favour the Malenkovs, simply because it that fails, we still have the political route in reserve. The other way round, that wouldn't work."

"Yeah, I can't disagree with you. Well, then, if we're keeping it at an aluminium level, not a political level, it should probably be you who approaches them, shouldn't it?"

"That makes sense. I'll get in touch with them, see if I can go up to meet them in Moscow. But just to be clear: if they're looking to get some outside shareholders in, we'd be keen, right?"

"Certainly. Obviously the terms would have to be good for us, but the principal is clear. We wanted that business before they grabbed it, and nothing since then has changed my mind. Call 'em up and see what you can do."

Moscow

Eisenstadt did just that, and a week later he was checking in to his hotel in Moscow on a dark, cold evening. The snow was still heavy on the ground, the people in the streets wrapped in thick clothing. The Swiss had a solitary dinner that evening; since the death of Alex Koch and the weakening of their position in Russia, Metalex had only maintained a small presence in Moscow and the head of that office was travelling in the Urals that week.

The next morning, as the sun rose in a cloudless blue sky over the frozen city, he made his way to the Malenkovs' office, just round the corner from the Kempinski. Leonid and Oleg welcomed him into their office. They had met before, but only briefly, so they were not well acquainted. Eisenstadt admired the view from the floor to ceiling windows, and then got down to business.

"Gentlemen, thank you for agreeing to meet me at such short notice. I know how busy you must be; your business is certainly very active. We share a lot of customers, and they are pretty much always complimentary about the efficiency and smooth-running of their contracts with Russo-European."

Oleg spoke. "Thank you. But actually the good operation of our sales business is more to do with our partner in London, Victor Lansky. He is responsible for ensuring our metal is sold and arrives promptly in our customers' works. Here in Moscow, my brother and I are more involved with the overall running of the business and maintaining production at our smelters. We also look after our internal Russian relationships."

Leonid cut in. "But I'm sure Mr Eisenstadt did not come to see us just to exchange pleasantries. We know each other in some ways as competitors – friendly ones I hope – but I guess you had something specific to discuss with us."

Eisenstadt was slightly taken aback. That was a pretty clear indication that they didn't have time to waste on Metalex, unless there was something important.

"Yes, I do. You know my company is one of the world's largest traders of metal, and that we also have fairly significant production facilities and offtake agreements with other producers." The two Malenkovs nodded. "Well, obviously we are always looking for new opportunities to add to our portfolio if good assets become available." Oleg began to get a nasty feeling about where this was heading; Eisenstadt's next words confirmed his suspicions. "We have heard from some of our contacts that maybe you are looking to secure more investment in Russo-European, or maybe some sort of partnership arrangement. If that is the case, then Metalex would very much like to discuss any such venture with you."

Sensing a rising annoyance in his brother, Oleg spoke quickly. "I'm not sure where you could have got that idea from, but it's certainly not the case. We are very happy with the way things are going, and we have no intention of changing the structure of our business. We definitely don't have any need of further capital or of bringing in outside shareholders."

Leonid interrupted. "May I ask if you heard that rumour from London?"

Eisenstadt paused for a moment, then replied. "Yes, I did. But I can't tell you any more than that. Obviously my informant had the wrong information. But look, if it's wrong, it's wrong. I have no intention of trying to push you into anything. Just please remember if you should change your minds, Metalex would be interested in talking to you."

Oleg was conscious that he had to get the visitor out before the inevitable explosion from his brother, so he hustled him through the door and out to the lift. When he got back into the office, Leonid's face was black as thunder.

"This bloody Lansky. What is he doing, talking to people about our business? We cannot just ignore this. He must be told."

"Relax, Leonid. We don't know for sure this information came from Lansky. It could have been someone else."

"Little brother, you're being stupid. Who else could it be? This is Lansky and his friend Feinstein. I tell you, they want to steal our company from us. And if Metalex have heard this, then so have others. It will not be long before word of this gets to the Kremlin, and if we have kept this from him, Ansonov will not be happy. This time, Oleg, we have to tell him."

Oleg nodded. "Yes, I agree we can't keep quiet now. Maybe I shall give Denis Menkov a call, just to let him know what has been happening." He sighed. "I'm disappointed in Victor. I thought he understood that this was not a subject for discussion. I don't know what he thinks he will gain out of it. And Metalex, anyway. I told him a long time ago that we could have no dealings with them. He must realise that the best thing for us all is just to continue as we are."

"He's a westerner, Oleg. He wants power, the money alone is not enough for him. He and his friend want to have control, they want to turn this into a western company. They don't understand that it can only function if it remains in Russian hands. And yet at the beginning, he seemed to understand so well. He can't be allowed to continue in this way, causing problems."

Chapter 23

The Kremlin
Moscow

Denis Menkov sat in the chair in front of Ansonov's desk in the palatial President's office in the Kremlin. "I had a call from Oleg Malenkov this morning. It seems there may be a problem with Lansky, their English partner."

"What kind of problem?"

"Apparently, he is talking to an English bank, Feinstein's, about floating Russo-European on the London stock market, so they can raise money to make some acquisitions of companies. He seems to think that Russo-European should become a major, diversified mining company in order to reduce its dependence on Russia."

Ansonov looked blankly at him for a moment. "But that's absurd," he said. "It has to remain Russian. That's the point of it. To control Russian raw material assets. Why would he think anything else?"

"I don't know. Oleg said that it's Leonid's belief that this is about power. He wants to be a big fish. Feinstein's have produced a scheme which, according to them, would make the two Malenkovs and Lansky some of the most influential players in the mining sector. It seems that Lansky is not happy with just the money, he wants power and influence as well."

"What do the Malenkovs say?"

"They understand that things are not going to change, because it's not in our interest that they should. By our, I mean Russia's interest, of course," he added hurriedly, just for the avoidance of any doubt. "Obviously, Lansky doesn't know that the Malenkovs have quite such strong links with the Kremlin, although he must realise that the whole deal started from here, with the very generous terms of the original privatisation sale of the smelter. But we have plenty on Lansky, anyway, if you recall. We should be able to dissuade him easily enough."

Ansonov leaned back in his chair and steepled his fingers. "We certainly have plenty on him, thanks to your efforts. We have pictures of him with a Russian girl who may or may not be a professional – that should be enough to embarrass him severely. And of course we have photographic evidence linking him to a multiple shooting. I'm sure we could persuade him to forget his new scheme if you went and showed those pictures to him, and explained that we intended to use one set to destroy his reputation, and the other set to extradite him to face a charge of complicity in murder. But I wonder if that's enough. Sure, it will stop this scheme of his, but can we trust him? We have always known that at some point Leonid and Oleg would need to ditch him; maybe now is the time." He leaned forward, and spoke more decisively. "Denis, I need to think this over. This could be the catalyst. We know the aluminium business is now strong enough to stand on its own, without Lansky. This could be the time to demonstrate to all those involved in our country that we will control our own destiny, and that they are only here as long as it suits us. Tell Oleg to say nothing to Lansky and to make sure Leonid doesn't, either. I will think about this, and we will talk again when I have made a decision."

Ansonov sat staring at the wall after Menkov had left the room. He had known from the beginning that there would come a day when Lansky had outlived his usefulness, but he had not really expected the Englishman to choose the moment. Yet, unknowingly, that seemed to be exactly what he had done.

Vienna, Austria

Eisenstadt had to report his failure to his boss, Roger Erlsfeldt. The latter absorbed the news calmly. "So do you believe them, Max? Is it really just a story, or is there some fact at the bottom of it?"

"I'm not sure. Leonid was very quick to ask if the rumour came from London. If it was all news to him, why would he pick London? Why not ask me if it came from New York, or Hong Kong, or anywhere else? If I had to bet on it, I think I'd say that it was not completely news to him, and that he had heard stories out of London from somebody else. Whether that means it's true or not" – he shrugged – "I just don't know. Look, we know they don't like us, so they were never going to be receptive first off. I think it may be worth persevering, just to see if anything comes of it."

"Mmm. I think we should put the rumour around ourselves; that way we can see if anything comes back from elsewhere. You could drop some hints to your contacts, couldn't you? Just quietly refer to hearing stories that the Malenkovs are looking to get some money into the company."

Eisenstadt nodded. "Yeah, that makes sense. See if we can smoke them out. The only problem is that that may let somebody get in ahead of us."

"I'm prepared to take that risk. If it comes to it, we'll just have to make sure we can show the best deal. Frankly, we would be in pole position anyway, because we have such a strong sales network."

Over the next few days, Eisenstadt started referring to the story in his phone calls around the market. A week or so later, he got a bite back. The editor of the Metal Bulletin, the trade's weekly bible, called him up and told him he'd been hearing a story that might have big implications for the aluminium business. Did Eisenstadt have any comment about a rumour that the owners of Russo-European were contemplating either floating the company or looking to bring in an outside shareholder ahead of going on an acquisition spree? Eisenstadt was careful to be non-committal, while trying to get the other man to reveal his sources. The journalist was too canny for that, and in the end got what he wanted, a quote from Eisenstadt, unattributable except to 'a senior industry figure', to the effect that he would not be surprised to see some action of that sort. That quote featured prominently in the article the magazine published three days later.

Moscow

Metal Bulletin wasn't required reading for Denis Menkov, but Russo-European and its oligarch owners, to say nothing of its international jet-setter Victor Lansky, held a wider interest than just the trade press. The story was picked up, first by the financial pages of the mainstream media in London, and within a week had reached Moscow. Menkov had to take the news in to his boss. Ansonov was sanguine, in contrast to the fury Leonid had shown when he found the story had still not been killed. Ansonov sat, elbows resting on the big desk, with Menkov facing him. "The time has come, Denis. We can't let this kind of thing go on any longer. The world has to understand that Russian assets are Russian, they will not be auctioned off to the international capital markets. Mr Lansky has become an irritant that we cannot allow to continue."

"You want something more terminal than just a chat about photographs?"

"Yes, but we have to tread carefully. There is a political dimension to this; we must do it in such a way that the British government accepts our reasoning. The last thing we need would be them probing into things after we have finished. I will need to speak to their ambassador, and through him to their Prime Minister. They will have to understand the position we take on this and that our actions are necessary to protect our national self-interest."

"But they're not going to be happy if our national self-interest demands that we take action against one of their citizens. Surely it would be better to keep it completely unofficial. I could mount a totally black operation. We could easily put the blame on some competitor, or just a random attack, next time he is in Moscow. Why take the risk of showing our hand to the British?"

"I understand your concern, Denis, but you must accept when I say that that is too risky. I don't doubt your ability to conceal our hand in anything that you do, but even if we know they would not find anything, we still do not want investigations and probing into affairs which belong in Russia. If I can handle this the right way, it will also demonstrate to them how serious we are. That will also, I trust, ensure that they do not try and meddle in any other issues which may arise in the future."

"You mean it will persuade them not to try and start games with their oil company and our oil."

"Exactly. We all know the aluminium is the template, and other things will follow. They need to understand where the boundaries lie. It will be unfortunate for Mr Victor Lansky, but he should have kept within the limits." He laughed harshly. "Anyway, he's half Polish, so he should be well aware of what happens if you take on Russia."

Menkov smiled back. "So I'll do nothing for now, until you give me more instructions?"

"Correct. Or almost correct. You must still make sure that Leonid doesn't do anything stupid. Let him understand it is in our hands; he should keep out of it for now."

That, reflected Menkov as he left the Kremlin, was going to require him to be extremely forceful. He knew from his conversations with Oleg that the elder Malenkov was working himself into a fury against his western partner. As he settled back into the leather seat of the official car taking him back to the FSB base at the Lubyanka, he pulled out his mobile phone to call Oleg. He needed to see the brothers sooner rather than later, to make sure he could keep a lid on Leonid's temper until Ansonov was ready to move. The President was already putting things in hand.

Two days later
Moscow

Sir Crispin Smith was the British Ambassador to Russia; as he sat in the back of the Rolls-Royce, wending its way through the Moscow traffic, he was musing on why he had received a summons to visit the President. The car swung across Red Square, finally clear of the traffic jams, and followed the high, imposing wall round until they came to an entrance gate, giving them access to the fastness of the Kremlin. In an official car, expected by the guard, the security was relatively light. A cursory glance at Sir Crispin, a word with the driver, directing him where to take his passenger, and then where to go to wait for him, and they were through, approaching the steps up to a set of ornate but solid doors. A uniformed officer welcomed the Ambassador, and led him through to an anteroom, where he asked him to wait a moment while he informed the President of his arrival. Ten minutes later, the door opened and he was beckoned in to the presence of the President. The aide closed the door behind himself, from the outside, and the politician and the diplomat were left alone in the huge office. Smith had been Ambassador for several years, yet this was the first time he had ever been closeted alone with the President, either this one or the last. There was something a little strange. He was on his guard.

Ansonov rose from behind his desk, and shook Smith warmly by the hand. "My dear Ambassador, welcome. Thank you for agreeing to come in to see me at such short notice. Come, let us sit down." He gestured towards the deep armchairs on either side of a low table.

"Mr President, it is a pleasure to see you again. I must confess, I am intrigued to know what it is that you wish to discuss."

Ansonov smiled. "There are just two of us here, this meeting is not being recorded" – not technically true, the little recorder mounted in the table between them was actually whirring away – "so let us be informal. I wanted to ask you about Victor Lansky, and his involvement with the Malenkov brothers and Russo-European Metals. I guess you are aware of them and their activities."

Smith was momentarily thrown off balance. This was certainly not what he had expected the Russian to ask him about. "Well, I'm aware of the names and some of the background. I've never met any of them personally, but they seem to be a good example of Russo-British co-operation in business. The company, as far as I am aware, has been very successful for the last few years."

"Yes, they are certainly successful. But I wonder how much you know about the background?"

Smith gave an open gesture with his hands. "Not a great deal. Lansky, obviously, is a British subject, but that doesn't mean we necessarily keep a close eye on him; I would only be aware of him if he had any problems here in Russia. Then perhaps I would be called in to help where I could. But I don't believe that is the case at the moment. Unless you tell me otherwise?"

Ansonov ignored the question. "I will explain a little of the background. Russo-European was created at a time when this country was nearly bankrupt. At that time, the state policy was to auction off certain previously state-owned assets, in order to convert them to hard cash. At that time, for the majority, in fact let's say for all, of these auctions the buyers had to be Russian. Foreigners were not allowed to bid, as it was felt that the assets in question should remain Russian. That posed a problem in some cases where the amount of investment needed was beyond the resources of the Russian entrepreneurs who wished to bid. This was the case for the Malenkov brothers, who had a very strong case to be allowed to buy the Krayanovsk aluminium smelter, but lacked sufficient capital. They came up with a novel solution, to bring in outside – non-Russian – money, but still comply with the rules of the auction. This involved creating Russo-European, and receiving a substantial amount of money from Victor Lansky. Effectively, Lansky handed over the money with no more assurance that his shareholding would eventually be recognised than the word of the Malenkovs. Given the reputation of the Malenkovs at that time, this was a brave, some might even say a foolhardy, step to take. However, all turned out well. As you know, the rules regarding foreign investment changed, and now, as long as there is a domestic partner, some international joint ventures are welcomed in my country. So the shareholders of Russo-European are all now fully identified and recognised and indeed have gone on to become some of our richest and most prominent citizens. The trust Victor Lansky showed at the beginning has paid off in spades. I think you will agree that he too has become very rich indeed."

Smith nodded. "Yes, that's certainly so. But surely you did not just invite me here to tell me how successful some of our citizens – yours and mine – have been in the Russian export business?"

"You are of course right. I didn't. I invited you here to discuss a problem which seems to have arisen. But, my dear Sir Crispin, please indulge me a little more. Let me finish outlining the background before we consider the problem and how we may resolve it." He stood up and walked across to his desk, from where he picked up a large brown envelope. Placing it on the low table and sitting down again opposite the Ambassador, he continued. "In a way, Russo-European has been too successful. It is clear to anybody who looks at it that this company makes a great deal of money. It has therefore attracted quite a lot of attention. While it remains as it is, it's difficult to see how it can expand further. They already control the bulk of the major Russian aluminium industry, so if they are to grow further, they would have to look at different products, or outside Russia, or both. The first, different products within Russia, is not an option. The way we foresee the development our economy means that individual industries will remain just that – individual. We do not foresee the creation of conglomerates here. We wish people to remain focussed on what they know. The result of that policy is that anybody looking to expand Russo-European would have to look outside Russia in order to effect that sort of change."

Smith was getting puzzled. Ansonov was sitting there spouting business-school speak at him. That didn't really seem right, from the hard line politician. He folded his hands together, and waited for the President to come to the point.

Ansonov went on. "Because the company is so successful, many people are looking at it, and for the reasons I have just explained, when they look at it they want to take it outside Russia, or at least inject a substantial element of non-Russian capital and maybe management."

Smith interrupted. "But surely that's exactly what Lansky was in the first place, so in fact wouldn't that just be repeating what happened before?"

"No. As I said, the circumstances at the beginning were unique. The Soviet system had fragmented and the Government had to hold the country together. The Malenkovs created a very clever scheme which kept the business Russian, even though they accepted capital from outside. That capital was on very particular terms, which could never be repeated. The world has moved on. Those who were weak are now strong; Russo-European does not need to bring money in from outside now. Look, right now we have very good evidence that there are people who would like to buy Russo-European. They believe they could use it as a starting point to build a substantial position in the global resource industry. We do not believe this is helpful to Russia, so obviously we do not approve of it. If it were just outsiders, then we would probably just ignore them. However, we have reason to believe that Victor Lansky may be interested in co-operating with those who wish to take the company over. He is very much an insider of the company, so obviously that concerns us much more." Smith began to think he could see where this might be heading. But surely the Russian understood that a British government could not intervene in the same way that his own would? Ansonov left his last remark hanging, obviously waiting for a comment.

"Well," said Smith, "I can understand your point – we would all like to keep our resources for ourselves. But you are in rather a different position from us. Whatever we may think of corporate takeovers or changes of ownership, we don't, or rather, our government doesn't, get involved. We would only do that if there were a competition issue – what the Americans call anti-trust; and that would only apply anyway in the case of a publicly-quoted company. So although I can sympathise, I couldn't really suggest any way in which we could help you. Lansky is a private citizen, and what he and his partners choose to do with their privately-owned company is really nothing to do with us."

"I understand the difference between our countries, of course. I am just outlining the position we find ourselves in, to help you understand the action we are going to have to take. My concern in all of this is for my country and its people. My mandate, my *duty*, as President of Russia is to ensure the well-being both now and in the future of my people. That means I have to protect the resources of the country which are the future wealth of its citizens. This mineral wealth is something I have to regard myself as holding in trust for the generations to come. It is not an easy task. The easiest route, the one which would perhaps be followed in the west, would be just to say to the foreign investors, 'yes, come in, develop our mines, our oil-wells.' They would pay high salaries to some people, there would be an illusion of riches, but in truth I would be giving away our heritage. This is something I will not, something *I cannot,* do." This last sentence was said with real vehemence. Smith was just beginning to glimpse the steel beneath the smooth exterior.

"Can't you just change the rules? Make it illegal again for foreigners to own Russian assets?" As soon as he spoke the words, Smith wished he'd phrased it differently.

"No, Sir Crispin, we cannot 'just change the rules'. I know many people in the west have difficulty in believing it, but this country follows the rule of law. No, that is not how it will be. Mr Lansky, frankly speaking, is not the sort of man we would wish to see influencing one of our major exporting companies. We will have to take action against him."

"But just wait a moment." Smith was just starting to get a bit irritated by the high horse the Russian was riding. Rule of law? Yeah, right. "What do you mean? 'Taking action' against an innocent British citizen is not something we could tolerate, even if his business involvement doesn't suit you. We all often have individuals who annoy us, but that doesn't give us licence to 'take action' against them. What are you suggesting?"

Ansonov sensed the Englishman was getting annoyed. He picked up the envelope from the table, and, tilting it, pulled out three or four photographs. "First," he said, "Mr Lansky is in fact not a nice man. One could, I suspect, find some similar pictures of many successful middle-aged men. But not, perhaps, those to whom one was thinking of awarding a knighthood. Have a look." He handed the photos across, then stood up and walked over to the window. Standing watching the soldiers in the courtyard beneath, he waited for Smith to speak. Smith's first thought was that the girl was really good looking. Putting that out of his mind, however, he said, "As you say, these do not make him unique. They're not the sort of thing to hand round at a dinner party, but we are in the twenty-first century. I don't think they're really too shocking. But how did you get them, anyway? Somebody must have been spying."

Ansonov turned back to face him, away from the window. "A few years ago, Lansky was at a private party at a chalet in Courchevel, in the French Alps. At that party were some Russians, and particularly some Russian girls. They were there with tourist visas, but they would be willing to testify that they were in fact invited there to satisfy the desires of the guests. That they were in fact paid to entertain Mr Lansky and the others. I agree; these things happen. Nobody expects a multi-millionaire businessman to be a saint, but this is a sordid story which I'm sure would not reflect well on anybody, including a government who was preparing to honour the man in question. I believe also he is a big donor to your ruling party? That would also not reflect well. However, this is only nibbling at the edges of what Lansky has been involved with." He crossed back to the table, picked up the envelope again and shook out the remaining half dozen or so pictures. "These photographs were taken in Siberia, at a rail crossing traversed many times by trains carrying aluminium from the smelter at Krayanovsk to the port of St Petersburg. Before you look, I warn you, they are a little gruesome."

Smith picked them up, and grimaced as he looked at them. They were very clear; Lansky was standing in a group, several of whom were holding Kalashnikovs and at whose feet were a number of corpses. Flicking through the pictures, he said nothing.

"Come, Sir Crispin, you have nothing to say? The first pictures were evidence of a little peccadillo, not, as you say, damning in the twenty-first century, but I think you will agree these are a little different. True, Lansky is not holding a gun. But he is clearly a part of the group who are, and those bodies would certainly appear to have been shot. I think one would be hard pressed not to conclude that he was at the very least a passive participant in this unpleasant scene. This, I think, would be seriously damaging, particularly if the Russian police force were to see these pictures. I am sure they would be persuaded to open an investigation of the events we see here in front of us, don't you think?"

Smith was thinking rapidly. This was all getting very unpleasant. Personally, he didn't give a damn whether Lansky was a nice person or not. Why should he care? Equally, he knew that what the Russian said was true – Lansky was being teed up for a knighthood, and he was definitely a useful donor to the Prime Minister's party. This could be extremely inconvenient. "Mr President, I agree this is very serious stuff, at least, the second series of pictures is. But unless you are simply giving me warning of what is going to hit the press soon, I'm not sure what reaction you expect from me. It would of course be deplorable if any British subject were to be involved in some form of unlawful killing, and we would of course expect the Russian police and courts to uphold the rule of law. Obviously, just like us, you adhere to the principle that everyone is innocent until proven guilty, but the initial evidence does look bad. As the Ambassador, it would be my job to ensure that my consular officials gave Lansky, or indeed any other British subject, such support as they could, while of course leaving him to face the legal Russian court. Beyond that, I can only express my outrage at such a crime."

"Yes, I'm sure. You make all the right noises. But, you know, Sir Crispin, there is possibly another way to solve this little conundrum. One that avoids embarrassment for your government and also solves my difficulty with the threat to Russia's resources. But first, there is one other issue." He smiled encouragingly, like a benevolent uncle. "Don't worry, there are no more photographs. I just thought it might be an appropriate moment to remind you that your North Sea oil is almost exhausted. I understand your oil company is in serious talks with their Russian equivalent about some of our deposits. This of course would be a very proper deal, maybe an offtake arrangement, but certainly in no way an attempt to own Russian resources." He looked quizzically at Smith, all innocence. "I guess it would be quite important for the United Kingdom that those talks would succeed?"

As a diplomat, Smith was impressed. The Russian President held all the aces. An exposure of Lansky of the type he was threatening would be a heavy blow, given how the government had been pushing him as a positive role model for British commerce, but it would be survivable. The oil deal, on the other hand, was in a different league. That was of vital national interest. With the decline of North Sea production, without access to Russian oil, the country would effectively be in the hands of some very unstable regimes. Russia may have its issues, but on the whole they were controllable. This was leading somewhere very nasty indeed. Time for some diplomat-speak.

"Mr President, this has been a very interesting meeting, and I certainly take on board the issues you have raised. I am concerned that a British subject may appear to have committed an offence on Russian soil – although obviously ahead of any investigation we cannot know for sure – and I can promise that Her Majesty's Government will do all in its power to assist the forces of the law to get to the bottom of it. I am also pleased to note that you are positive about developing a strong relationship between our two countries in the oil industry. I will report the contents of this meeting back to the Foreign Office."

"No, no, Sir Crispin. We have not finished yet. You have not yet heard my solution to our mutual problems." Ansonov paused, then began again. "Violence, sadly, has become part of Russian life, in the years since the end of the Soviet system. I hope very much that by the time I step down from this role I have that I will have set the country on the course to wipe it out. It is like a cancer in our society. However, sometimes - rarely, but sometimes - violence has its place. Just think for a moment how our problem would disappear if Mr Lansky ceased to exist. I would not have to worry about one of Russia's major enterprises being taken away and put in the hands of foreigners. You would not have to worry about the potential fall-out of your governing party accepting funds from a potential serious criminal. And we could both be comfortable in the knowledge that our relationships in the oil industry would be solidly founded. Truly, Russia and the United Kingdom would be the staunchest of allies. Is that not an appealing thought?"

Crispin Smith was literally lost for words. He simply stared at the Russian, his mind racing. It was almost unbelievable. He had been in the diplomatic service since he left Oxford twenty-five years ago. He had been through a fair few embassies before ending up with one of the plum jobs, in Moscow. But never, in Africa, in the Middle East, in the Far East, had he ever heard the leader of a country calmly proposing murder. Or, he thought since Ansonov was ex-KGB, it would probably be called liquidation, with extreme prejudice. If he were watching as an onlooker, this would have been a great scene. As a participant, he didn't know what to say.

"Come, don't look so shocked. I'm simply describing how everything would fall into place, if we make one small decision." Ansonov's eyes hardened, and his voice dropped. "I'm serious, Sir Crispin. I know you are not like us, at least on the surface. But do not underestimate the desire of the Russian people to control their own country. Mine are a hard people. Don't forget, the Second World War was won between Stalingrad and Berlin, not in the Battle of Britain or Normandy. Those were a sideshow to the brutality of what went on here. Millions died, in a welter of blood and savagery. The world has never seen its like. And the Russian people bore it all, not for the cause of the Party and the apparatchiks, but for the cause of Mother Russia. Do you seriously think I am going to let some half-Polish Englishman walk away with Russia's riches? This *will* happen. Lansky is an irritant we do not need. With or without your agreement, Sir Crispin, I will get my way. And you will agree, because you know it is the best solution for you as well. You do not need to create problems between our countries for this. Listen to your head. You need, I know, to discuss this with your Prime Minister, but please impress on him that what I have proposed will happen and that all you have to do is sit quietly, make the appropriate noises of sympathy, and leave the rest to us. Can I suggest we speak again in two days time?"

A few minutes later, the Ambassador found himself back in his Rolls-Royce, being driven out through the gates of the Kremlin. He knew he would have to discuss this face-to-face with the Foreign Secretary and the Prime Minister. There was no way they could use even a scrambled phone line to talk about the Russian state threatening, quite coolly and calmly, to execute a British subject, and expecting the British government to acquiesce to their plan. He pulled out his mobile phone to call his masters in the Foreign Office to arrange an urgent visit to London.

Chapter 24

February 2000

Mayfair

London

Victor Lansky was unaware of the waves he was creating He had had a couple more discussions with Jacob Feinstein, which were slowly convincing him that the course outlined by the banker would be the best one to follow. He knew there was work to do in persuading the Malenkovs, but he was actually confident that the potential profit was so huge that they would be unable to resist – rather like he was himself. He knew well the obsession they had, particularly Oleg, with developing Siberia's mineral wealth for Russia, but he really didn't understand the political dimension to their business. How could he? He had no knowledge of it, beyond a vague recognition that without the assistance of the Kremlin, the original purchase of the smelter would never have got off the ground. But Lansky's head was turned by his riches, and although he knew if he wanted to move this thing on he would have to raise the whole deal with not only Oleg but also Leonid, he was actually more interested in planning his yachting season, so he didn't do anything. It was just in his 'to do' list, waiting for the appropriate moment. He carried on with his plans, excited about the first cruise he had in mind, from Jamaica to the British Virgin Islands, accompanied for the first part just by a very attractive American heiress. After that, he was expecting the Malenkovs to join him in their own yacht at Bitter End, with the intention of cruising in company down to Barbados. In so far as he thought about it, he had in mind to use that opportunity to discuss the future financing of Russo-European. He anticipated ultimately winning the argument.

No 10 Downing St

London

Crispin Smith had been inside No 10 Downing Street a handful of times during his career, but he still felt a frisson of awe as the policeman on duty outside opened the famous shiny black door to admit him and the Foreign Secretary, in the deepening afternoon twilight of the winter's day. Inside the Prime Minister's residence, they were shown immediately into the ante-room before the leader's office, where a smart-suited Civil Service aide asked them to wait for a moment while he informed the PM of their arrival. A moment later they were ushered into the presence of the head of the British government. Crispin Smith was momentarily taken aback. What had happened to the fresh-faced, youthful politician with the bambi eyes who had walked through this front door so full of enthusiasm only a few short years ago? The man now standing in front of him had gaunt features and a receding hairline. Smith was relieved he had worn the years better than his Oxford contemporary.

"James, Crispin," the PM greeted them, "how are you both? Not too cold in Moscow at the moment Crispin? Or is that why you're here, to warm up? Please, gentlemen, sit down." And he ushered them towards a group of leather chairs around a low ebony coffee table.

Smith smiled. "Not really, Prime Minister. I'm here because there is an extremely delicate issue that came up with the Russian President, which, I think you will agree when I tell you what it is, needs face-to-face discussion, rather than risk the phone lines."

"How intriguing. With you coming from Moscow, that almost sounds like we're going back to the cold war." He glanced at the Foreign Secretary. "Do you know what it's about, James?"

"Yes, we discussed it briefly this morning, when Crispin arrived. I can confirm that it is a matter of the utmost delicacy."

The Prime Minister became serious. "OK, Crispin, why don't you tell me what Ansonov wants now?"

In for a penny, in for a pound, thought Smith. "Well, actually, he wants to kill somebody."

The other two stared at him. Then the PM said, "But that's hardly new for him, is it? I mean, I imagine he has had it done before. Wouldn't be where he is if he hadn't, if we're being frank. Why should that concern us? Beyond our concerns for Russian human rights, of course," he added hurriedly, almost as though he was expecting a journalist to jump out from behind the curtains.

"It should concern us, Prime Minister, because the putative victim is a British subject."

That brought the Prime Minister up short. "Ah. Did you tell him he couldn't? I mean, that there would be serious diplomatic consequences, not only with us, but with our European, Commonwealth and North American friends. And with the rest of the world."

"I think I had better tell you the story, and the way he put it to me."

"I think you had." He glanced at the Foreign Secretary. "And you know about this, James?"

"Listen to Crispin. It's not a hollow threat. There's a genuine issue to discuss here." He turned to his diplomatic colleague. "Go on, tell the PM the whole story."

Smith did, giving the PM an accurate report of his meeting with Ansonov. He was careful to keep his voice neutral, and to offer no opinion as to how they should respond. He was aware that the other two would have a different view about the fact that any exposure of Lansky would also expose the party, to whom he had been a substantial donor. Smith was acutely conscious that he was a civil servant, whereas the others were career politicians. They stood to lose if the party took a hit.

When the Ambassador had spoken, the Prime Minister sat for a moment seemingly staring into space. Then, as though clearing his mind, he said, "That's an interesting story. We knew Ansonov was a tough guy, but this seems quite extreme. As I see it, there are two problems. The first is the problems Lansky can cause if the pictures and the story are made public. Incidentally, Crispin, I suppose there is no chance the photos have been faked?"

"I'm not a technical expert, but to me they seem only too real. I don't think Ansonov would risk doctoring them."

"No, I guess that would be clutching at straws. OK, so that's the first problem. The second one is that he knows where our weakness is. We need those oil negotiations to be successful. We would struggle without some sort of supply deal from Russia. We don't want to end up dependent on some flaky West African or left-wing South American bunch for our oil supply security, and we already take as much as we can from the more obvious places. No, we have to get a long-term Russian deal signed up as soon as we can. So, it looks like Ansonov has managed to manoeuvre us into the position he wants. But, "he continued emphatically, "he would appear to be asking rather a lot in return for giving us what we need. Killing a British subject is not something we take lightly."

"And," interrupted the Foreign Secretary, "if we think he's got us by the balls now, where would we be left in the future if we acquiesced in this? He'd have a hold over us for ever."

"Actually, I don't think that is the case. What he's asking us to do is ignore something, not actually participate in it."

"That's true, Crispin," the PM continued, "but it would look very odd if we just ignored the death of a prominent citizen, and we can't deny that Lansky is prominent."

"Yes, but I think Ansonov would maintain that they could dress it all up in such a way that we could actually do nothing, while making all the right noises for public consumption."

"Mmm. Look, before we go any further, Crispin, there is clearly a party political element here, to which you cannot be exposed, as part of the Diplomatic Service. I don't know how critical it is, but would you mind waiting outside while James and I discuss that? It's for your own good," the PM added, "you wouldn't want any accusations that you had been involved in discussion of political funding."

Smith was quite pleased to escape. As the door closed behind him, the PM said "OK, James, tell me the bad news. How much have we had from Lansky?"

"Well, I haven't got the exact figures, we'd have to check with the Party Chairman and Treasurer for that, but it's a lot. You know it is. He was introduced to us through Jacob Feinstein and for the last couple of years he's been right up there at the top of the list. That's why we're putting his name forward for a knighthood."

"Yes, and we've been using his success as a good news story. God, the way these things always seem to come and bite you back! Wouldn't it be nice to have a clean, straightforward party donor for a change?"

"It would, but we've both been in politics long enough to know that it isn't going to happen. They give us money because they want something back. The fact that they want something back really means they're not in fact suitable to be giving us anything in the first place. It's the old, old conundrum of political finance versus influence."

"Yes, thanks for the philosophy, James, but it's not really helpful, right now. On a more immediate level, what are we going to do? I suppose nothing is the most attractive option, but can we really just abandon him? We really can't afford to be tarred with any sleaze coming out of Lansky's Russian business. And we do need that oil. Ansonov is a clever bastard. He's got us just where he wants us. We've known all along that he wasn't going to let anyone trespass on Russia's ownership of its resources; I suppose we should have paid more attention. But you don't. You just listen to all this crap they come out with and try and run your own shop as well as you can and let the others take care of themselves. Well, this is going to bite us in the neck. OK, are we agreed we can't let Lansky be exposed because of his ties to our funding?"

"Yes, I think that's right. How we resolve it though, I don't know."

"That is the problem. Anyway, no more specifics about the funding; let's get Crispin back in, and see what we can all come up with." He took off his gold-framed glasses and rubbed his eyes. "I could really do without this. In the end it's going to come down to one of those decisions about the individual versus the greater good. I didn't climb the greasy political pole to be in a position where I'm asked to sanction the killing of one of our citizens."

At that moment, for the first time in his political career, the Foreign Secretary realised that perhaps he didn't want the top job, after all. "It's a no-win," he said. "Whatever we decide, we lose something. As you say, it's a question of whose suffering can we best tolerate. Not an easy decision." This last was just to emphasise that in the end, it was the PM who had to make the choice. All anybody else could do was to act as a sounding-board. He got up and, crossing the room, opened the door and beckoned the Ambassador, who was sitting outside, back in.

His moment of self-doubt passed, the Prime Minister was again his normal brisk self. "OK, we have to try to settle this. First of all, I don't see any point in involving anybody else in this discussion. If it comes to a point where we have to deny anything, the less people who know about it, the better. So, let's just recap. Victor Lansky has made a shed load of money out of his involvement with a bunch of Russian gangsters." He held up his hand to stop interruptions. "I know that's not politically correct, when describing Russia's new entrepreneurs, but between ourselves let's be honest. Now, the Russians have got wind of the fact that he wants to sell the company, or at least part of it, to the open market. That worries them because they see it as a loss of their own national sovereignty in the way they organise their resource sector. They have photographs which incriminate Lansky in some fairly dubious and/or sleazy situations. Fantastic though it may seem in this day and age, they seem to believe that the way out of their dilemma is to kill Lansky and therefore resolve their problem that way. They want us to do nothing about it, not to protest in the way we would normally do if a foreign power were threatening the life of a British subject. The quid pro quo that they offer is not to put in the public domain those self-same photographs, and not to put the knockers on the oil supply deal currently being negotiated." He stopped and looked at the other two. "Is that right? That's also your understanding of the situation?"

"When you put it like that," said the Foreign Secretary, "it sounds utterly ludicrous. It's like going back to the worst excesses of the Stalin era, or Nazi Germany. Can they really behave like that, in the twenty-first century?"

Crispin Smith answered him. "Having had the conversation I did with Ansonov, I'm convinced that they will go ahead with this, whether it looks like harking back to the old days or not. The main plank of Ansonov's political support is precisely this form of patriotism. He believes that his voters will keep supporting him as long as he defends the interests of Mother Russia at all costs. I'm sure that in his eyes, if he let Russo-

European, which after all owns a big chunk of Siberian industry now, become anything other than a genuine Russian enterprise, the electorate would turn against him. And that matters, because although Russian democracy is not the same as that in the west, it is a democracy, and he does have to consider voters. So for him, it's one life – a foreigner – to be weighed against his political future. And he has this almost messianic belief that it is his destiny to rebuild Russia's position in the world after the corruption endemic under the last President. Also, don't forget there has been a lot of violence in that country. They're a bit more inured to it than we are."

"Yes, I see all of that. Bizarrely, I have to admit I do understand his motivation. And, of course, the truth is that a strong, friendly Russia is very much in our interests as well." He stopped for a moment. Then, resuming more quietly, almost in a whisper, he went on, "I can't believe we're having this discussion. We are part of the Government and Diplomatic Service of what claims to be one of the freest, fairest, most decent countries in the world, and we're sitting here calmly debating the pros and cons of letting one of our citizens be killed because he has become an inconvenience. We can't do this, can we?"

The other two stayed silent, neither one of them prepared to make any comment that might be construed, now or later, as giving advice. They knew whose decision it had to be. The Prime Minister stood up, and began pacing the room. "And yet, we have a responsibility to the greater good. The people of this country need energy security, and it's one of the things we have pledged to give them. And, James," he said, turning to face the Foreign Secretary, "you and I have to believe that the continuation of our Government is in the people's interests; that's why we are in this job. And frankly, we couldn't withstand another Party funding sleaze investigation plastered all over the press. We would have to resign." He turned away again, to stare out of the window at the No 10 garden below, already half-hidden in the deepening twilight. Such a small thing, to do nothing; and he did have the greater good to consider. He looked up, at the portraits of some of his predecessors staring down at him, mostly stern-faced, the odd smile here and there. They'd all had tough decisions, as well. Most had taken them, a few had shirked them. He knew which ones history had judged more kindly. Right now, he would have given anything to be able to swap jobs with either of his two companions. But he couldn't. He'd forced his way to the top, and this was his bitter reward. He made the decision.

"Gentlemen, we have to go along with the Russians. I can't pretend I'm happy about it, but I have to let this happen. I have considered the wider interests of the British people, and I have weighed those interests against the alternative. Regrettably, I can't see how we could let the welfare of one man destroy what we are trying to achieve for the country. I would also make it quite clear to you both that this is entirely my decision and no blame attaches to either of you. It's between me and my conscience, and you are both completely absolved from involvement." Actually, Crispin Smith doubted that; for him, any politician could change his mind, if necessity dictated.

"Crispin," the Prime Minister continued, more briskly, "when you get back to Moscow, perhaps you would convey in person, and in private, to Mr Ansonov that although my Government would naturally be saddened by the death of any British subject, we would nevertheless not expect to intervene in the investigation of a crime committed outside our jurisdiction. We would leave such an investigation to the local authorities where the events occurred and we would see no reason to doubt their findings."

That was smart, thought the Foreign Secretary. Phrasing it like that virtually guaranteed nothing would be done within the United Kingdom and if questioned, the Prime Minister could always say he had full confidence in the investigative powers of the (presumably) Russian police force. As a politician, he had to admire his boss's nimble thought. As a human being, he found it repulsive.

The Kremlin
Moscow, Russia

When he got back to Moscow, and was in front of Ansonov, Crispin Smith was still sickened by himself and the message he had to relay. He hadn't joined the Diplomatic Service to be a party to a shabby deal like this, but nevertheless he had to comply with his Prime Minister's orders.

"Mr Ansonov, I am instructed to convey to you the view of Her Majesty's Government, that they would not consider it appropriate to intervene in the investigations of the murder of a British citizen by a responsible local domestic police force. The British Government does not as a rule become involved in matters outside its jurisdiction, unless there are particular circumstances which suggest that any case is not being correctly pursued by the relevant authorities. I think that may answer the debate we had at our last meeting."

"Yes, Sir Crispin, I think that makes the attitude of your government perfectly clear. I feel we can now put that issue satisfactorily behind us, and move on. Perhaps you would convey to your leader, my good friend the Prime Minister, that I believe it may now be the appropriate time for the two of us to meet, together with our oil industry advisors, to try and finalise the agreement which I know we both see as in the interests of our two countries. I would be delighted to extend to him an invitation to

Moscow, or if he would prefer it, I should be equally happy to come to London. This is a matter on which I believe we should act swiftly. All the necessary preliminaries should soon be in place."

That sent a shiver down Smith's spine; presumably, it meant the clock was ticking for Lansky.

"Mr President, I shall pass your thoughts and comments on to the Prime Minister. I am sure he too is keen to move the oil talks forward as soon as possible." He rose to leave.

"Just one point, Sir Crispin. Understand well what it is you have agreed. You can be sure I shall not break my word on this. I would not advise you or your colleagues to do so either, no matter how distasteful you may find it. It is after all just another positive step forward in the ongoing friendship between Russia and the United Kingdom."

Crispin Smith felt physically sick as he made his way back out to his car for the ride back to the Embassy. He knew there was no stepping back from the deal, and that by his silence in London and by communicating the message back here to Moscow, he was complicit in a very sordid political stitch-up.

Chapter 25

Ansonov lost no time in calling Denis Menkov in. "How were our friends down in Siberia?"

"It'll be OK. I had to endure some shouting and screaming from Leonid, but eventually Oleg and I between us managed to make him understand that dealing with Lansky involved more than just his ego. He now sees that he is far better to allow others to take care of the issue and that his best policy is to behave as if nothing untoward had happened. I could suggest that they might like to get Lansky out to Krayanovsk again, which would give us a chance to finish it?"

"No, that won't work."

Menkov looked quizzically at the President. "But that will be the easiest place for us to arrange things," he said, "and make it look like Siberian gangland squabblings."

"Denis, I understand that, but I want this to take place outside Russia. I want it in a jurisdiction which the British cannot argue with. I am of course assuming we can do what needs to be done in such a way as to ensure the culprits will never be traced." Menkov smiled and nodded, as the President continued, "So it needs to be somewhere where the local police can make a full investigation, and that their findings will be accepted by the British. It has to be very clearly not an obvious Siberian gangster squabble. Let them draw that conclusion if they want, but keep it well away from Russia."

"Lansky will be in the Caribbean in his yacht for the spring season. Maybe one of the British's own former colonies there would serve the purpose?"

"That sounds perfect. Now, as I said before, you should not be personally involved. Prepare the plan, certainly, but do not take part. Use some illegal heavies."

"Maybe the Malenkovs' Chechens? They will do anything, without questioning, so all they have to do is follow the orders I will have prepared for them. We can get them in on Kazakh or Uzbek passports, and then back into Moscow on Russian ones. That will muddy the trail." Menkov paused, then asked the question that had been bothering him. "There's one thing I'm curious about. When Lansky is gone, and by whatever legal means they need, the Malenkovs have got a hundred percent of Russo-European back, what then? Are they just to keep it all? That would make them very powerful, maybe the most powerful industrialists in Russia."

Ansonov looked hard at his side-kick. Then, speaking very deliberately, "That's not decided yet. The first stage is to get it back into Russian hands, entirely. Then we can think about what to do with it. As long as Leonid and Oleg remember that it's not really theirs, that they are just the caretakers, all will be well. Where things may go wrong for them would be if they were to begin to believe the story, or to forget that this fantastic wealth was just given to them for safe keeping. They always need to remember who can pull the strings. If they forget that, things will not go so well for them. But Denis, don't concern yourself with that for the moment. Focus on dealing with the Lansky problem and leave the future to me."

March 2000

Ocho Rios
Jamaica

Still blissfully unaware that he was now "the Lansky problem", Victor Lansky sat contentedly up on the flying bridge of his yacht 'Sea Gem' moored in the bay of Ocho Rios on the north coast of Jamaica. He had flown in to Montego Bay the evening before, meeting up with his companion, who had caught her flight down from New York. She was to cruise with him as far as the BVIs, from where she would return to New York, and Lansky would be joined by the Malenkovs and their own yacht. Lansky was excited; in front of him on the table was a chart on which the captain had drawn their route, initially hugging the north coast of Jamaica, and then skimming the south of Hispaniola and Puerto Rico before sailing up the Sir Francis Drake Passage to their next port of call, the fashionable Bitter End Yacht Club on Virgin Gorda. Lansky might have a short while on his own there after his current companion left and before the Russians arrived. That didn't worry him; he was in his element, totally in love with his new toy. The American heiress down in his stateroom could vouch for that – waking at six a.m., she had expected a bit of activity before getting up. Instead, Lansky had slipped straight out of bed, and up to the bridge, to play with the navigation equipment before they weighed anchor and set off.

He looked round, to see the captain climbing the companionway up to the bridge. "Morning, Mr Lansky, you're bright and early."

"I'm keen to get going. I want to see how this boat goes, at last."

"Well, if you look here," – the captain reached across and punched a couple of buttons on the Raymarine chart plotter fixed in front of the helmsman's position – "you'll see that I estimated our time of departure for about ten o'clock. I anticipate our voyage time to Bitter End will be just over forty-eight hours. We could do it quicker, if we did twenty knots all the way, but the boat is new and although the rest of the crew and I got pretty familiar with her crossing the Atlantic last month, I'm scheduling in some time for you to play around and get to know how she performs. I'm assuming from all our conversations that you are the kind of owner who wants to be involved in sailing the boat? If you'd rather just sit on the sun deck with your lady friend and drink cocktails all day, just let us know."

"No, I definitely want to be involved. I want to learn to handle this boat; I want to learn how to navigate her, how to get her in and out of port, everything."

"Ah, you want to learn my job, then," the captain laughed. "OK, we'll get you there. Right, I'll just go and get the chef and steward geared up for a bit of breakfast. I would suggest about half an hour's time, and they'll serve it on the aft sun deck. Will that be OK for the young lady, do you think?"

Lansky glanced at his watch. Although the sun was up in the sky and the air was warm, it was still only seven thirty. "Make it forty-five minutes. Give her a chance to wash New York out of her hair." As he spoke, the American girl, Lara, climbed up the companionway on to the bridge behind them. She was stunning in a white sundress, long blonde hair floating in the gentle breeze. "Already done, Victor. New York's well and truly washed down the plughole in the shower. Good morning, Captain. Ignore Victor, here, I'd say breakfast in thirty minutes sounds just perfect." And as the captain nodded to her and stepped down off the bridge, she continued, "Victor, I love your yacht! And however many times I've been to Ocho Rios, I've never seen it from the sea like this before. This is going to be a great few days."

A couple of hours later, the anchor chain rattled up and with a deep throb from the diesel engines, the captain steered them out of the bay. There was a cruise ship heading in to the jetty, which caused them to head out to the west to begin with. The captain pointed. "If you look over there, you can see the old disused bauxite loading jetty; that was used in the film Dr No, as Crab Key. And beyond it, if you can see where all those people seem to be crowding, that's the waterfall at Dunn's River – one of Jamaica's big tourist attractions."

"Bauxite, huh?" said Lansky. "Very apposite. Aluminium's what I deal in." Lara looked uncomprehendingly at him. "It's the raw material you make aluminium from," he explained. "Jamaica's been a big producer.

Used to have a huge deal with the Soviets, when Michael Manly was the Prime Minister."

They swung out in a big arc behind the stern of the cruise ship. The captain spoke again. "I'm going to keep us between a quarter and a half mile offshore for the moment; there's plenty of depth of water and at that distance we can see the shore quite clearly. Sticking with the James Bond theme, just further along the coast here, after we pass Boscobel and Oracabessa, if you take the binoculars and look hard in amongst the trees you can see Goldeneye, which was the house where Fleming wrote all the books. I think it's an exclusive hotel now. That's Boscobel there" – he pointed – "just around the big hotel you can see. So past another couple of headlands, then we'll be level with Goldeneye."

The day was perfect. The trade wind blew true out of the north east at about ten knots, ruffling the surface of the gentle swell. The water was intensely blue, reflecting the brilliance of the Caribbean sky. Lansky took over the helm of his yacht for the first time, creaming along at a steady twenty knots; Lara sat next to him on the helmsman's seat, her long blonde hair flowing. Lansky couldn't imagine anything better. A 120 foot Sunseeker is a lot of boat, but it's not a superyacht; it's designed so that the owner as well as the professional crew can handle it, and Lansky pretty soon settled in to helming. The captain hovered on the bridge, though; after all, the vessel was his professional responsibility. But he was happy enough. He'd worked for a number of owners before, and he knew they came in two types; those who had the yacht simply to be seen, and to spend the day eating and drinking, and those who genuinely enjoyed the possession of a beautifully-created piece of engineering and wanted to be involved in it. He could tell Lansky was one of the latter, which would make his life as the skipper a lot pleasanter. The stunning coastline of the island of Jamaica slipped past on their right hand side, the mountains growing taller as they headed east. Again, the captain pointed to the shore. "Up there, near the top of that hill, is Noel Coward's house, Firefly." He grinned, embarrassed for a moment. "Sorry, I'm behaving like a tour guide. I'll keep quiet."

"Not at all," said Lara, "I want to hear all you know about it. It's so gorgeous. I've been to Ocho Rios and Montego Bay, and occasionally to Kingston, but I had no idea it was so pretty here from the sea."

"I love it. I work here in the Caribbean most winters and springs, and Jamaica is by a long way my favourite. Up there in those mountains is one of the most beautiful places on Earth."

They ran along the coast for about five hours, then as Jamaica slipped away behind them, they altered course a few degrees to the south and the captain called one of the other crew members up to the bridge to take over while he joined Lansky and Lara on the rear sun deck for a late lunch of grilled Jamaican lobster. Later in the afternoon, the captain gave Lansky some lessons in handling the boat, demonstrating how easily she could be manoeuvred at low speed. "This is what you need to be confident with," he pointed out. "Anybody can steer her in a straight line at twenty knots, but until you understand how she responds to the propellers and the rudder at two or three knots, you'll never be able to bring her in to a port." Lara joined in enthusiastically as well, and they had a great afternoon. Later, as the sun dropped over the horizon and the brief tropic dusk fell, they began to see the lights of Haiti, the western half of the island of Hispaniola, twinkling off their port side. "That's a bit of a contrast to Jamaica," said the captain. "One of the poorest countries in the world. Still, it was the first to abolish slavery and the first of the Caribbean islands to overthrow colonialism. I've only been there once, and frankly I wouldn't recommend it as a destination. If you look on here now," he continued, pointing to the chart plotter, "you can see that we'll pass quite close to land at the Cabo Beata in the Dominican Republic, then we've got a pretty straight run towards St Croix. That's where we go in amongst the islands, up the St Francis Drake Passage to Bitter End. When we get into the Passage, we can decide whether or not you want to drop in to Road Town, on Tortola, which is the capital."

"So we'll be passing Puerto Rico tonight, will we?" asked Lara.

"That's right, but we'll be too far off shore to see it."

The evening spun on. They dined, chatted, relaxed in the warm Caribbean night, and eventually retired to the owner's stateroom. The crewman at the helm overnight cut the engines back until they were doing about twelve knots, the yacht riding the swell smoothly and comfortably.

Charlotte Amalie

St Thomas, US Virgin Islands

The next morning, four powerful, heavy-set men disembarked from a flight into Charlotte Amalie from Mexico City. Contrary to popular belief, carrying a weapon on an aeroplane is not impossible; try and take it into the cabin, and every alert on earth will go off. Pack it carefully in hold baggage, however, and unless you are very unlucky, it will get through. Just to be on the safe side, the four men who had boarded in Moscow had not taken the obvious route via New York, but preferred the more relaxed Mexican airport for their flight change. They were not unlucky and their bags, including the Glock pistols packed in them, came through to the carousel with no alarms. Stepping out through the airport doors, they picked up a cab which took them down to one of the marinas. There, they made their way to the office of a boat charter company. They were expected. The paperwork was simple. The leader simply showed his Kazakh passport, the yacht charterer confirmed in his system that the funds to cover the charter and insurance had hit his company's bank account, and after a couple of signatures, he led them out onto the pontoon where a smart red and white 42 foot Cigarette sportsboat lay at her moorings. The leader and one of his men sat in the cockpit with the charterer while he gave them a full briefing on the controls of the boat; the other two headed for the store near the marina gate to pick up some provisions. When they returned, and the briefing was over, the leader started the two big 400 horsepower Mercury engines, his comrades cast off and the speedboat eased out of her mooring. The man at the helm had handled powerboats before, as a member of the Russian special forces, and, although that had been mostly on rivers, since there is no tide to speak of in the Caribbean and the navigation was pretty much line of sight, he was confident he could get them to where they were going. Nevertheless, just to be on the safe side, he switched on the chart plotter and entered a waypoint just to the south west of Norman Island with his final destination set as Road Town harbour. The schedule they had been given indicated that they should have a day or two's wait before carrying out their operation. Grim task they may have had ahead of them, but they'd all done that before; what they hadn't done before is ride a Cigarette boat. In the 1920s Prohibition, rum-runners from the Bahamas had developed very high speed, very low profile boats to evade the US Customs. That delta shape, with a low freeboard and big engines had been developed by Don Aronow in the 1970s and 1980s into his World Championship-winning Cigarette Racing Team boats. For the rum-runners progeny, the drug-smugglers of the 1980s and 90s, they were perfect; very fast, and, equally important, with a very small radar signature due to their low-in-the-water profile. Built in Miami, lots of them had found their way into the Caribbean, either still used for smuggling, or, like this one, chartered out to playboys as the ultimate thrill, with their eighty-knot top speed potential. The four men who had chartered her had a whale of a time in their boat that day, only eventually rumbling into the marina in Road Town harbour slightly before dusk fell.

Lara had insisted on the Sea Gem stopping way out offshore so they could bathe in the clear blue Caribbean. They'd launched the tender, and dived over the stern of the yacht, plunging deep into the warm water. They stayed hove-to for lunch, which pushed their arrival time back, so that by the time they slipped quietly into Road Town, where they had decided to overnight, it was already dark. There was a pontoon berth big enough for them in the Marina, and Lara persuaded Lansky to dine ashore. As they walked down the pontoon towards the shore, they passed the red and white Cigarette sitting quietly at her moorings, the crew having already taken themselves ashore to find some activity for the evening. They wouldn't need to leave the harbour until the next evening, unless they wanted to play in their boat again.

Lansky and Lara sat at a table in Road Town's best restaurant, overlooking the harbour. She sighed. "It's been a fabulous couple of days, Victor. I've absolutely loved it. Seems a shame to be going home tomorrow, but I've got a lot of things to do back in the city."

"Yeah, it's a pity you can't stay longer. But actually, I've got my Russian partners arriving soon, and I don't think you'd really want to be here then. We've got a lot of business things to discuss."

She spluttered over the sip of wine she had just taken. "Victor, don't talk bullshit! You may have some business to talk about, but you know you're also going to have a great time. I was talking to the crew today, and they said there are some wonderful places between here and Barbados. I bet you do more yachting than business! You've always told me the Russians really like to have fun. Anyway, I'm looking forward to my next invitation on board. It better not be too long."

"Of course not. You'll always be welcome. We'll be in the Mediterranean in the summer – you should come over then. But actually, you're being slightly unfair. I do have some serious business to talk to Oleg and Leonid about. We're thinking about the whole future direction of our business, and a few days on board will just give us the opportunity to discuss everything without outside interruptions."

After they had finished dinner, just for sentiment's sake, Lansky had them make a short detour on their stroll back to the yacht to walk past the office of a certain lawyer. There, in all its glory, amongst a field of others, was the brass plate proudly bearing the words Russo-European Metals Ltd, Registered Office. That was the little sign that had come to be worth hundreds of millions of dollars to him.

The next morning, the Sea Gem slipped quietly out of the harbour for the short trip across to Bitter End. The sun was high in another perfect blue sky as they sailed up the Passage and into Gorda Sound. Sea Gem was too long for any of the marina berths, so they moored a couple of hundred feet off and lowered the tender to go ashore. As they climbed down the gangplank into it, a couple of hundred metres away they saw a red and white Cigarette picking up a buoy; the bass rumble of its engines was clearly audible across the water. As they pulled away from the Sea Gem and rounded her bows, the line of sight to the other boat was blocked, and they couldn't see the binoculars one of the crewmen was training on the yacht. The tender bumped up against the mooring dock, in front of the imposing three storied, balconied club house, its bright red roof glaring in the tropic sunshine. Lansky and Lara stepped ashore as the crewman made the boat fast. Lansky turned back to him. "We'll be lunching ashore in the club, so don't stay here if you would rather go back to the Sea Gem. We can always call you when we want to go back aboard."

"That's OK, Sir, I'll probably stay ashore and have a wander around. I'll be here when you're ready."

Lansky nodded. "Come on, then, Lara," he said, "we're going to walk round the corner there before lunch. From there, we can see the Atlantic Ocean. Brisk stroll will build up the appetite." The water in front of them was crowded with boats. It was the height of the spring season, and as well as the big privately-owned boats, the harbour was alive with yachties in their 35 and 40 foot charter boats homing in to the sheltered anchorage to moor up for lunch. They walked a bit further than just round the corner, as far as the beach facing out across the Ocean, where the big Atlantic breakers crashed against the shore in complete contrast to the quiet of the Sound on the sheltered side of the island. When they returned for their late lunch, the red and white Cigarette had slipped its mooring and was rumbling back across to the entrance to the Sound. The men on board had seen all they needed. Lara had a pick-up arranged by a light aircraft from the Virgin Gorda airstrip to take her back to Charlotte Amalie and her connection with her evening flight back to New York. They loaded her baggage into the tender and motored across to the south-west corner of the Sound where a car was waiting to take her to the airstrip. She gave Lansky a lingering farewell kiss, and reminded him to invite her back to the yacht soon. In the tender on the way back to Sea Gem, the captain, who had accompanied them to the landing, nodded across the open water of the Sound and said "I think that must be your Russian friends arriving" He pointed, and, following his finger, Lansky saw a big, dark blue yacht heading in through the entrance at the narrows.

"Yep, looks like them. The 'Siberian Princess'. She's actually a bit bigger than Sea Gem." He grinned. "Not that it's a competition; at least, not for me. For the Russians, well, let's just say size matters to them. But she's a year or so older than Sea Gem."

"Should be a fun cruise down to Barbados – I'll go over and have a chat with their skipper tomorrow morning to talk about the route and so on. Give me a chance to have a look at their boat, as well."

By the time they got back to Sea Gem, the other yacht had dropped her fore and aft anchors about two hundred metres away. As he climbed up to the bridge, Lansky's mobile phone went off in his pocket. It was Oleg.

"Victor! We have arrived. We just sailed down from San Juan. Come over and see us!"

"OK. Give me hour or so, and I'll come over in the launch."

After the fun interlude of the cruise down from Jamaica, Lansky had to focus his mind again. He sat for a while thinking about how he was going to persuade the Malenkovs to agree to go ahead with letting outside money into the company. He knew it would be a tough argument, just from the conversations he had previously had with Oleg. But he was still convinced it was the right thing to do. He was realistic; he knew the wealth he now had was as much due to luck as hard work. He had been the right person at the right time for the Malenkovs' plans. He'd been a core part of the way the whole thing had developed, but the last few days had reinforced his view that these days he got more fun out of spending it then earning it. But to get to that, he had to convince the Malenkovs as well. He leafed through the papers he had outlining Feinstein's proposals, reassuring himself that he could answer any rational questions about the plan; his problem, though, as he could foresee, was that the questions may not be rational.

Picking up his papers, he called to one of the crewman to take him across to the Siberian Princess in the launch. As they approached the dark blue hull, he could see Oleg and Leonid sitting in the shade on the aft deck; Oleg came to the head of the companionway steps as Lansky's launch bobbed alongside and he stepped aboard. The warmth of Oleg's greeting was badly matched by the iciness of Leonid's demeanour.

They sat at a table under an awning; Oleg tried to keep the atmosphere calm, with small talk about the trip down from San Juan, but Leonid soon interrupted.

"Victor, why are you trying to destroy everything we have? Are you stupid or just greedy?"

Lansky sighed. "Neither, Leonid. I am just suggesting that we try and maximise the value to us all of what we have." He gestured around him. "We've all worked hard to get to where we are; why can we not at least talk about how we can take the next steps?"

Oleg spoke, before Leonid had a chance. "Victor, we know this is what you suggest; but do you not understand when we say it is not possible? The ownership of our resources cannot move outside Russia. We cannot give it away, no matter what is offered."

Leonid spat over the side of the yacht. "Forget it, little brother. Our friend is a fool. He refuses to understand."

Lansky was becoming annoyed. "No, Leonid, I'm not a fool. I'm the man who made this all possible for you. Never forget that without my money to finance the beginnings of our business you would still be a cheap Siberian gangster. I made this company possible, by fronting up the initial cash. I think that gives me an equal right to make decisions about the future. Why don't you stop being so pig-headed and just listen?"

Leonid stood up, muscles clenched in his hairy forearms. He swung at Lansky, catching him a blow across the cheek. "Don't ever call me pig-headed!" He stalked off into the saloon, slamming the glass door behind him.

Oleg looked across at Lansky. "You see? Whatever you say, you will not change his mind on this. I'll go and calm him down." He followed his brother.

Lansky rubbed his hand over his sore face; as he did so, he saw Olga appear from the sun deck below. "Victor! Are you OK? I heard the argument and the door slamming."

"What are you doing here?"

"I'm joining you all for the cruise down to Barbados. Some of my friends will be arriving tomorrow." She slipped into the seat vacated by Oleg. Dropping her voice to little more than a whisper, she spoke hurriedly. "Victor, I don't know exactly what you want to do, but you should stop it. I heard them talking yesterday; they will not allow you to continue. They have been talking a lot to that man you met in Courchevel, Denis Menkov. You remember – I told you to be careful. Victor, I like you, so listen to me. These people are dangerous – not to me, my parents are their friends, we are all like an extended family. But from what I heard, they are cutting you out, they are throwing you away. They do not play games. Just agree with what they want, and it will all be like it was before."

Except that I will always be marked, Lansky thought to himself. Out loud, he said "Why are you telling me this? If you're part of the 'extended family'?"

"Victor, don't be stupid. I like you. I know you have other girlfriends; you had that American girl on the boat the last few days. I don't mind that. You are a kind man, we always have fun. I don't want you to get hurt. Look, the first time I slept with you, in Courchevel, that was because Menkov told me to. He paid me for it. But it wasn't like that afterwards, all the times since."

"Why? Why did he pay you?"

"I don't know. Menkov is part of state security in some way. You don't know why they do things. But don't push them any further. I'm really frightened for you. Look, you must go now, back to your own boat. I know Oleg will calm Leonid down, and then you can come back and agree whatever they want tomorrow. It will be better that way. Honestly, Victor, it can't be that bad; you're all very rich men. Just carry on as before."

Lansky looked sorrowfully at her. "Did they ask you to do this as well? To convince me if the threats didn't work?"

"No." She spoke sharply. "They did not. I am telling you this because I don't want you to be hurt. They would be angry if they knew I was speaking to you of this. Now, go, before Leonid comes out here again."

She stood up, and pushed him towards the rail, hustling him to the top of the companionway below which his launch was bobbing in the breeze.

Lansky was shaken. However much he'd always known Leonid's violence lurked close beneath the surface, he'd never expected to be the target of it himself. The smack in the face hadn't really hurt too much, but it emphasised an unpleasant truth to him.

Out of sight, in the open water of the Passage, the Cigarette rolled gently in the swell. The crew were occupied in extracting a Zodiac dinghy from its bag and inflating it. Once done, they carried an outboard up from the cabin under the foredeck and hung it on the stern of the rubber boat. A petrol tank followed, and one of them tugged on the starter cord to check that the motor fired. No problems. They tied it off from the stern and settled down to wait for darkness. The helmsman kept the engines turning over gently and the bow pointed into the wind. It was boring, just waiting, but a lot pleasanter in the Caribbean sunshine than in the bombed-out wreck of a house in the blighted city of Grozny. They kept each other amused with soldier's talk and playing cards.

Chapter 26

Bitter End, Gorda Sound, British Virgin Islands

The tropic night had fallen, and with it the breeze. In a dead calm apart from the swell rolling up the Passage, three of the crewman on the Cigarette dressed themselves in black – black trousers, black sweatshirts and black windbreakers. They climbed over the stern of their boat into the Zodiac and carefully the helmsman handed over to each of them as they settled against the tubes of the dinghy a pistol and a silencer. They put these in the waterproof pockets of their windbreakers. The man at the stern started the outboard and let it run for a minute or so before they cast off. He opened the throttle and, bobbing gently on the swell, the inflatable picked up speed until it was bouncing over the surface of the dark water. The man at the helm pointed them towards the opening into the Sound. They could see lights twinkling on the shore each side, from the villas built up the slope just behind the beach. They didn't speak. Even if they had wanted to, it would have been a struggle over the buzzing of the outboard and the slap of the water against the rubber hull. As the land got closer on either side, the helmsman cut the throttle right back, until the engine was making no more than a whisper. They crept forward, invisible against the black sea. As they rounded the point and entered the Sound proper, they could see the lights of the Yacht Club at the far end. As yet, the bulk of the Sea Gem wasn't distinguishable amongst all the moored boats. The man sitting in the bow of the dinghy put a pair of night-vision binoculars to his eyes; the scene became clear as day to him, and he waved with his left hand, pointing the direction they needed to his colleague on the helm. On they crept; it was a desperately slow business, but taking time was preferable to opening the throttle and being noticed by one of the other boats. They had all night to achieve their goal.

Victor Lansky had sat chatting to the skipper after dinner, but his mind was not on the talk about boats and cruising. Finally, after a last brandy, he called it a night and went down to his stateroom amidships. He showered, and then lay tossing and turning, fitfully dozing. He'd been relaxed talking to Lara about the business he had to do over the next few days, but the argument with Leonid and Olga's pleas to go along with the Russians had focussed his mind again. He was sure he was making the right decision to split now from the others; he had to capitalise, to take the money and run. The reaction he had got from Oleg when he had suggested opening the company up had made it plain that if he didn't push for what he wanted now, if he let the opportunity pass, he would always be at the beck and call of the Malenkovs. This was his one chance to be free, to take what he had earned and enjoy it without the spectre of the Russian connection. He thought also back to his father, and how the old man would have enjoyed the spectacle of his son milking Russia for billions; that would be revenge for what had gone before.

Upstairs on the bridge, the crewman on watch sat playing on his Gameboy. They were in a safe anchorage on a calm clear night; he did no more than cast a cursory look at the world around him every half hour or so. The Zodiac crept closer. Its crew exchanged a whisper and each donned a mask, pulled from the pocket of his windbreaker. Slowly, slowly, the outboard barely popping and burbling, they nosed up to the stern anchor chain.

Lansky had eventually fallen into a deeper sleep, and only groggily awoke when he heard the door to the stateroom opening. He had no time to react; the bullets ripped into his head and throat. One of the gunmen grabbed his watch from the bedside shelf, another swept up the briefcase lying on the table and then they were sprinting back down the deck and re-boarding their inflatable in seconds. It was as if nothing had changed; the yacht still sat, lights darkened, at anchor, the watchkeeper sat on the bridge, engrossed in the electronic toy in his hand; but down below, the owner lay dead, blood and brains spreading slowly across the bedclothes. Once back on the Cigarette, the Chechens carefully slashed the buoyancy chambers of the Zodiac, leaving the weight of the outboard to drag it down into the depths. The nine millimetre pistols and silencers followed, dropped over the side along with Lansky's watch and briefcase as the speedboat picked up its pace on the way back to Charlotte Amalie. Before they entered the marina there, the helmsman collected the Kazakh passports from his colleagues and issued them each with a Russian one, all with a carefully-forged US Virgin Islands entry stamp, dated a few days previously. The Kazakh documents went to the bottom of the Caribbean. The men had never registered crossing between the US and the British islands, so the trail would be sufficiently confused to hinder any investigators who might have been interested in four eastern Europeans blasting around the islands in a high-powered boat.

The next morning, the body was discovered by the crew when Lansky didn't appear as usual; there was uproar through the yacht club and the moored boats as the news spread. The general consensus amongst the yachties was that this was probably another case of armed robbery, not unknown in Caribbean waters, although more usually restricted to less well-occupied anchorages. Lansky being a British subject, the local police informed the High Commission, who as a matter of course, made a report back to their masters in the Foreign Office in London. The London press pretty soon became aware of what had happened, as well, and the story of the murdered tycoon, as the red-tops called him, was splashed all over the front pages. The Prime Minister could hardly have claimed to be surprised, but nevertheless seeing the result of his decision brought him up short. He called the Foreign Secretary across to Downing Street.

"James, come in. Sit down. I guess you've seen the press?"

"Yes, and I've had the preliminary report from our people in the BVIs. The first reaction locally is that it is the work of a gang of pirates – armed robbers, we'd probably call them. There's a story that some of his personal possessions are missing, but the crew can't be too sure, as this is the first time he's used the yacht. Nobody is that familiar with what he had on board, but they seem pretty certain there's a briefcase missing, and possibly his watch – no doubt big, vulgar and worth a small fortune." His tone changed. "I know we knew it would happen, but that doesn't make it any less shocking. You're going to have to comment, aren't you? Big party donor, major commercial figure – all that sort of thing."

"Yes, I'll have to make a statement." He stood up, walked across the room to the window. Looking out at the garden bathed in early spring sunlight, with his back to his colleague, he continued: "This is the worst thing I've ever done. However much I tell myself I had to sacrifice one man for the greater good, I keep thinking of what that platitude has meant to Victor Lansky. He's dead, James, and I killed him, just as surely as if I'd pulled the trigger." He turned to face the other man. "And now I'm going to have to go in front of the cameras and give him a eulogy."

The Foreign Secretary nodded. "And then you'll have to sign an oil supply deal. That's what you'll be giving the people of this country – security in the energy supply. You know what, even if the voters knew how you'd got them that security, I'd bet they'd still support you in the ballot box, whatever they might say out loud."

"James, that's the most cynical thing you've ever said to me." He shook his head, as if trying to clear it. "And you know what, I think you're right. God, we're a self-interested species. Well, what's done is done. I'll mouth the trite words of sorrow; and I guess we'd better prepare for a trip to Moscow."

The Kremlin, Moscow

Once again, Denis Menkov sat in the chair opposite the President's desk.

"You have done well," said his boss. "The Lansky problem is solved. I assume nothing will link it with us?"

"No, absolutely not. The Chechens did their work well. The press in the Caribbean, and more importantly in London, are convinced it was a robbery – there have been many from yachts in that part of the world. They will find nothing." He grinned. "The sea is such a convenient place to dispose of things. The fact that the Malenkovs were also there is an extra confusion. It is apparently quite clear to the police that nobody on their yacht is implicated, but it just muddies the waters."

"Have you spoken to them?"

"Yes, they were obviously sorry to hear of the death of their associate and business partner, but I suspect their sorrow will be short-lived."

The President gave a thin smile. "When they remember that they can buy back the other fifty percent of their company at the original cost price, I guess they may live with their grief. I told them at the time they would be grateful to me for helping them to write their agreement with Lansky." He sighed. "We have succeeded, Denis. We've used the foreign investment, but control is once again totally in Russia. It just remains to be seen what we do with the Malenkovs. I think it might be a good idea for you to join the Board of Russo-European."

Menkov looked quizzically at him. "My expertise doesn't really lie in the boardroom, Yuri. I'm normally more use as a practical man."

"I know what I'm doing, Denis. There are still some moves to be made in this game before I can say check-mate. You have another part to play. Now, go down to Krayanovsk and make sure our friends can keep everything together."

Menkov left the room, and Ansonov leaned back in his chair. He could sense that he was very close to his ultimate goal, which might be the point at which the interests of Yuri Ansonov, personally, trumped those of Mother Russia. On his personal, unrecorded mobile phone he dialled a number in Vienna, Austria, and when he got through spoke at some length.

A couple of weeks later, Ansonov requested Crispin Smith to pay him a visit.

"Sir Crispin, how delightful to see you again. The circumstances seem to have changed since our last meetings. If you recall, then we thought there might be a problem with the future of Russo-European Metals, and the development of our aluminium industry down in Siberia. I understand now that the issues which were creating that potential problem seem to have resolved themselves. But I'm getting ahead of myself. First, let me express my sorrow about the death of your countryman, Mr Victor Lansky. Such a loss; he was a true friend of Russia, and we shall be eternally grateful for the help he gave with that development, particularly in Krayanovsk. He will be sadly missed; I know his partners will regret no longer having his wide knowledge and experience to call upon."

Smith fought down an urge to punch the Russian. Instead, as a true diplomat, he said: "Yes, a great loss. I suppose his partners will have to get used to working with whoever inherits his stake in the company, assuming they want to keep an involvement."

"I don't think that's quite right. I understand that there was a deal in place that, should a shareholder die, the other partners had a pre-emptive to right to buy out the stake. I don't know, but I suspect the Malenkovs will exercise that right." His voice became harsh. "You will recall, Sir Crispin, that I made it clear to you that Russia would control her own resources." The two men stared at each other for a moment. Then Ansonov resumed, the good humour back in his voice. "Now, the reason I asked you to come to see me is this. We have been doing a certain amount of work in preparation for our two countries to conclude the oil supply agreement of which we spoke before. I believe that from our side we are largely ready to make that formal agreement. We would like to invite your Prime Minister to Moscow in order to finalise this arrangement, which we believe will create such a positive relationship between our two countries. Of course, I know that the respective Trade Ministers, and the heads of the various oil companies who will actually execute the arrangement, will also have to be involved in the fine detail. But I believe that a firm commitment, made by your Prime Minister and me, will be a fine demonstration of the regard in which our two countries hold each other. I believe we can make an announcement, here, in Moscow, the two of us, which will ensure the success of the deal. So I would like to request you formally to pass my invitation on to the Prime Minister. Tell him that I am eagerly awaiting his visit to Moscow. This will be the beginning of a whole new era of co-operation between our two countries."

Once again, Crispin Smith found himself in his official Rolls-Royce riding back from a meeting with Ansonov, aware that the Russian had completely outplayed them. The right the Malenkovs had to buy out Lansky's share was a master stroke. They had used Lansky's money for as long as they has needed it, and then killed him to get the company back. In Smith's eyes, that meant they had known all along how it would end. And all it had cost them was an oil supply deal, which would probably end up being at something very close to the market rate anyway. Smith sighed. While the big boys had been playing the truly global game, the British politicians had been worried about their source of party funding drying up.

Chapter 27

British Embassy, Moscow

Two weeks later

The harsh Russian winter was over and spring was beginning to show in the buds of the flowers and trees starting to emerge in the Embassy gardens. The Prime Minister sat with his colleagues, the Foreign Secretary and the Moscow Ambassador in the latter's palatial office. He had arrived in Moscow the previous evening, with an entourage of oil industry representatives and specialists, to say nothing of the hordes of the press corps. Talks, ostensibly to finalise a "forward-looking energy trade agreement" (as the press briefings described it), but actually to rubber-stamp what the two leaders had already agreed over the phone, were scheduled to begin the next day. "So, Crispin," began the PM, "our man is pleased with himself?"

"Very; he's got what he wanted, I think. Certainly, he's got his people in sole control down in Krayanovsk. Effectively, they just made use of Lansky for as long as they needed him, and then..........well, we all know and then what, don't we?"

"Yes. James tells me that you believe it was all pre-planned."

"Well, look at it rationally. That clause giving them pre-emptive rights makes it look very much that way."

"Yes, but it applied in both directions, so it would have given Lansky the same advantage if the circumstances had been reversed. I don't think you can automatically assume that they'd planned all this in advance."

"That's true; it may be that it was there just in case, and it was only later that they realised what a huge benefit it could give them. Look, I don't know when they planned everything, but I do know Lansky was dead meat from the moment they decided they didn't need him any longer. And that, I believe, was the case from the outset. In their eyes, I think they thought he was getting a free ride, and they would only let that continue as long as they had to. Look, if it wasn't premeditated, how come they'd got those photographs? Those weren't just the holiday snaps of a man who happened to be there with a camera. Somebody made a conscious decision to get those pictures taken; whether the motive at that stage was to blackmail Lansky or, as eventually happened, to blackmail HMG, I don't know. But it must have been one or the other. And here we are, waiting to be allowed to get our reward for not upsetting the Russian applecart." Smith and the PM had been contemporaries at Oxford and had known each other ever since; they were friends, of a sort. For that reason, Smith had a bit more leeway in speaking frankly to his leader than the majority of his diplomatic colleagues. "Honestly," he continued, "I think we've been played like a salmon on a line."

"Crispin, we had this discussion already. We all agreed that there was nothing else we could do. I don't like it any more than you; but that's the way it is. Anyway," – he got up from his chair – "I need to go upstairs to think a bit about the meetings tomorrow, so you'll have to excuse me for a bit."

There was silence after he left the room. Then the Foreign Secretary broke it. "Crispin, you have to cut him a bit of slack. It was a horrible decision he had to make, and he's still struggling to come to terms with it. He knows it was in the country's interest, but he also knows the human cost. Some of his predecessors have started wars that have killed lots of people, but somehow we all accept the necessity there. He has secured energy supplies for the country for years to come, without conflict. And yet, because of the nature of it, he's got to carry that guilty secret about with him for the rest of his life. You've known him for a long time – you know he's a decent man, trying to do the best he can."

"Sadly, James, with politicians, when expediency drives, decency gets forgotten."

"I should take that personally, as a politician, but I can't altogether disagree. But trying to do the best for the majority all the time is tough. Hell, he's the same age as you; he looks at least ten years older. It hasn't been easy."

"Wasn't easy for Lansky, either. Look, I know in reality we all agree. It's just that I find it tougher to accept. I'm also acutely aware that we have been turned over by Ansonov. Yes, we've got our oil supply, and I know how vital that is, but we've also just opened up and shown him how he can walk all over us. I just hope this isn't the first in a series of shabby accommodations we have to make with him."

"Crispin, I understand your concerns, but we are where we are. This is the hand we've been dealt. It's not the first shabby accommodation, as you call them, that democratic politicians have ever had to make, and it won't be the last. It sticks in the throat so because it's so personal. How do you think Chamberlain felt when he backed out of protecting the Czechs against Hitler in 1938? Or Churchill, when he agreed to let the Russians rape what the Germans had left of Poland in 1945? It's never easy. The measure of the man is that he *can* have the clarity of mind to understand the greater good. In the grand scheme of things, this is such a small thing. Lansky was no angel, either."

"I know, but it's not what I signed up to. Honestly, James, I don't know if I can continue with it. I'm seriously thinking about quitting. But don't worry, I'm not going to tell anybody our grubby little secret. Whatever my own views, I know that wouldn't help anybody."

"You must make your own decision, James, but you would be sorely missed. We need honourable people in the diplomatic service, even if, as politicians, we sometimes want them to behave in a different way." And there, thought Smith, was the problem encapsulated.

The Kremlin, Moscow

Three days later, the two leaders, Yuri Ansonov and the British Prime Minister, Tom Blake, stood next to each other at a pair of lecterns in a big conference room in the Kremlin. Facing them were the world's news media. The press secretary introduced them and Ansonov began speaking, in deference to his guest in English.

"Ladies and gentlemen, today marks an important milestone in the relationship between two great nations. The United Kingdom and Russia have had their ups and downs over the years, but our leaders over the generations have striven for similar ideals – peace and economic prosperity for our peoples. At times, we may have had differing approaches to these goals, but I am proud to say that, together with my colleague - no, let me now call him my friend - Mr Tom Blake, I believe that today we have taken a huge step along that road. You may say we have just signed a trade deal. You may say such things are two a penny, that this is no different from other agreements. I would tell you you are wrong. This historic agreement we have today signed marks a departure from what has been done before. We have agreed to a long-term sharing of the resources of one country for the benefit of its friend and ally. Our agreement covers the long-term supply of Russian oil to the United Kingdom at prices dictated by the international market. This represents a secure supply of a vital commodity; for Russia, it guarantees a consistent major customer, who will take the product at a predetermined annual rate. This gives security to Russian producers, enabling them to plan their development with confidence." Some of the financial journalists exchanged glances. International market prices, guaranteed rate of offtake? Plenty of scope for their columns tomorrow to speculate on who this arrangement really favoured. Ansonov spoke on for a few more minutes, then handed over to Blake, who spoke some more about Russo-British friendship, economic growth, stability and so on. Some of the journalists started to drift out of the room, vying to get the story out first. Then, as he was winding up, Blake indicated the two leaders would take questions. Third or fourth question in, a tall, balding reporter stood up and addressed them. "Mr Blake, Mr Ansonov. Nigel Roberts, BBC TV. With all this talk of Russo-British co-operation, have you any news on the investigation into the death in the Caribbean of Victor Lansky, who was intimately involved in just such co-operation in the resource area?"

Blake spoke first. "Obviously, we are very sorry about this issue. Victor Lansky seems to have been the victim of a violent robbery aboard his yacht in the British Virgin Islands. The local police continue to investigate, but as yet, as far as I am aware, they have uncovered no substantive leads pointing to the guilty party. I can't really say any more than that, except to re-iterate my sorrow. Mr Lansky was indeed a friend to both countries and in his business advanced the cause of co-operation. We have every confidence that eventually the BVIs police force will track down the guilty and that they will be punished."

As he stopped speaking, Ansonov indicated that he also had something to say. "Ladies and gentlemen, history will judge Victor Lansky as a great man. By his foresight and his trust and belief in potential, he was instrumental in enabling the revival in our industries to proceed at the pace from which we have all benefited since the change in system in this country. We all owe him a debt of gratitude for showing such trust in what is possible here. We deeply regret his death and trust that the perpetrators of such a crime will be brought to justice."

At the back of the room, unnoticed, Crispin Smith got to his feet and walked out, his decision made. His letter of resignation would be written before Blake and the Foreign Secretary got back to the Embassy. He would keep his word and never divulge what had happened, but he could no longer be a part of it.

Krayanovsk, Siberia

The Malenkov brothers sat in front of a blazing log fire in the living room of the new dacha they had had built on the outskirts of Krayanovsk, on the side opposite to the smelter to keep it away from the fumes roaring out of the chimneys. They spent increasingly less and less time in Siberia, being seen far more often in Moscow's restaurants and clubs, where they mixed with the other super-rich of Russia's developing society. They were in Krayanovsk now because Denis Menkov had asked to meet them there, preferring to keep things out of Moscow this time. The large flat-screen TV on one wall of the room was tuned to a news channel, showing coverage of the Ansonov/Blake press conference. When he heard Ansonov refer to Lansky as a great man, Leonid cackled with laughter. "So, little brother, our leader confirms we chose our partner well. A great man. Would he be saying so if Victor had not been so co-operative as to die? If he still owned half of our business? I think probably not. It has all worked out very well. We have our company back, we are financially as strong as any in the world; and Yuri Ansonov can tell his people he is keeping their interests at heart by holding Russian resources in Russian hands. And then when he chooses, like now, he can flick his fingers and the foreigners will come to take what he gives them, like dogs from a feeding bowl at their masters' feet. And all the while, Oleg, we get richer and richer. I couldn't have written the story better if I had done it myself."

"No regrets for Victor? We worked with him for a long while. He was a kind of friend, as well."

"In a way, but he should have been happy with what he had, not tried to get some sort of control from us. He caused his own downfall."

"Do you think so, or do you think our friends always had this in mind?"

"Oleg, I don't know. I just know we have come a long, long way. We are rich beyond anything we could have ever dreamed, and I'm not going to let anything risk that. Victor was silly. He tried to be the player of the game, rather than just a chessman."

"Mmm." Oleg gestured through the window, where they could see a car approaching up the slight slope from the main road. "That will be Denis. No doubt he has something to say on behalf of him." He pointed back at the screen, where Ansonov was still answering questions in the press conference.

A couple of minutes later, Menkov was shown into the room. Old habits died hard. In his hand he held a couple of bottles of vodka, and as Oleg reached for three tumblers, he greeted the brothers and said: "Ah, it's such a pleasure to be out of the formality of Moscow. We can relax here, just the three of us, and discuss the things that matter without worrying about being overheard, or without some press photographer constantly trying to get our pictures." He gestured toward the TV screen, the sound now muted, but still showing the press conference. "I see you're watching our President and his new best western friend. What do you think?"

Oleg replied. "We just heard the kind words he said about our former partner. He described him as a great man, with his contribution to the relationship between his country and ours and his efforts to help with the development of our Siberian industry."

Leonid laughed. "We were just saying he would have been less full of praise if Victor had not had the foresight to die when he did."

Menkov smiled back thinly. "Yes, events have worked out conveniently. So you two now have on the surface full ownership of the company. That is good. But Yuri Ansonov has some small changes in mind, which he has asked me to explain to you." Seeing the quizzical looks on the brothers' faces, he hurried on: "Nothing that will cause you any problems, I am sure, but just a way of making certain that his interests can be adequately represented."

Oleg looked hard at him. "His interests have always been kept in mind, but obviously there can be no overt reference to them. Does he have it in mind that that should change?"

"No, no, of course not. As far as the world is concerned, his only interest in Russo-European is as the President of Russia, to see that one of the country's resource giants is continuing to develop satisfactorily."

"And so? What should change? I don't really understand what you are getting at, Denis."

"It's simple, really. Yuri wants you to appoint me to the Board of the company, and he wants me to take responsibility for re-shaping the way our product is supplied into the western market since Victor Lansky is no longer available to do that job."

Oleg looked across at his brother, a puzzled expression on his face.

Then he said: "I see. Or at least, up to a point I do. But we believe that we are in any case able to do that job ourselves; we are in a position now where we can just continue as before, even without Victor. Our sales channels are very robust."

"Mmm. But you know how it is. This is how Yuri Ansonov wants it to be. It's not really a matter of debate."

Leonid spoke for the first time. "Of course, Denis, we have no problem with you joining the board of our company. In fact, we would welcome it, as yet more proof of the continued interest your boss, Yuri Ansonov, has in our enterprise. But before we can really judge anything else, we would need to know how you propose to change our sales policies."

Menkov reflected for a moment on how the rough, thuggish Siberian gangster had become the smooth-spoken businessman; well, such were the effects of money. "It's more to do with concentrating on what we do well. We are able to produce a good product at a very competitive price; this is in essence the strength of the Russo-European smelters. Our product is in demand by the customers. Up until now, we have really relied on one man – Victor Lansky – to distribute our metal into the market. But it is time to move on. The size of the company really demands that we cannot rely on one man. Victor Lansky was a particular case – he had grown up with the business, he knew it inside out. In that sense, he is irreplaceable. To move forward, we need to use a corporate sales operation, one which has in place a network able to absorb our material and disseminate it into the marketplace. I'm sure you agree we would not be able to find one man who could replace Lansky."

Oleg nodded. "Yes, I can see there may be some merit in what you – or rather, the President – are proposing, but do you really think there is anyone strong enough to undertake what you suggest?"

"Oh, yes. We have a name in mind. But we have to have some more discussions before we can be completely clear. I suggest we do this in two stages. Let us announce my joining the Board, then you should come to Moscow in a couple of weeks time, where we can get together with the President and finalise all the detail."

Oleg looked hard at him. He took a swig of vodka. Then he said: "We don't really have a choice, do we?"

"Not really. You know how Yuri is when he has made a decision. But don't worry. The money will keep rolling in. Now, are we going to get some old friends together and visit the Turkish bath this evening? I always look forward to that here in Krayanovsk."

The Kremlin, Moscow

As he prepared for the state banquet with the British delegation that evening, Ansonov received a call from Menkov, confirming that all was moving according to plan in Krayanovsk. He pulled out a mobile phone, and dialled the Viennese number. When it was answered, he said, "Roger, my friend, I believe our deal is ready to be done. Just a couple more weeks, and everything will be in order. We need to meet somewhere quiet very soon after that." He listened to the reply, and terminated the call. He mused for a moment on the disadvantages of having a well-recognised face. It would be so much easier if he could meet Roger Erlsfeldt without worrying about being observed. Still, for the benefits that were going to accrue, he could afford to hide in the shadows, occasionally.

Chapter 28

Three weeks later

A Dacha outside Moscow

The guards at the entrance to the estate saw a black Chevy Suburban approaching rapidly down the road. As it came level with them, the driver swung the wheel and pulled up by the guardhouse. The windows in the back of the vehicle were dimmed-out and the passenger no more than a shadowy figure sitting back in his seat. The driver handed over his identification, which the guard took back into the building. A brief phone call later, he opened the heavy, barbed-wire topped gates and the Suburban eased forward up the long drive which led a couple of kilometres uphill through dense woodland; the passenger in the back spotted several armed, black-clad guards half-hidden among the trees. Eventually, they came to another set of gates, with another guardhouse protecting it, and the entry procedure was repeated. Roger Erlsfeldt, the passenger sitting in the back of the SUV, had been to the White House in Washington before now. The security there, he reflected, was a doddle compared with this. Finally, the drive curved round in a semi-circle in front of a substantial wooden dacha. Yet more security guards clustered round as Erlsfeldt climbed out of the car, and eventually he was shown into a big, wood-panelled room with a log fire blazing at one end of it. Sitting in front of the fire, relaxed, in casual clothes, were Yuri Ansonov and Denis Menkov.

"Roger, welcome", said Ansonov, getting to his feet and advancing across the room, hand outstretched to receive his guest with a handshake. I'm glad you could make it out to the countryside. Was your flight OK?"

"Yes, fine. Obviously, I didn't use the liveried Metalex jet. I chartered something anonymous. I don't think the world need to speculate about this meeting."

"Indeed. What we have to discuss is really of no concern outside this room. But please, sit down. The staff will be taking your baggage up to your room. Would you like to go and freshen up, or shall we get straight down to the things we need to discuss?"

Menkov reflected to himself that it was almost the first time he had ever seen Ansonov show any deference to anybody else.

"No, I'm fine Yuri. It's not that long a flight from Vienna. Let's get on."

"At least let me offer you a drink." He gestured towards the open vodka bottle sitting with three glasses on the table." Erlsfeldt nodded his thanks, and Ansonov poured a good shot for each of them.

"OK," he said "we have one issue to discuss, which I think we can resolve to the satisfaction of all parties. As you know, we have many natural resources in my country, and we are always interested in exploring better ways to exploit them to the benefit of the Russian people. You may be aware that we have recently concluded a very powerful oil deal with the United Kingdom." Erlsfeldt nodded, as Ansonov continued. "Well, that is the kind of thing we are keen to do – to ensure that the natural wealth of the country is not stolen by foreigners."

"Well, you've certainly done that in that case. I haven't – obviously – seen the full details of that deal, but it seems to me the Brits have signed something far more beneficial to you than to them. As I understand it, they've *got* to take the stipulated quantities at market price; great when things are good, but when their economy turns down, and for sure it will at some point, then they'll find themselves awash with your oil, which they have to pay for, even if it's more than they need." He grinned. "It's the sort of deal I would be proud to have written myself."

Ansonov grinned back. "I have no comment; but my friend Tom Blake was more desperate than me. But let's leave that there. We're here to talk about how we may co-operate, specifically in the aluminium business, not to discuss what mistakes may have been made by other politicians. Of course, we know that in the past my predecessor in this office had some very close ties to Metalex." Erlsfeldt looked hard at him at that comment. "Come, Roger, there's no point in hiding things between friends. One of the reasons we had to cut off relationships between Metalex and the government was precisely because they had become ....let us say, too close."

"That's as maybe. But I thought the purpose of this meeting was to try and strengthen our links, not hark back to what may have happened in the past."

"But of course it is. That's *exactly* what we are going to do. I merely mention the past in order to make the point that things will be done in a different way this time. Look, there are only the three of us here. We can be frank. My predecessor was happy to take money in order to deliver our wealth into the hands of your company. He was unable to create a strong, resilient base in this country, no matter what he may have said publicly. In fairness, in his time the country was effectively bankrupt, and it was difficult to know which way to turn. The way he turned, in the end, was the way of the venal man. Now, we are in a different position. We have been fortunate, not only to have had money to make the necessary investments, but also to have lived recently through a period when demand for our resources has been strong. That enables us to be in a position where we can look upon an alliance with Metalex more as a partnership of equals." He paused, while he threw another log onto the fire. "You will know that Mr Victor Lansky, who was an important part of the sales success of Russo-European, died tragically in the Caribbean recently. This has created a gap for the company. They relied upon him; but as a founder of the company, as a man who had grown up with its business, it will be very difficult to replace him. Indeed, they believe that it would be nigh-on impossible to replace him with one individual. They believe that it will prove far more effective to utilise the benefit of a strong company, one who already has a powerful position in the market, which, if added to Russo-European, could be almost invincible."

Erlsfeldt sat back in his chair, a smile playing around his lips. He steepled his fingers, and paused a moment before replying. Then, he said, "And you believe we could be that company. It's possible. But what I don't understand altogether is with whom I'm negotiating. I know from our previous talks that you are involved because this is a big deal for Russia, not just the company involved, but I don't understand why the Malenkovs are not here. Surely they would need to be part of any discussion?"

"Things are changing all the time, Roger. Denis, here, who I think you may have met before, has recently joined the Board of Russo-European. I can also tell you, although it is not yet public knowledge, that he will be appointed Chairman and Managing Director in the next few days. The Malenkov brothers, having created the success that is Russo-European, now wish to step back from active involvement and enjoy fully the fruits of their labours. They will still be involved, as shareholders, clearly, and as non-executives. So going forward, it will be Denis with whom you deal."

Erlsfeldt was himself a ruthless man – the road to the top of Metalex was not for the faint-hearted – but he found himself doffing his metaphorical hat to the man opposite him. Like many others, he had been suspicious when he heard the rumours of Lansky's death that it was not a coincidental robbery gone wrong. Now, learning that the Malenkovs were also departing the stage to be replaced by a known associate of the President, he could work out the pattern. Ansonov's next words confirmed it.

"Of course, as ever, I do retain a strong interest in the continued success of the company. Although clearly, as President, my concerns are with the whole of the Russian state and its people, it would be unfair of me to deny that I have a strong wish to see this business continue to prosper. So I am always available to offer assistance – as now, for example, in arranging this meeting."

"For which, I guess, there is a cost."

"Crudely put, Roger, but to the point. Yes, my assistance does not come for nothing. Let us be frank with each other; I know the level of profitability of this business, and I know how much Lansky earned from it. I also know that Metalex would bite our hands off to secure the sole sales rights of the company outside Russia for only half of what Lansky was taking. I think that makes our arithmetic very easy, don't you? Gentlemen, I think we are reaching an area of commercial negotiation between two corporate leaders. I am not sure if I, as a politician, have a role to play in those detailed discussions." He looked straight into Erlsfeldt's eyes. "I think we all know what the parameters are. I will leave you to your discussions. I have some matters of state to attend to. We should meet again at dinner. Denis, perhaps you could take Roger through to the library to talk about details."

As they left the room, Ansonov moved from the armchair he had been in, across to the desk under the big window, through which he could see the woodland stretching away into the distance.

Predictably, coming to an agreement wasn't too difficult. Erlsfeldt knew what he wanted – access to the production of the smelters. In an ideal world, he would have liked to own them as well, but he was a pragmatist and he recognised what was and was not possible. And Ansonov had been right; he would certainly do the deal for half of what Lansky had been taking. That left plenty for the President; millions of dollars a month, to pour into his hidden accounts. At dinner, the details tied up and therefore in a celebratory atmosphere, Erlsfeldt had idly speculated to himself about how much the President was also taking out of the oil deal. The difference was, Metalex knew what was going on; he doubted if the British had a clue. He was developing a healthy respect for Yuri Ansonov; he was a true player.

The next morning, the black Suburban whisked the Metalex man away to his anonymous flight back to Vienna. In his pocket was the heads of agreement document tying everything up. Showing that to his senior management team would certainly let them know there was still life in the boss. It had been a good couple of days.

There was one last piece of Ansonov's jigsaw to complete. The Malenkov brothers had been summoned to come to the dacha in the afternoon after the previous guest had left. They arrived to find the same scene in the big drawing room – Ansonov and Menkov sitting in front of the roaring fire. Smiling, Ansonov welcomed them and they too settled down before the fireplace.

Oleg began. "So, Yuri, I guess you have called us here so we can all discuss how things will be going forward, with Denis now joining us as a colleague on our board of directors. We were a little surprised when he told us that was your intention, but we all know each other well, so I guess we can all make it work well. But Denis wasn't really clear about whether or not he was going to be an active board member, or just looking generally after certain interests."

"That's right. He was just conveying my instructions. In some ways it would maybe have been nice to have had this discussion before appointing Denis, but in the end it makes very little difference. But let's take the opportunity to review where we are with Russo-European and how we can see the future developing."

The Malenkovs looked slightly surprised; Ansonov didn't normally make such clear statements about the company – normally, he preferred to stay in the background, obviously pulling some of the strings but not being so overt as this.

Ansonov continued. "Things have changed, now, with the death of Lansky. Whatever his faults, it cannot be denied that he had done a good job in getting our metal to the customers."

Leonid interrupted. "It was not that difficult. The price means that it can almost sell itself. And the price is a factor of our cost of production."

"But of course, Leonid, we all know that. That's what made the whole project interesting in the first place. But the fact remains that Lansky was the one who handled the sales side of the business. He's now dead, so we have to reassess how we do that. We could simply continue on the basis that you handle it all from here, that all sales and logistics are run from Moscow; we could try and find a replacement for Lansky, but without Lansky's financial commitment, would such a person be anything more than a functionary? Could we rely on such a person, who would not have the same depth of involvement, who would effectively be simply an employee?" He answered his own questions. "I do not believe either of these solutions would be acceptable. We need to do something more innovative to make sure we continue to see our business develop in a healthy way." He paused, looking into the fire, then carried on speaking. "Things must change. Russo-European is now wholly Russian-owned; we must focus all our efforts on ensuring it continues to maintain its ability to produce at low cost. Rather than attempt to replace Lansky, we will make a deal with a western trading company to deliver all of our metal to them, and let them have the issues of dealing with the end customers." He held up his hand, to prevent Oleg interrupting. "Denis Menkov has signed a memorandum of agreement to that effect with the head of the trading company Metalex. From now on, they will be the sole sales agent of Russo-European production."

Leonid jumped in before Oleg had a chance to speak. "What do you mean, Denis signed? It's not Denis' position to sign. This is ridiculous. Why should we give all this away to Metalex? You know what they have done in the past, the corruption of your predecessor."

Ansonov continued. "There are two other things I should tell you. Please do not interrupt again; remember who I am. As from yesterday, Denis is the Chairman and Managing Director of Russo-European. You, Oleg, and you, Leonid, will continue as board members, but you will be non-executive. Denis will manage the company, and you will turn up for board meetings and vote how you are told. Fifty-one percent of your shareholding will be transferred to a nominee company; Denis will take care of the details. The other forty-nine percent you may retain. You will be paid, just as Lansky's estate was paid. You will continue to receive dividends, when they are paid, so you will still be very rich men. But you will not control the business any more."

Leonid sat there with his mouth drooping in shock. Oleg looked shaken, but tried to argue. "But, Yuri, what are you doing? We have always looked after your interests. Why do you need to make things change? Why are you throwing us out? What have we done wrong?"

Ansonov shook his head, almost sadly. "You never really understood, did you? Did you really think you were being given this? You were a pair of hard-line Siberian gangsters. You are now amongst the world's super-rich; and you're there because I have let you benefit as an aid to something I needed to do. But you should never have believed that you had achieved this by yourselves."

"Yuri, we understand that." Oleg was beginning to sound panicky. "Why change now, when it's been working so well? Sure, Victor's gone, but why change everything else? We can work with Metalex, if that's what you want. We know how to do it. For Denis, it's all new; if you want him there, we can help him."

Leonid had been staring into Ansonov's eyes as his brother gabbled. Now he put a restraining arm on the latter's shoulder, and said, almost wearily, "Relax, little brother. It's over. He's used us to get what he wants, but why resist?" He turned to Ansonov. "You win, Yuri, we'll do what you want."

But Oleg continued, wheedling. "You can't do this; it's not fair! All the effort we put in! What are we going to do?"

Ansonov's temper snapped. "You stupid little man. What effort did you put in? You've been given such a free ride that most people in the world would kill for. Just take the money and run, before I think of sending the taxman to audit your affairs. You wouldn't like that, I'm sure. Now get out while you're still ahead. And as for what do you do now? What do I care? You're being allowed to keep all the money – go and buy a football club in Europe or something. Enjoy yourselves, and thank God for the day you met Yuri Ansonov. But don't get in my way."

Leonid nodded, put his arm round his brother's shoulders and walked him out of the room.

As the door closed behind them, Ansonov looked at Denis Menkov, who had remained silent throughout. "That's it. We've done what I wanted." Silently, Menkov promised himself never to let himself get carried away and think that he was really important to the man facing him.

Epilogue

May 2003

Stade de France, St. Denis, Paris
France

The high point of the European football season is the Champion's League Final between the two survivors of a season-long elimination competition amongst the previous season's national champions of the major footballing powers of the Continent. It's the biggest event in football, after the World Cup, and for some fans, seeing their club team picking up the Championship trophy is an even bigger thrill than seeing their national side win. So it was that year, when the final, contested at the spectacular Stade de France in the northern suburbs of Paris, was between the Spanish and the German champions. For the supporters of the Spanish team it was extra exciting; until a couple of years ago, their club had languished mid-table in La Liga; then, rich new owners had stepped in, and used their millions to buy the best coach and the best players. Their reward had come at the end of the last season, with a stylish romp to the Spanish national championship; a spectacular run in the Champion's League had followed through this last winter, and here they were, on the brink of history. One more game to play and they would be hailed as Europe's finest. Not that the German side and its supporters were giving up easily. With their blend of German and East European stars, they still presented a formidable hurdle. More workmanlike perhaps than the international jet-setters of the Spanish team, but in the eyes of the cognoscenti, it was going to be a well-matched game. The European press was drooling with anticipation.

All week, the fans had been rolling into Paris. In the warm spring sunshine, they meandered about the centre and the Grands Boulevards, their gaily coloured flags and clothing lighting up the city. The banter between the two groups was good-natured, much to the relief of the gendarmes, who had been cautioned to prepare for the worst. Now, finally, the day had come, and the fans were streaming out of the centre towards the drab suburb of St Denis and the temple to rugby and football that dominates it. As well as carrying their club colours and flags, many of the fans also sported their national flags; illogical, maybe, for a club

202

game, but nevertheless the way of the world. It was a little strange, therefore, to see amongst the bright red and yellow Spanish flags that many of the supporters were also clutching flags with the distinctive white, blue and red horizontal stripes of Russia. And in the suites and private boxes high in the stands above the centre line, amongst the VIPs already beginning their pre-match lunch, there was a noticeable buzz of Russian conversation.

The Kremlin
Moscow

The time difference meant that the afternoon kick-off in Paris was an early evening game in Moscow. Yuri Ansonov was alone in his huge office in the Kremlin; he was watching the flat-screen TV mounted on the wall opposite his desk as the whistle blew and the Germans kicked off. A pattern of passing, the ball played across the pitch, and suddenly the centre forward was free, unmarked on the edge of the Spanish team's penalty area. Turning, he smashed the ball passed the despairing dive of the goalkeeper into the top corner of the net, before wheeling away in triumph to receive the plaudits of his team. As his name flashed on the screen, the camera focussed on one of the boxes in the stand. There, head in hands, was Oleg Malenkov, next to him his brother, with a shell-shocked expression on his face. The goal was the fastest in the history of the competition, its scorer the German team's ace Polish striker. His name was Alexander Lansky, whose grandfather's brother had left in 1939 to fight for his country's freedom.

When Ansonov had moved into the President's office, the walls had been adorned with portraits of the leaders of the Soviet era. He had felt that unsatisfactory, and now, staring down at him as he silently raised his glass of vodka to the memory of Victor Lansky, who had helped make it all possible, were what he felt to be far more appropriate: pictures of Russia's Czars.

Truly, there is nothing new under the sun.

Lightning Source UK Ltd.
Milton Keynes UK
UKOW051355280412

191679UK00001B/1/P